*Portrait of a Woman
in Love with Love*

Helen Miley stepped into the warm city sunlight and
smiled. On days like this, when the whole city was in
ecstasy, Ohio was more than just miles away. Life
was indeed a bowl of cherries, bursting with promise
and ripe with opportunity; a pirate ship sailing to
adventure, a smorgasbord of sweet male flesh...

Join Helen in her love affair with life. Come and
discover

THE PLEASURES OF HELEN

Lawrence Sanders

The Pleasures of Helen

BERKLEY BOOKS, NEW YORK

This Berkley book contains the complete
text of the original hardcover edition.
It has been completely reset in a typeface
designed for easy reading and was printed
from new film.

THE PLEASURES OF HELEN

A Berkley Book / published by arrangement with
G. P. Putnam's Sons

PRINTING HISTORY
G. P. Putnam's Sons edition published 1971
Berkley edition / January 1979

ISBN: 0-425-10168-1

A BERKLEY BOOK ® TM 757,375
Berkley Books are published by The Berkley Publishing Group,
200 Madison Avenue, New York, NY 10016.
The name "BERKLEY" and the "B" logo
are trademarks belonging to Berkley Publishing Corporation.

PRINTED IN THE UNITED STATES OF AMERICA

20 19

1

THE PHONE RANG. Charles Lefferts squirmed as if someone had goosed him with an icicle.

A voice came from under the sheet—muffled, furious: "Don't answer."

He picked up the phone. "Yes?"

A stuttered squawk.

He reached for the stub of his cigar. "Who is this?"

The hand under the sheet dug sharp nails into his thigh, then inched thoughtfully upward, nail over nail.

"The Death of a Thousand Cuts," the voice under the sheet said hollowly.

The voice on the phone burbled.

"Bob!" he roared. "Bob Cranshaw, for heaven's sake! How are you?"

A small head, covered with a toque of tight blond curls, popped out from under the sheet. Two blue eyes, expressionless as bagels, stared at him through horn-rimmed glasses.

"Hang up," she growled.

The phone made anxious noises.

Cool fingers tightened remorselessly. He showed his teeth in a death's-head grin. She held him fast.

"Can't talk now, Bob," he gasped. He fumbled around for his lighter. "Listen, old man, why don't you let me call you tomorrow, and maybe we can get together. Bob. Old man."

The phone yapped away.

He found the lighter. It didn't work. He shook it upside down and tried again. A little blue flame flickered, then went out. He set the cigar butt carefully back in the ashtray.

"Listen, Bob," he said. "Noonish. I'll call you, old man."

Helen Miley leaned across him, put her mouth close to the phone. "C'mon back to bed, white boy," she drawled in a horrible plantation accent.

The silence on the phone was deafening.

"Righto," he said rapidly. "Will call, Bob. Noonish. So long, old man."

He hung up. He looked at her.

"Thanks so much," he said bitterly.

She released him, rolled onto her back, stared at nothing.

"That was Bob," he insisted. "Bob Cranshaw."

"Son, you've got more crap than a Christmas duck. That was one of your randy women. You know it, I know it, and God knows it."

He lifted his chin, looked at her sternly. He really was a snot-nose, she decided.

"Hereafter," he sniffed, "when I am on the telephone, I would appreciate your not manipulating me in that disgraceful fashion."

She sat up, put her back against the headboard, folded her arms across her perky breasts.

"A crotch-clutcher," she said dully. "My God, I think I'm becoming a crotch-clutcher."

"Ohmydarling," he groaned. He took her in his arms. He put his wondrously cunning tongue to her nose, her ears, her pink nipples and grinning navel.

"You bastard," she gasped.

He bounded out of bed, raced across to the dresser, stared at himself in the mirror, began busily combing his hair. "Up!" he shouted. "All up and out! Everyone out for the potato race! Let's go! Up and out!"

She looked at him coldly.

"Up is right." She nodded. "That's just where I'm getting it. Up."

"I'll mix you another drink," he said hopefully. "I'll play Chuck Mangione. You want to shower first?"

"Oh . . . I may not get up," she said dreamily. "I may decide to be a problem. I may just lay here and let you try to get me out. Maybe I'll just move in with you. Maybe I'll scream and yell until someone sends for the cops. Maybe I'll break up the joint, dump all your jars of spices, and smash your African masks. Or maybe I'll just swallow a few sleeping pills and pass out."

He looked at her in horror, whimpering softly. "But why would you want to dump my spices?"

"Oh, God." She sighed. "Where were you when they were passing out brains? Don't tell me—I know. You were waiting in line at the tool shed."

"Oh, bacon and eggs," he caroled. "Bacon and eggs and toast and jam and pots and pots of coffee. Let's go! Chow down!"

Then she was weeping, head bent over, face hidden in her hands. Her shoulders jerked. Hoarse coughs came out of her. Suddenly she thought of a Model T her grandfather had owned. AhOOOgah, the horn went. AhOOOgah.

He sat on the bed. He gathered her into his arms. He touched her ears teasingly, kissed her lips timorously, drew wispy fingers lovingly down her naked back.

"Babybabybaby," he crooned. "Don't cry. It hurts me to see you cry."

"I want to die."

"Of course you do, dear," he said, nodding.

She sat upright, stared at him. She wrenched her face into a half-ass grin.

"The great lover," she said sourly. "Go powder your armpits, for Chrissakes."

She heard him in the shower, singing, "Mammy's little baby loves shortnin' bread!" and she wondered how many signatures you needed on a petition to have a man committed.

She lighted a cigarette, lay spread wide on his fuchsia sateen sheet. She propped two pillows behind her head, looked down at her naked body. Graceful, slender, pure of line.

"You've got it, kiddo," she breathed. "Now all you've got to do is find a guy who wants it."

When it was her turn to shower, the bathroom was clouded

with steam; all the towels were damp. She made do and considered dumping all his colognes, lotions, scents and powders into the sink. She settled for using the point of his toenail clippers to poke a little hole in the bottom of his toothpaste tube. When he squeezed . . . hoo-whee!

She dressed quickly. Pulled on an inflatable bra she had purchased by mail order from a company called Paris, France, Fashions, Inc., of Lobo, Arkansas. There was a slow leak in the left pouch, giving her a depraved, lopsided look.

Then on with panty hose in an open-weave pattern that made her legs look like a Rand McNally road map. And a shiny Qiana chemise that clung to her good ass. She slashed her mouth with plum lip gloss, then smacked her lips. Tousled her blond curls and was ready for Destiny.

Thirty minutes later they were seated in a restaurant on Sixth Avenue. The waitress knew Charles Lefferts; she put the check in front of Helen when she served the coffee.

"Oh, no," Helen said when he made a crippled gesture toward the check. "Let me get it. I got paid yesterday. Besides, you gave me two drinks and a plum."

"That's true." He nodded happily.

"I must call you again sometime," she said, pushing her luck. An evening with him was two weeks in never-never land.

"Oh, sure. Anytime. Even if I can't see you, at least we can chew the fat."

"On the telephone?" she asked. But it was wasted on him.

"Well, you know . . ."

"I can understand, Charles," she said, patting his hand. "I can understand hangnails and diaper rash."

"Want a cab?"

"Sure," she said cheerfully.

He dashed into the middle of Sixth Avenue, halted a cab. He attempted to give her the fare but discovered he had left his wallet at home.

He poked his head through the window. "Call me soonish!" he sang. She nodded.

She didn't look back.

2

THE CORPULENT DIRTY-WHITE spaniel lay sleeping just inside the bedroom. He breathed in coarse, asthmatic gasps that fluttered his lips. Occasionally he moaned; his stubby tail twitched.

A key turned in the outside door. Rocco lifted his head, yawned, stumbled to his feet, went padding into the hall to investigate.

Helen Miley slammed the door behind her, headed directly for the bathroom. "Honey baby Rocco boy," she said, "my back teeth are floating."

Rocco staggered after her into the bathroom. He stood yawning and sneezing. He waited until she flushed the toilet, then put his paws up on the seat, and lapped the fresh water gurgling into the bowl.

"Must you do that?" Helen asked him. "*Must* you?"

She went into the bedroom, undressed swiftly, pulled on a white terry cloth robe. It had "Killer Miley" embroidered across the back in red thread. She mixed a scotch and water in the kitchen, took it into the living room. She went directly to the parakeet cage, yanked off the night cover. The greenish-blue bird cowered away from her.

"Listen, you," Helen growled, "forty-five ninety-eight for you and sixty bucks for your cage. Now *talk*, dammit."

The bird huddled back into a corner, turned its head away. She gave up, flopped down on the couch. Rocco jumped up beside her, tried to lick her face. He was very old and had bad breath. Helen pushed him away, took a long swallow of her drink.

"You smelly scoundrel," she said. "Do you love me?"

He began to pant, showing rusty teeth, a tongue that was almost black.

"Of course you do." Helen smiled. "How could you help it? I'm so fucking lovable."

She poured part of her drink into a shallow ashtray. She held it under Rocco's nose. He lapped it slowly, belching occasionally.

"The son of a bitch," she said. "The dirty, cotton-picking bastard. You know what I'd like to do, Rocco? I'd like to take one of his ankles and you take the other and we run him along a picket fence." She chuckled evilly. "Him and his goddamned Bob Cranshaw," she added bitterly.

Rocco finished his drink, curled up in the corner of the couch. He lay panting, watching her with rheumy eyes.

"Why did I call him?" she asked. "Why do salmon go upstream to spawn? I called him because I was bored. I was lonely because it's been so goddamned long since I've been to bed with a man. He's got a loverly body, really beautiful, and in bed he's a tiger. But he's *so* spacey. Oh, God, how awful I was. How *awful*." She grimaced, shook her head. "I called him. Rocco, I *called* him!"

She took another swallow. "Why did I call him? Because I'm fed up to the balls with spending nights reading schmucky books or seeing dirty movies or watching *The Incredible Hulk* or walking into strange bars with Peggy. That's why. I like men. Goddammit, I like to be with men. Oh, such a flip. Rocco, you have no idea. But so spacey!"

She went into the kitchen, for a refill, brought a dog biscuit back for Rocco. He sniffed at it, licked it once, then put his head down between his paws, and went to sleep.

"My head is splitting," Helen told him. "It's cracking right down the center. I swear to God, Rocco, it's just peeling open like an old onion."

She lay back, closed her eyes.

"Bastard," she muttered. "Up and out. Up and out. All out for the potato race. Bozo."

She felt sleep coming, finished her drink quickly. She went over to the parakeet cage. "One more day," she vowed. "You talk by tomorrow, or it's all up with you. Either you say something nice to me, or I'll give you to Rocco. He'll chew you up and spit you over the left-field fence."

The parakeet cringed back into a corner of the cage. She pulled on the night cover. She went into the bathroom and took four aspirin and a Librium.

Rocco stumbled after her into the bedroom. He curled up on his blanket, put his head down, began to snore.

"Honey baby Rocco boy," Helen Miley murmured. "Good night, dear."

She took off the robe, slid naked into bed. It was a double bed with two big pillows. She closed her eyes. Silently she recited the prayer beginning "Now I lay me down to sleep..." She finished by asking God to bless her brothers and their families, Peggy Palmer, Rocco, all the men she had ever loved, the parakeet, a stranger who had smiled at her from a Madison Avenue bus two years ago and whom she had never forgotten, her dead parents, and finally—after some consideration—she also asked God to bless Charles Lefferts and make him call her occasionally.

She lay on her back, one arm thrown across the other pillow. After a while she turned on her side, pulled the other pillow to her breast. She bunched it up, put her arms around it. Then she moved it down, clasped it between her legs.

Just before she fell asleep, she said, "Please."

3

HIS NAME WAS Jo Rhodes. It was really Joseph Rhodes, but he changed it to Jo one day when he happened to be reading a dictionary and discovered that Jo was a term of endearment in Scottish.

Joseph Rhodes would meet people, and they would ask, "Why do you call yourself Jo?" He would say, "A Rhodes by any other name would smell as sweet," and they would look at him.

He was a fizzy little man who chain-smoked Gauloises (blue) ferociously and occasionally said, "Bless my soul!" He had a fringe of white hair around a pointy skull, wore a pince-nez attached to his lapel with a black ribbon, and in a year when every man in New York was dousing himself with Stud, Brute, Stallion, and King Kong, Jo Rhodes was using Ed. Pinaud's Lilac Vegetal.

Helen Miley was wandering through the portrait gallery on the upper floor of the New York Historical Society at Seventy-seventh Street and Central Park West. She paused before a 150-year-old portrait that looked exactly like Don Ameche, and she laughed.

A wheezy voice at her elbow said, "It looks just like William Powell, doesn't it?"

"No," she said, without turning around, "it's Don Ameche."

"Ah, yes," he said. "Don Ameche. To be sure."

Then she turned around, her head tilted back to look up at the man speaking to her. Then she looked down. He was a few inches shorter than she and couldn't possibly have weighed more. He was wearing a suit of beautifully cut gray flannel, somewhat marred by food and wine stains on the double-breasted waistcoat. There was a tiny pink sweetheart rose in his lapel.

An hour later they were seated in a dim Italian restaurant on West Seventy-second Street, drinking chilled white wine from a green bottle shaped like a fish.

"I like the bottle, and I love the wine," Helen Miley said, "but there is something about having your wine come out of the mouth of a fish. . . ."

Jo Rhodes smiled mysteriously, touched her hand. He motioned to the proprietor, and a long, staccato conversation followed in Italian, which Helen did not understand. Their voices rose until they were almost shouting. Then Jo Rhodes got up; the two men embraced and kissed each other on the cheek. Helen found this mildly amusing.

He lighted Gauloises for both of them, then said, "This is what I have ordered: small chunks of filet mignon and small chunks of shrimp cooked together in a red wine sauce. Also, for each of us, a portion of spaghetti *al' la ōlla*. And for each of us, a salad of romaine and pickled mushrooms, with oil and vinegar dressing."

"I love you," she said.

For a very small man, he had a very large appetite. She watched, fascinated, as with great economy of movement he cleaned all his plates (wiping up the excess sauce with pieces of crusty bread) and consumed at least two-thirds of their bottle of Valpolicella. Then he patted his lips delicately with his napkin but scrubbed roughly at his white Adolphe Menjou mustache.

"It takes the wax out," he acknowledged, "but I must rid it of the garlic in case you wish to kiss me later."

She was delighted with him.

He ordered espresso and cognac for them, explaining that his doctor had recommended one or two brandies a day for his heart condition. He then had four cognacs and said, "Now I won't have to drink any tomorrow." But she did not believe him.

He lived on the top floor of a Murray Hill brownstone—but it was more studio than apartment. He was, he explained, a fashion and portrait photographer in "semi-retirement."

There was one big whitewashed room, an aquarium of light, sweet-smelling and clean. The floor was old-fashioned wide boards waxed to a high gloss. Cane screens divided the room in half. The front portion was blessed with floor-to-ceiling windows. Here he kept his photography equipment, including a huge old studio camera on a massive tripod. The camera itself was a wooden box bound in brass. There were smaller, more modern cameras, lights, reflectors, props, rolls of seamless paper in an eye-shattering rainbow of hues.

The rear portion of this enormous room, the living portion, was surprisingly designed with modern furnishings—steel and plastic, chromium and glass. Even an inflated chair and ottoman.

"When my wife died," he said, "I got rid of everything. We had some lovely pieces—would be worth a fortune today. But I didn't want any of it. I sold out. Now I redecorate every three or four years. I try to keep up."

"When did your wife die?"

"Oh," he said vaguely, "years ago."

There was a small bedroom, a smaller bathroom, and an unexpectedly large kitchen—big enough to accommodate a stretcher table and four chairs. There were hanging racks of copper pots and pans, a modern refrigerator-freezer, an electric oven.

"I don't like it," he said crossly. "Doesn't cook as well as gas. You can never adjust the thing properly."

He had a bottle of California champagne cooling, and they drank that, sitting on a leather and brushed-steel sofa, putting their glasses on a slab of plate glass that appeared to be floating in the air.

He showed her a fat portfolio of his prints, all black-and-whites, all characterized by a romantic softness, as if they had been taken by candlelight or through a screen of cheesecloth. Most of them were fashion shots that had appeared in *Vogue* and *Harper's Bazaar* during the 1930's. He had also done a great deal of work for a dead magazine called *Stage*, and there were signed photographs of Bert Lahr, Norma Shearer, W. C. Fields, Gertrude Lawrence, and many others. They all looked incredibly young.

"Did you know all these people?" she asked him.

"Oh, yes," he said softly. "Yes, I knew them."

"You must have had some wonderful times."

"I think so," he said, puzzled, "but memories are deceitful. You remember the good times and can't remember the bad. I'm sure I had many miserable experiences in those days, but I can't remember them."

He put the book away, refilled her glass.

"I would like very much to photograph you, Helen," he said.

Ah-*ha!* she thought. "Nudes?" she asked.

"Bless my soul!" he cried. "Of course not. Portraits. Head and shoulders. You have the head of a young Greek boy. About the fourth century. Those tight blond curls are exquisite. Against a black background, I think. Someday... when you have the time."

"All right," she said happily. "I'd like that. I haven't had my picture taken in years."

The sun had shifted. It was dimmer in the studio... a little. The light was muted, paler. The soft light soothed Helen, rounded her bare legs.

Not a beautiful woman, he decided. Maybe not even pretty. Her chin was too audacious; the boniness of her face was accented by the way she wore her hair. But it was a strong face with a look of steady purpose. Time would help. Time would carve wrinkles and slashes, cuts and bruises. He was certain this face would age well, becoming sweet, mocking, old...

The body was good. The body looked as springy as new turf. She surged with juice; she moved well. He thought she was perhaps thirty-five or thirty-six. Around there. Her skin was fine, unblemished. He had already admired the plump curve of her buttocks in the New York Historical Society.

"You must weigh almost as much as I do," he told her.

She turned and grinned at him. Then she took off her shoes, sat far back on the couch, tucked her feet under her. They sat there side by side, arms almost touching.

"I bet I outweigh you by ten pounds, baby," she said. "They'd have to peel you off the ceiling."

He chuckled and slapped his knee.

"Could be," he said. "Could be."

They lifted their glasses to take a sip. A drop of icy

champagne slid off Helen's glass, down into the neckline of her linen dress, down between her breasts, down, down, down. . . .

"JEE-rusalem!" she gasped, and he smiled at her. They sat some moments in silence, not wanting anything more.

"You are not married?" he asked—and then was ashamed of himself when he saw her face freeze.

"No."

"I don't understand that."

"I have bad luck with my men."

"Yes." He nodded sadly. "Like old ones . . ."

She turned, looked at him gravely. Then she leaned forward, kissed his lips and Adolphe Menjou mustache. Her mouth was warm, wet from her drink, and so sweet that he made a sound in his throat: a little cry, a sob.

She pulled back, winked at him.

"That's for nothing," she said, "so watch yourself, buster."

She watched him inherit the world. He smoothed his mustache with one knuckle and then, in a fit of wild bravado, twirled the tips.

"It's important not to expect too much," he said.

"I know." She nodded. "I keep telling myself that. A slice of the cake. Not the whole cake. Just a slice."

"Yes. Just a slice."

The small bedroom had a skylight. It seemed to him the evening light was violet, soft, perhaps scented. She brought her glass and the remainder of the champagne in with her; he switched to a small balloon of cognac.

He sat on the edge of the shiny brass bed, sipped his brandy, watched admiringly as she undressed. He laughed delightedly when he saw her naked. Tears came to his eyes; he took off the pince-nez and let it dangle.

"Oh, oh, oh," he said, almost spluttering. "So lovely."

She leaned back against the cool brass headboard, pulled the satin sheet up to her waist. She sipped her glass of champagne and didn't care.

"Where are you from, Helen?" he asked her. "From your accent I would guess the Middle West. Not New York. I would guess Indiana."

"Close," she said, "but no cigar. Ohio."

"How long did you live there? When did you come to New York?"

"Oh, baby." She sighed. "Looking back is a mug's game. I mean the surest way to bug yourself is to keep thinking of how things were with you and what you would have done differently if you had to do it all over again."

"Yes," he said wonderingly, "that is so."

He took off his jacket and waistcoat and hung them neatly on the polished arms of a wooden valet.

"After I left Ohio and came to New York, I met this man in the service..."

"When was that?"

"Oh...I don't remember exactly...around 1971 or 1972 ...about then. He was training to be a pilot in the Air Force when I met him. Then he made lieutenant. I had this big thing for him, and every time he got to New York he'd stay with me. This went on for a year. He was from Boston, and I didn't know he was married until the night he got sent overseas."

"How is it possible to be intimate with a man for a year and not know he is married?"

"Well, I never believe in asking men questions like that. If they want me to know, then they'll tell me. Besides, it didn't make any difference to me. I really loved that guy, so when he told me he was married, I said it was okay, the joke was on me."

"Or on his wife."

"Yes.... or on his wife. He said his wife didn't understand him, and I laughed at that. He said he wanted me to wait for him, and after he got back from overseas, he'd divorce his wife and marry me."

He bent over to unlace his shoes; his voice was muffled.

"Did you believe him?"

"I treated that as a big buffola. I told him we'd had a lot of laughs together, a lot of laughs, and I would have appreciated knowing he was married, but it really didn't make any difference. That's what I told him. He swore that if I'd wait for him, he'd get a divorce and marry me. 'Oh, sure,' I said."

"I gather, then, that you didn't wait for him?"

"You gather right. I didn't even answer his letters. What the hell. Then I heard he came back and actually did divorce his wife and marry a woman he had only known a week or two."

"I'm sorry, Helen."

"Sorry? What for? But it shows you. I suppose if I knew then what I know now, I would have waited for him. But like I said, what's the sense of looking back? You just end up bugging yourself."

He placed trees inside his shoes, set them neatly under the bed.

"You came directly to New York from Ohio?"

"That's right. I was working as secretary to an office manager in Lower Hotchkiss. That's my hometown. It's near Toledo. He wasn't a bad guy—about average, I'd say. Every payday he'd chase me around the desk, and about once a month I'd let him catch me. I was bored as hell with Lower Hotchkiss. He had a wife, a nice home, and two children. His son was my age, but I never met him. This man's wife had cancer. She died from it, and it really broke him. On the day he buried her—that night, that is—he asked me to spend all night with him in a motel, and I did. But that was the end of it for us. He never wanted to shack up again. I left for New York right after that."

He took a sip of cognac and slowly, slowly, began to unbuckle his garters.

"What did you do before the secretarial job?"

"Before that I was going to a business school and learning typing and shorthand. And I was slinging hash at a local beanery."

"You were a restaurant waitress?"

"What the hell, baby—am I talking Eskimo or something?"

"I just wanted to make certain I understood you, Helen."

"Yes, I was a restaurant waitress. If any girl wants to learn how to handle men, I suggest she should take a job as a waitress. First of all, you get so the sight of a man eating doesn't make you sick to your stomach. It's very important for any girl who eventually wants to be happily married. Second of all, you also learn when a man is making a serious pass or when he's just talking. Most of them at the Kitty Kat were just talking—about ninety percent, I'd say."

"Do you feel this proportion holds true for men in New York as well?"

"Maybe ninety-five percent in New York. But let's talk about you for a while, Jo. What kind of life have you had?"

"Oh, no," he protested. "I find this fascinating. My life has been very uneventful compared to yours. Much longer, but not as full. Please, tell me more."

He rolled his silk socks into little balls, tucked them inside his shoes.

"All right," she said, raising her knees and hugging them. "I'll confess all. I haven't even thought about these things for years and years. Well . . . I met a lot of guys at the Kitty Kat and had a lot of laughs."

"Was there any one man in particular?"

"There were a few I was interested in for one reason or another. There was Joe Fossley—he owned a garage. He was an older man, almost old enough to be my father."

"Do you like older men?"

"Older men? Sure. And younger men and all those in between. What has age got to do with it? Then there was Eddie Chase, a boy I went to high school with. He was working in his father's furniture store, and he had a car. We had a lot of laughs together, but it was nothing serious. Eddie wasn't about to get married—just waiting for the draft to get him. Then there was a traveling salesman who came through occasionally. His name was Smith—John Smith. I know it sounds phony, but it really was John Smith. He showed me his birth certificate, driver's license, everything."

He removed the gold links from the cuffs of his striped shirt, placed them carefully in a small leather box atop his oak dresser. He began to unknot his tie slowly. Helen watched him, bemused by this ballet.

"And what kind of a man was this John Smith?"

"Strange. Real strange. He was about forty, a little roly-poly guy, part bald and false teeth. He was separated from his wife."

"What was so strange about him?"

"Well, Johnny looked exactly like a traveling salesman. I mean he was always trading jokes with the men in the diner, and he carried fountain pens and cigars in his breast pocket, and he was loud and liked to drink it up. But then I'd go out on a date with him, and he'd change completely. He was quiet and loving and very tender. He was just nice—a very nice guy. We'd drive out on the highway and shack up at a motel, and, son, this guy was the greatest. This little old roly-poly, baldy, false-toothy guy was really something. He taught me what sex could be."

Jo Rhodes paused, his shirt half unbuttoned.

"You're not just saying that to give me confidence?"

"Does a guy who can pick up a girl half his age in the New York Historical Society need a boost? Don't be silly. No, what I'm saying is that I had been going out with boys ever since I was nine years old. By the time I met old Johnny I knew what the score was. One to nothing. But it never meant anything. It was like scratching a great big mosquito bite—you know? But it had meaning for Johnny. It was really his whole life—the only thing he lived for. He showed me what it could be. I learned a lot from him, but it was more than just sex. That's only a word. Johnny was the first man I ever slept with who gave me the feeling that I was needed, that I was wanted, that it took *me* to complete a guy. Not just any woman, but *me*. You still with me?"

"Yes, Helen. I think I understand."

He hunched out from under the straps of his silk suspenders, took off his shirt, shook it out. Then he hung it on the knob of the closet door. He was wearing a light weight ecru undershirt with short sleeves and three buttons at the neck.

"And what did you do before you became a waitress at the Kitty Kat diner?"

"Before that? Well, I had been out of high school for about a year. I was just staying home and helping Mother. She had been feeling poorly since my father died. I have three brothers, all older than me. Alfred was married and in California. Earl—he's the middle one—he's in the Army. A captain. Lewis—he's the young one—he got out of high school a year before I did. He was in the bank. That's how we were living—on what Lewis made at the bank and my father's insurance money. And sometimes Earl would send us some money from his Army pay."

"Did you have a happy childhood?"

"Oh, yes! I did. Very happy. We lived on a farm outside of Lower Hotchkiss. Before my father died, he and my uncle—my father's brother—ran the place, and my brothers helped. Yes, it was a lot of laughs. My father and my uncle were hard workers, but they liked to relax, too. They liked to yak it up. They were always pulling jokes."

"What kind of jokes?"

"Oh, God, Jo, I must be boring you to tears with all this shit."

"No, you are not. It really gives me great pleasure. I want to know about you. Please don't stop."

"All right. Well, you know what kind of jokes farm people pull. Once my uncle brought me a little bitty rabbit from town. A little white rabbit. I didn't know it, but he had bought four other white rabbits, each one a little bigger. Every morning for four days he'd sneak down to the cellar and take my rabbit out of the orange crate and put it in a bigger one. Every day my rabbit got bigger and bigger. I was so excited that it was growing so fast that I took it all over and showed the neighbors. Then, after it had grown to full size in four days, he reversed the whole thing, and my rabbit kept getting smaller and smaller. Jesus, I didn't know what was happening. I was afraid it would get real small and disappear. Then, when I started to cry, my uncle hugged me and kissed me and told me what he had done and gave me all the rabbits for my own. Jokes like that."

He pulled his undershirt over his head. His torso was thin, white, quite hairless. His nipples were two tiny pink sweetheart roses. Helen was charmed.

He took a maroon silk dressing gown from the closet, donned it, knotted the belt, turned his back to her, began removing his trousers and underpants under the gown.

"Maybe I'm not telling it right, but it was a very happy home. Very happy. My parents always liked a lot of company. Every Sunday evening there'd be a crowd over for supper—on the lawn if the weather was nice. People would bring things. Baked beans, potato salad, cucumber salad, pecan pie, a chocolate layer cake, maybe a big baked ham. Every woman would bring what she was famous for. You know? My uncle played the mandolin, and my brother Earl, he played the guitar. A lot of fun. My brothers would ask the girls they were going with. It was nice. We'd sing songs. No one knew what was going to happen."

"What happened?"

"Well, my father and uncle went into town to make a payment at the bank. I guess they had a few drinks. On the way back they piled up our Ford pickup truck. They were both killed."

"You loved your father?"

"Oh, God, yes! Very much. My uncle, too. They were both big men. Real men—you know? Different from the kind of men I meet in New York."

"Yes. I can imagine."

"No, you can't imagine. You can't know unless you're a woman. They were real men. Even my brothers aren't like them. A little maybe, but not really like them. I guess they don't make men like that anymore. Oh, shit, what's the use of talking!"

He set his glass of brandy on the bedside table. Then, in one swift, dexterous movement, he ripped off his robe, let it fall to the floor, and slid naked beneath the sheet, close to her but not touching her. It happened so fast she couldn't even look at him. He was just a rapid white ghost. He lighted a Gauloise, but she had one of her filter tips.

It was darker now. Through the skylight she thought she could see a star. They blew plumes of smoke toward it. Somewhere, faintly, music was playing. It was a John Philip Sousa march: "The Stars and Stripes Forever."

"What happened after your father and uncle died?"

"What happened? Oh...everything broke up. Alfred got married and moved to California. Earl enlisted in the Army. Mother just went downhill, and we sold off most of our land. All except the house. Everything broke up."

"What kind of a woman was your mother?"

"Mother? She had beautiful eyes. Mother was all right. A hard worker. She never complained. Jesus, she worked hard. She didn't laugh it up as much as Dad, but she'd sort of look down, and you could tell she was laughing inside but didn't want to show it. She was a lot quieter than my father and Uncle Barney. She let them make the noise and sing the songs and play the clowns. But she ran that home. She was what held us all together—until my father got killed. Then she changed. Then she hardly spoke at all and never even smiled. That's the way it went. Then she died. Maybe you're thinking they don't make women like that anymore either. Maybe you're right."

"What kind of a child were you, Helen?"

"Oh, hell, I was all legs and buckteeth. I ran wild. I cut my hair short and wore pants and tried to keep up with my brothers. I wasn't much of a sweet little girl. I guess I was a disappointment to my mother. She tried, but then she gave up and said she figured I was just born to be a tomboy."

He turned to stub out his cigarette, then rolled his way farther down in the bed until the sheet was up to his chin. The back of his hand touched her naked thigh. It was a cool, soft hand. He stroked her thigh lightly with the back of his hand.

"Were you good at school?"

"About average, I'd say. If I was interested in something, I was good at it. History and economics and things like that bugged me, so I wasn't very good at them. But I had a crush on our science teacher, so I was pretty good at that. I was in the dramatics club, too. We didn't have enough boys in the club, so when we put on *Othello*, I was Iago. What are you laughing at?"

"Oh...I don't know. Were you popular in school?"

"I'd say I was popular with the boys and not so popular with the girls. I dated a lot. They used to call me Hot Pants when I wasn't around. They thought I didn't know about it, but I did. My brothers were always getting into fights about it."

"What did they mean by Hot Pants?"

"Where you from, kiddo?"

"I was born and brought up in New York. Why?"

"Sometimes I think you must be from outer space or somewhere, the things you don't know. They called me Hot Pants if you must know, because they thought I was always hot for a little loving."

"And were you?"

"Sure."

"Bless my soul! Helen, who was the first—the first—"

"My first lay? That was with Eddie Chase in the icehouse. Christ, I was picking sawdust out of my—out of my ears for two weeks after."

"How old were you then?"

"I was thirteen, and Eddie was fourteen."

His fingertips touched her thigh lightly, not moving. She turned closer to him, kissed his cool shoulder. Then she lay on her back, watched the night come into the room.

"Listen, dear," she said dreamily, "it's been a wonderful day, and I'd like to give you a gift. I have this darling little parakeet, and I bet you'd love it. I love it myself, but I'm not home enough to give it the care it should have."

"Oh, I couldn't, Helen."

"I'll even throw in the cage."

"Does the parakeet talk?"

"Just a few simple, heartfelt phrases. He's very intelligent. You could teach him a lot, I'm sure."

"Thank you, Helen, but I don't believe..."

Then he was silent.

"Jo?" she said.

But he was silent.

She had a moment of panic, remembering what he had said about his heart condition. But she put her ear to his chest, heard his heart thumping away determinedly. She bent close to his lips, smelled wine, champagne, cognac, and a bit of garlic. She smiled.

"Good night, darling," she said aloud and kissed his bald pate.

She rose and dressed. She left him a note, thanking him for a wonderful afternoon, giving him her addresses at home and at the office and her telephone numbers.

She took the tiny pink sweetheart rose from the lapel of his jacket and ate it thoughtfully as she descended the stairs to the street.

4

HELEN MILEY ENTERED the offices of Swanson & Feltzig, Public Relations, at nine twenty-four Monday morning. Susie Carrar was at the reception desk, weeping noisily into a small bunch of handkerchief.

"What's the matter, baby?" Helen asked anxiously. "Did you miss again?"

Susie sobbed.

Helen hiked up the skirt of her Adolfo suit, put one hip on the edge of Susie's desk.

"Okay," she said, "stop crying. The world hasn't come to an end."

Susie wept.

"First thing is to go to a doctor and make sure," Helen advised. "Then I'll give you the address of this marvelous clinic in Brooklyn. He gives penicillin and even has you come back for a checkup. How much money has your guy got?"

"He's a shipping clerk," Susie said mournfully.

Helen nodded grimly. There goes the mink, she thought. "Well, let me worry about the bread."

"Thank you, Helen," Susie said gratefully.

"Have Loeb and Leopold called in yet, baby?"

"Mr. Swanson will be in at eleven. He wants to go over this month's luncheon schedule with you. Mr. Feltzig said he's having lunch with a client and won't be back until maybe two or two-thirty."

"All right." Helen nodded. "Any answers to our ad?"

"Three calls so far. I told them to come in at ten, ten-fifteen and ten-thirty."

"That's fine, sweet. I'm going down for coffee. And don't worry about it. I've had more abortions than you've had permanents. Believe me, it's no worse than a high colonic. See you later."

The Sam-Al Luncheonette was crowded. The only empty seats at the counter were directly in front of the short-order cook working furiously at a sizzling grill. Helen slid onto one stool, put her alligator purse on the other. She was there only a moment before Peggy Palmer removed the purse, slid onto the stool, grinned at her.

"Buttered corn muffin," the cook roared. "Pick up."

"Hello, ducks," Peggy said, dimpling. "How was the weekend?"

"It had its moments," Helen said. "And yours? Did you make it with the Camel?"

Peggy rolled her eyes. "I got the curse. Imagine. Saturday night, and I had finally decided to blast."

"What a sell," Helen said sympathetically. "After all your worry, too. What did he say?"

"I didn't let on." Peggy giggled. "I asked him what kind of a girl he thought I was."

"What did he say to that?"

"He said he thought we were two normal adults with normal desires and normal ways of looking at things. J'order yet?"

"Normal?" Helen scoffed. "Mr. Nose normal? That's a laugh. Just coffee for me. I don't see how you stand that creep."

"Oh, Helen, he isn't so bad. He brought me a bunch of violets. I think I'll have coffee and a toasted English. Wasn't that sweet?"

"Toasted English, two down," the cook screamed.

"What did you do?" Peggy asked. "Did Bob call?"

"Bob? I haven't seen him for weeks. Didn't I tell you that was all over? Yesterday I met this sweet old gaffer who's one year younger than God. His name's Jo Rhodes. I thought he was going to be a dirty old man, but he turned out to be sweet, just sweet. We had a marvelous dinner at a wop restaurant on West Seventy-second Street. Lots of vino. It was marvy. He holds his socks up with garters."

"You're kidding?"

"I'm not, I swear. And Charles called me Friday night."

"Charles?"

"Side of rye," the cook yelled. "Scrambled working."

"You know—Charlie Lefferts. I was all undressed and ready for bed, and I had this stinking headache, but I figured what the hell."

"Did you go out?"

"No," Helen said, smiling, "not exactly."

Peggy giggled. "Did he suck your toes again?"

Helen looked shocked. "My God, did I tell you about that? Pass the cream, please, dear. Yes, he's a shrimper. I tell you that man hasn't got a brain in his head, but when it comes to bed, he's the guy who wrote the book. Really incredible. I'd introduce you, but I don't want to make you dissatisfied with the Camel."

"I don't think the Camel will ever suck my toes," Peggy said forlornly. "Sugar, darling. He's very conservative."

"You're not telling me anything I don't know. Listen, Peg, do you really think you're playing him the right way? Maybe you should—you know—sort of dangle him?"

"Large OJ," the cook shrieked. "Side of wheat with."

"I wish I knew," Peggy said worriedly. "If I decide to go all the way, he might just decide to make it with me and then drop me. If I don't, maybe he'll get sore and drop me anyway. What should I do, Helen?"

"It's too important to let anyone else decide for you. But I guess you're right. You ought to swing. After all, if you do get married and then discover he's just a drip in bed—then where are you? I really think it's better if you go all the way now and find out."

"I don't know," Peggy said doubtfully. "I'd hate to lose him. My God, I'll be thirty-four next month. How old are you?"

"I'm thirty-two," Helen said.

Both women sipped their coffee silently for a few moments.

"Scramble two with French," the cook screeched.

"Lunch?" Peggy asked.

"Can't, dear. We have such a rough month coming up—two new product introductions—I finally talked the Rover Boys into hiring a temporary for a month. We had an ad in yesterday's *Times* and Susie Carrar told me she got three answers so far, and they're coming in this morning for interviews. Jesus, I need someone to help out with the releases and mailings. On Friday we've got this big luncheon at the Bixby."

"The Bixby? How come you have it at such an unchic place like that?"

"Old Hot Hands gets a kickback from the manager," Helen explained. "Besides, the drinks are big, even if the food is lousy. And all those reporters and editors are so loaded by the time they sit down they don't know what they're eating."

"God," Peggy said enviously, "all those men."

"Not a chance." Helen shook her head. "A one-night stand maybe, but nothing serious. They're all from Nyack or lushes or both. Anyway this thing at the Bixby is for a new electronic broiler, so a lot of editors from women's magazines will be there, too. You know—the bitches with the big hats."

"Still," Peggy said. "God, all those men. I don't get to meet any. You know what my office is like. Fifty girls and Mr. Nussbaum. Do you think I should change my job? You know—go somewhere where there are eligible men?"

"Eligible?" Helen asked. "Alive, you mean? Why not, baby? You could get two hundred anywhere. I'd change, too, but where could I do better than two seventy-five?"

"Ham and egg on a roll," the cook bellowed.

"You run that whole office," Peggy said.

"Damned right," Helen said stoutly, "but where do I go from here? In another few years I'll be making three hundred—maybe. And that's it. That's practically tops for women anywhere."

"It's not fair," Peggy complained.

"What is?" Helen shrugged. "You've just got to be hard and shiny and ride with the punch. Oh, my God, I almost forgot to tell you—Susie Carrar is knocked up."

"Oh, my God," Peggy said. "Is she sure?"

"Pancakes and sausage," the cook shrilled. "Side of white down."

"She missed again," Helen nodded. "It's practically certain."

"What's she going to do?"

"What can she do? Get it knocked. Some schnook shipping clerk. He's way beneath her."

"He couldn't have been too far beneath her," Peggy said, giggling.

"You can say that again." Helen grinned. "Here, let me have the check. You got it on Thursday."

"But you paid the tip at lunch," Peggy said.

"But you got the cab from the bar," Helen reminded. "Oh, hell, let me take it. You get the next. So what are you going to do about the Camel, Peg?"

"I know what I'd like to do, but beggars can't be choosers. Honest to God, ducks, it's been so long since I've had sex that every time I sneeze dust comes out my ears."

"I know exactly how you feel," Helen said sympathetically. "If it wasn't for Charles calling me every now and then, I'd be climbing walls. He's wonderful for me. You know that pain I had in my neck and shoulder? It went right away."

"You make him sound like a doctor." Peggy laughed.

"Yeah," Helen growled. "Him and his injections."

"Poach one on toast," the cook muttered.

"Call me tonight, Peg," Helen said. "We can discuss more about the Camel. I really think you should consider all angles carefully. He's such a nudnick."

"I know"—Peggy sighed—"but what are you going to do?"

"Yes," Helen Miley said with wonder in her voice, "what *are* we going to do?"

"Burn two," said the cook.

5

THE FIRST APPLICANT was waiting when Helen returned to the office. He was, she saw, a plump youth with blond sideburns down to his mandibles. Princeton '77, she thought, nodded to Susie, and marched into her private office.

It was a small, crowded room, the walls lined with cork. Push-pinned to the cork were press releases, schedules, newspaper clippings and magazine stories, publicity photos, business letters, memos, addresses, a swatch of tweed cloth, a photo of John F. Kennedy, and a white card that had the word "LOVE" printed in the center in 24-point Bodoni Bold caps.

But all Helen could see was the long florist's box balanced on the clutter that hid her desk. She ripped it open. Two dozen lemon-yellow mums and a small card engraved in English script. Jo Rhodes. On the back he had written, in a precise bookkeeper's hand, "I thank you. Jo."

She called him immediately.

"You shouldn't have," she told him, "but I'm glad you did. It's the dearest, nicest, sweetest thing that's happened to me in years."

"Helen," he said," I must—ah, it's rather embarrassing—but I must ask you."

"What is it, baby?"

"I wasn't—well, you know—I wasn't too brutal, was I? I didn't hurt you in any way, did I?"

"Kiddo, you were just marvelous," she assured him. "You were incredible."

"Bless my soul!" he said. "Ah!" he said. "Hah!" he said. "I was, was I? Well, well, well! Just one other question: You did—did you not?—uh, take the proper precautions?"

"Of course. Don't worry about a thing, Jo."

"Splendid," he breathed. "I do not, of course, want you to suffer on my account. It was a lovely afternoon, and I thank you for it. May I call you later this week?"

"Please do, baby. Either here or at home. Anytime."

She hung up, plopped down in her swivel chair, leaned back. She pulled up her skirt, parked her feet on the desk. She lighted her fourth cigarette of the day. She stared at the golden mums catching the soft morning light coming through her single window.

"Bless my soul," she said aloud.

The first applicant was, as she had judged, a recent graduate (Brown, not Princeton). He had a great deal of personality—perhaps a little too much for his age—and was bubbling with a hundred ideas, one of which had merit. But he had no acquaintance with the New York press, had never worked for a public relations firm before.

Helen explained that for this temporary job she needed an experienced man capable of moving right in and taking over without on-the-job training. Undaunted, he gathered up his samples of short, humorous essays published in magazines she had never heard of and thanked her courteously for her time. He then asked her if she would have lunch with him—an offer she politely declined.

The second applicant had held several jobs in as many months, and she could smell the reason why. She tried not to stare at his efforts to control his shaking hands. She was tempted to offer him a shot from the bottle of scotch she kept in her lower desk drawer, then thought better of it.

The third man spoke with a South London accent so thick she could hardly understand him. The fourth was actually a hairdresser who wanted to get into "more creative work." The fifth had a dreadful smirk. The sixth refused to work for a woman and stalked out.

So it went.... At twelve thirty Helen sent Susie Carrar downstairs to the Chinese restaurant next door for a large order of fantail shrimp and a double Rob Roy.

"One Rob Roy and I can feel it," Helen said. "Two Rob Roys and anyone can feel it."

Susie smiled wanly at this jape, which she had heard several times before.

Interviews began again after lunch. By three o'clock Helen was tiring, not so much from asking the same questions, cutting her way through the thicket of lies, half-lies, and exaggerations, but from a depression brought about by this parade of obsolete men.

She buzzed Susie on the intercom. "Next," she said.

He had to duck his head to come through the door. He was black and built like an Eberhard-Faber #3. His rusty hair was combed in waves from a side part.

"My God," Helen cried, "it's got to be basketball."

His smile warmed the room.

"Only in high school," he said. "I wasn't fast enough for college."

"How tall are you?" she asked, reaching up to shake his hand.

"A little under six-seven."

"And you still meet people who say, 'How's the weather up there?'"

"That's right." He nodded. "I still do."

"I'm from Ohio," she told him. "High school basketball is very big in Ohio. Not as big as it is in Indiana, of course, but still plenty big. Sit down and have one of these cigarettes while I go over your résumé."

Harry Tennant; thirty-eight; single; in good health. Etc.; etc. Education. Etc.; etc. Graduate of Columbia. Night courses in marketing at NYU. Etc.; etc. Six months here; two years there; then six years with the *Amsterdam Gazette* covering new products, research and development, marketing, advertising. Weekly column for four years. Etc.; etc. Free-lancing for *Advertising Age, Printer's Ink*, etc., etc. Lead article in *Rolling Stone* in 1976, etc.; etc.

"Look," Helen said, "you know this is just a temporary job? Just for a month? We're paying two-fifty a week for a month because we're in a bind. Everything's piling up. But if no new work comes in, then there's no job at the end of the month. You understand that?"

"I understand."

She scratched her ear as she stared at him.

"You know," she said, "I've had a lot of jobs. And every time I'd get interviewed, some bastard in personnel would give me one of those sick smiles and say, 'Now tell me all about yourself.' And I'd want to say, 'Well, I smoke opium in elevators, I dig little girls, and I've got this tattoo on my stomach that says: AMERICA—LOVE IT OR LEAVE IT.'"

"I know, I know."

"But now I'm on the other side of the fence, and I've got to say it. So tell me all about yourself."

"What do you want to know?"

"Why did you leave the *Gazette*?"

Yea, in measured and stately tones did he speak; for a moment she had an insane notion that he had written it all out and memorized it—a kind of private psalm.

"The *Amsterdam Gazette*," he said carefully, "is a daily newspaper published in Harlem and concerned with the activities and aspirations of black people. Rightly so. About a year ago, Mr. Thomas Aguin, publisher and owner of the *Gazette*, decided that the paper should take a more active role in black organizations devoted to the betterment of the black community in America, and particularly in New York. Mr. Aguin called a meeting of all employees—executive, editorial, printers, pressmen, advertising salesmen, sweepers, and so forth—and proposed that the *Gazette* strive to become a major force in Harlem life and in New York City politics. Specifically, he proposed that representatives of the *Gazette*—the employees—become more closely associated with Harlem organizations—militant outfits and block groups and anticrime groups and drug cure outfits and church and new black business associations. Things like that. He wanted us to join these groups and open the pages of the newspaper to them and talk about them in our columns. And he wanted us to address these groups, to make speeches, and to help organize things. I mean, take an active part."

"And what did the employees of the *Gazette* say to that?"

"They thought it was just great."

"And what did *you* think of that?"

"What did I think of that? Well . . . of course, I thought it was great, too. But what happened was . . . what happened was. . . ."

He bent his head, raddled his fingers. His face had a soft sheen to it, so hairless that he looked as if he had never shaved in his life. He looked up at her, a man trying to fly a kite in a tunnel.

"I guess," he said, "I've got no fucking charisma."

If he meant to shock her, he didn't succeed. But she was curious about why he wanted to get his ass kicked out so fast.

"What does that mean?"

"I wasn't good at the speeches. I wasn't even good at the writing—and that's my trade. I couldn't seem to get involved. That's my problem—I just can't get involved."

He threw one hand into the air. His small ears lay flat to his skull; his gestures were a delight to see. His eyes had the sad, baffled look of a chess player.

"You know many people in New York? I mean on newspapers and magazines?"

"Most of them in my field." He nodded. "I met them at press parties and meetings and interviews over the years. Do you want references?"

"No . . . that's all right. You know references don't mean a damned thing."

"That's right," he agreed.

She tapped her pencil on the desk. It was an Eberhard-Faber #3. Tap point. Tap eraser. Tap point. Tap eraser.

What am I doing? she thought. *What in God's name am I doing?*

"There's a lot of pressure," she warned. "Sometimes I blow my cork and scream. Sometimes the bosses scream. There's no room in my office for you. You'll have to work at a desk outside with the receptionist. You'll probably have to run errands—you know, deliver photos and releases. You'll get the shitty end of the stick."

He nodded.

"It's just for a month," she said desperately, "and then you'll get canned."

He nodded.

"Still want it?"

"Yes, I do."

"Can you start tomorrow morning?"

"Yes, I can."

She sighed, rose, stuck out her hand.

"All right, Harry," she said. "It's yours. You better call me Helen."

"Thank you, Helen," he said.

"Just be here tomorrow morning at nine."

"I'll be here."

He started for the door.

"Harry, wait a minute...Do you need an advance? I could get you your first week's pay in advance if it's important. Do you want it right now?"

"You trust me?"

"Of course I don't trust you," she shouted angrily. "You'll take the two-fifty and immediately book passage on the *Queen Elizabeth* and sail away to Europe. Do you want the money, goddammit?"

"You're some hard-nosed woman," he said admiringly. "Yes, I want it."

"Wait here a minute."

She went out to Susie Carrar's desk, got the firm's checkbook, made out a check to Harry Tennant for two hundred and fifty dollars. She ripped it out, stalked over to Mr. Feltzig's office, walked in without knocking. He was on the telephone.

"Of course I love you, baby," he was saying. "Didn't I buy your brother a violin?"

She plunked the check down in front of him, held out a pen. Still talking on the phone, he looked up at her, raising his eyebrows. Grimly she pointed at the check. He signed it.

She marched back into her own office, handed the check to Harry Tennant.

"Here," she said. "You owe us a week's work."

"You'll get it," he said. He looked at the check, and for a moment she was afraid he might weep.

"Beat it," she growled. "I've got work to do. I'll see you tomorrow morning."

Suddenly, he bent far down and kissed her cheek. Then he walked out, ducking his head as he went through the door.

"Jesus Christ," Helen said to Susie Carrar, "what a day. What the hell am I—a cross between Little Orphan Annie and Mother Macree?"

"What are you talking about?" Susie wanted to know.

6

THE KNITTED SHIFT accented her solid ass and Uncle-Sam-Wants-*YOU* breasts. She moved slowly through the crowd, all jaw, leg and horn-rimmed glasses. Six Rob Roys played a roundelay for glockenspiel inside her skull, and she showed her teeth in a deep-freeze grin.

A hand reached from the throng, lightly touched the knitted dress at the shoulder.

"Plum-colored," he said. "A divine shade."

She took his arm. "Marry me," she said. "At once."

He looked at her reflectively. He was a big, fleshy man, soft in the seat. Reddish bags looped down under his eyes. She was charmed to note that he had forgotten to zip up his fly. He held a full glass that was, she decided, either his specimen or pure bourbon.

"I have a terrace on my apartment," he told her, "and yesterday I found a folded slip of paper on it. Someone who lives

33

above me had thrown it down. It said, 'I hate you, Mr. X.' What do you think of that?"

"Listen," she said, "I know this woman, and she's married. Her husband lays her twice a year, on Thanksgiving and Arbor Day. And every time, after it's over, he looks at her and says, 'It's so wonderful, why do I deny myself?' What do you think of *that?*"

"My name is Richard Faye," he said, "but friends call me Uck."

"That's very funny." She nodded. "I'm laughing all over. Do you like women, Uck?"

"Some."

"Are you married, Uck? You don't have to answer that."

"No. Are you wearing anything under that dress?"

"Skin. My name is Helen Miley. I'm with Swanson and Feltzig. We're giving this luncheon. I am thirty years old and my fighting weight is one-o-seven. I wear a bra you have to blow up, and I like my drinks weak and my men strong."

"Who doesn't?" He shrugged.

"Uck, I shouldn't tell you this because I like you just the way you are—but maybe I should tell you."

"Do," he said.

"Your fly's unzipped."

"Again?" He sighed and zipped.

She looked around vaguely. It had been a successful luncheon. The client had made an effective speech. After they had eaten, he rose and said, "We have a new electronic broiler. The bar is now open." Reporters and editors applauded. Across the room Helen saw the head and shoulders of Harry Tennant. He was surrounded by a circle of harpies from women's magazines. He caught her eye and waved. She waved back with the hand that held her drink.

"That's all right," Richard Faye said. "It's a drip-dry suit. I have two cats. Did I tell you that? Their names are Moishe and Pincus."

"Men cats?"

"Denutted," he said gently. "Do you like cats?"

"I love cats," she said. "Actually, I hate cats, but I said I love cats because I love you. I have a dog named Rocco and a parakeet that won't talk, the little sneak. Uck, you *are* going to marry me, aren't you? Even if it's only for a night?"

"Um," he said.

"You're getting to me, buster," she said. "I go for those sacks under your eyes and your great big yellow teeth and the way your hair grows over your collar. I really adore you—honestly."

"I'm a wee bit drunkie," he said softly.

"No," she said seriously, "if you can say you're drunk, then you really can't be drunk, can you? I mean, if you were, you wouldn't really know it, would you?"

"I think you're absolutely brilliant," he said admiringly. "But I should tell you right now—I snore."

"I couldn't care less," she said. "Oh, God, I'm so happy. You know what I like about you? Usually there's a war between me and men. I mean we're always fencing, and they're pretending to be hot rods, and I'm pretending to hold them off, and it's all pretending—know what I mean? It's a game like. But I feel comfortable with you. I don't know what it is, but I can relax with you. We don't have to play that stupid game, do we?"

"No," he said sadly, "we don't."

"Listen," she said anxiously, "you don't collect African masks, do you?"

"No."

"You don't think you're the greatest cook God ever made, do you?"

"No."

"You don't say 'soonish' and 'latish' and 'eightish,' do you?"

"Neverish."

"And women aren't always calling you up, are they?"

"Very few women call me up—if any."

"I want you to know all about me," she said earnestly. "Every little thing. I want you to go over me with a fine-tooth comb. Did you know I can touch my nose with the tip of my tongue? Very few people and no gorillas can do that. See?"

He stared, fascinated.

"You're the girl for me," he said hoarsely.

"I can do other things like that, but they can wait till later. What can you do?"

"I can play 'My Country, 'Tis of Thee' on a fine-tooth comb and toilet paper. And I know a lot of divine limericks."

"Divine," she said. "I'd just as soon you wouldn't say 'divine.' But what the hell—I probably bug you, too. I mean, do I bug you?"

"Not too much."

"I'm sorry," she said humbly. "I'm sorry I mentioned

it—'divine,' I mean. It doesn't really bug me. You don't drag me at all. Honest you don't, Uck."

He touched her face with soft fingers. "Don't press," he whispered. "Take it easy. Just don't hurry it."

"I've got to hurry it. You don't understand. I lied to you. I'm not thirty years old; I'm thirty-two. Oh, hell, I'm thirty-three. Or is it thirty-four? I keep forgetting. I get all wound up inside. I don't know what's happening to me. Only nothing's happening to me. Nothing. That's why I press. I want something to happen to me. What's it all about? Do you know?"

He was puzzled. His face sagged. His meaty shoulders drooped. His carp eyes stared at her, wondering.

"All the girls I grew up with are married and have children and are miserable. I want to be miserable like that, too. I have this girlfriend, and she's going to marry a jerk. I mean a *jerk*. But what can I tell her? No? I can't tell her no. Listen, Uck, it's not all a big, dirty joke, is it?"

"It may be," he said thoughtfully. "It may very well be."

"I don't want things from men—honest I don't. I just want to love a guy. Is that so bad? I'm a freak maybe? That's what a woman's supposed to do, isn't it? But all the men I know are bent. None of them fit. Except you. Old Uck Faye. You fit. Uck, I'm a patient woman, but I really think you ought to say something now. You know, something like 'Are you doing anything Saturday night?'"

"Can we have lunch next Friday?" he asked.

"I accept," she said promptly. "That's all right. You're taking it slow. That's okay. I don't mind. The slow and easy type. That's fine. Friday. Lunch. That's great. I won't push. I won't hurry it."

He nodded approvingly.

"Listen," she said, almost breathless, "do you think this might be something?"

"What might be something?"

"This. You and me."

"Oh . . ." he said slowly. "You and me? Well. How can you tell?"

"Sure," she muttered. "That's all right, Uck. How *can* you tell?"

I could nail his balls to a stump, she mused, and push him over backwards.

"See you Friday," she said, and gave him a smile as brave as a bonfire in the rain.

7

She bounced into Jo Rhodes' apartment, filled with love and dry Rob Roys. She had rushed home from work and let Rocco plod around the block, waving a leg dispiritedly at a few trees and parking meters.

Then Helen mixed the first of three Rob Roys, gulped down as she undressed, showered, dressed again. She wore the white silk blouse Jo had suggested when he invited her for an evening of dinner and picture taking.

He wore a crimson velvet smoking jacket with wide black satin lapels trimmed with white piping. Perched on his little skull was a black fez decorated with jeweled brocade.

"It was the fez of the Grand Eunuch in a sheikh's harem in Mecca," he told her. "He gave it to me in return for a photograph I took of him reading the *National Geographic*."

"When was this, Jo?"

"Oh . . . years ago. Well, my dear, I hope you're hungry."

"Famished."

"Good. I have an enormous Caesar salad, a cold lobster for each of us, garlic bread, and for dessert I have been soaking fresh strawberries, peaches, pineapple chunks and grapes in a mixture of white wine and brandy for two days. How does that sound?"

"Yummy."

"We'll eat in the kitchen. It will make things easier."

He had covered the wooden table with a stiff damask cloth. The silver was heavy and ornate. Two slender blue candles were thrust into crystal holders.

"You have such beautiful things," she told him. "Did your wife buy these or did you?"

"Oh, I did. I don't have anything of my wife's. Now you sit here, Helen, and we will start with a champagne cocktail."

He busied himself at the serving board, his head tilted to avoid smoke drifting from the Gauloise stub stuck in the corner of his mouth.

"Jo," she said anxiously, "don't you think you smoke too much? I mean, your heart and all . . ."

"What about my heart?"

"Your heart condition."

"What heart condition?"

"You told me you had a heart condition."

"Nonsense," he said. "My heart is as sound as a bell— whatever that means. Here you are, my dear—just try that. Too much bitters?"

"Mmm. Just right."

"Here's to our new friendship." He smiled, tinking her glass with his. "Long may it wave."

"Well, why did you tell me you had a heart condition?"

"You must have misunderstood me, dear. I had a complete examination just the other day, and I'm in tip-top condition. Tip-top. A-Okay and All Conditions Go. The candles," he shouted. "Bless my soul, I almost forgot."

He lighted the candles, turned off the overhead light. He swooped suddenly, tickled the nape of her neck with his mustache.

"You lovely!" he cried. "I just can't forget how you looked when—well, you remember, I daresay. This *is* nice, isn't it? I'm so glad you could come."

They each had another champagne cocktail. Then he opened

a large bottle of Muscadet. He poured a little into a fresh glass, sipped cautiously.

"Ah," he breathed, rolling his eyes wildly, "dust on the tongue. Now then. . . ."

Everything had been prepared. He served the salad deftly. Then he placed a platter of two lobsters, halved and cracked, in the center of the table. He filled their wineglasses, sat down opposite her, unfolded his starched napkin with a gallant flourish.

"Fall to!" he commanded.

They finished the salad, finished the lobsters, almost finished the fruit, and sat back contentedly, finishing the wine.

"Coffee later," he promised. "Perhaps inside, before we get down to work. Brandy now? A liqueur? I have some funny things I think you'll like."

"Not another thing. The wine is fine. Oh, Jo, I can't move. What a wonderful cook you are."

"Cook?" He laughed. "The only things cooked were the lobsters, and there's no trick to that."

"But you know so much about food and wine and everything. I loved the way you screamed at the owner in that Italian restaurant. I suppose you had to learn all those things after your wife died."

"Died?" he said, puzzled. "My wife isn't dead. She's living in Palm Beach, Florida. We're divorced."

"Jo Rhodes," she said angrily, "you told me she died years ago. I distinctly remember it, and I did *not* misunderstand you."

"Of course, of course." He chuckled, patting her hand. "But what I meant was that she was dead as far as I was concerned. Good heavens, I haven't seen or spoken to the woman in over ten years. She remarried. She thought he was a French count, but he turned out to be a soccer player. It made me believe in God. That alimony was killing me. Shall we go inside for coffee?"

He served the espresso in little cups of white translucent china decorated with tiny bluebells.

"Oh, God," Helen breathed, "they're so beautiful. If I break one, I'll never forgive myself."

"Yes, they are nice, are they not? Carole Lombard gave them to me about a month before she was killed. I had done some informal portraits of her, and *Life* used one on a cover. Naturally, she was delighted."

"Was that before you were divorced or after?"

"Oh, before, long before."

"You must have been married a long time."

"Yes. A long time...."

"Do you have any children, Jo?"

"We had a son, a wonderful boy. He looked just like Leslie Howard. But he was killed in the war."

"Vietnam?"

"Oh, dear me, no. World War Two. He was in the Navy, in command of a torpedo boat. He sacrificed himself. He turned his boat into the path of a Japanese torpedo and saved a battleship. It was in all the newspapers. I keep his medals in my safety deposit box."

They sat in solemn silence for a few moments.

"Jo," she said, frowning, "you must have been married at a very early age if you had a son old enough for World War Two."

"Oh, yes. I was very young, very young indeed. Well, I think I will now have a small cognac. Would you like one?"

"I think I better." Helen Miley nodded.

He perched her on a high stool before a black background, wheeled up his big studio camera. He chattered as he took film packs from a cabinet, began switching on the bright lights.

"First we'll take some conventional poses, and then I want to try backlighting to halo your hair. Try to keep your chin down. Not down on your chest, but tucked in a little. Lick your lips before I shoot. Lips slightly parted. Not wide open—just parted."

He ducked under the black cloth, shoved the heavy camera forward and to the left a bit.

"All right." His voice came muffled and indistinct. "Turn your body to the left. No, the other way. That's it. No, that's too far now. Turn back toward me a little. That's it. Fine. Now keep your shoulders and body in that position and turn your head to face the camera. Look right at me. Excellent."

He came out from under the cloth, his fez tilted over one ear. He trotted up to her, fussed with the frilled collar of her white silk blouse.

"May I open the top button?"

"As many as you like," she assured him.

But he opened only the top one, tugged her neckline a little wider, ran back to his camera, disappeared under the cloth again.

"Beautiful," he said, emerging. He whipped off the cloth, inserted the film holder, and stood to one side, holding a rubber bulb attached to the shutter with a long tube.

"Here we go. Lick lips. Lips slightly parted. Just a bit more. That's good. Chin down a bit. Straighten up. You're slumping. Shoulders back. Arch your back. Chest out. That's it. That's it. Move your right arm back just a bit. A little more. Fine. Fine. Hold it. That's it. A smile. A small smile. Yes. That's—got it!"

He worked rapidly and efficiently for almost forty-five minutes. Then, when he saw Helen beginning to droop, her face shiny with sweat from the heat of the floods, he called a break. He switched off the lights; they moved into the living area to smoke a cigarette and have another brandy.

"That's hard work," Helen said. "I feel like I've been parboiled. Did you get anything good?"

"I think so. You're a very good model. Very patient. And you're relaxed. We'll see what comes across on film. Some people project; some don't."

"Did you ever photograph your wife, Jo?"

"Very rarely. She wasn't photogenic. In any event, I tore up all the photos I had of her. One night, in a drunken rage, I destroyed everything that might remind me of her. I was brutal. I even smashed her wedding bouquet that had been kept in a glass bell from which all air had been removed. And I threw away our son's baby shoes, which had been bronzed and mounted on bookends."

"What kind of a woman was she?"

"Dreadful," he said promptly. "Just dreadful. I could tell you stories you wouldn't believe."

"I'm sure you could."

"She made my life a living hell," he said morosely. "A living hell."

"What did she do?"

"Well, my dear—it's of a rather delicate nature. You see, she had a sexual appetite that simply could not be satisfied. At least, I could not satisfy it, and I doubt if any one man could. She was constantly unfaithful to me—constantly. I expect it may have been a psychic thing, you know. Anyhow, she just could not control herself. It was a sad thing—this rather handsome, educated woman throwing herself at actors, doctors, shoe clerks, the iceman (we had iceboxes in those days)—even strangers she met on the street."

"Did she drink?"

"Not to excess. Hers was a different kind of madness. I will never forget the afternoon John Barrymore came to my studio for theatrical portraits. My wife was present, took one look at him, and was lost. He was a man of great charm, you know, although frequently intoxicated."

"I loved him in *A Yank at Oxford*."

"That was Lionel," he said crossly. "Anyway, my wife followed John Barrymore back to his hotel room and didn't return to me for three days—and then with stars in her eyes. Our life was a succession of unsavory incidents like that. We once gave a party, and I found her in a mop closet, in *flagrante delicto*—vertically, you understand—with the delivery boy from the delicatessen. It was horrible."

"What a shame. But why didn't you leave her, Jo?"

"Why?" he asked hollowly. "I'll tell you why. Because I was in love with her. Oh, my dear!" he cried passionately, leaning forward, clasping her two hands between his. "Love is blind indeed. We bestow our greatest blessing on the most unworthy persons because we cannot help ourselves. We live a life of horror and pain because of our love. But we cannot give it up because it is all we have." His head dropped. "It is all we have," he repeated in a low, choked voice.

"Oh, Jo," she murmured, moved close to him, put an arm across his shoulders. She felt him tremble slightly, and tears came to her eyes.

He looked up at her, took off his pince-nez, wiped the glass slowly on his sleeve.

"So you see, my dear, when she met the man she thought was a French count, but who later turned out to be a tennis player, she—"

"A soccer player."

"Ah, yes, a soccer player. Well, she said her happiness lay with another, and she asked me for her freedom. It was anguish to let her go, but if it meant her happiness, then I had to do it. That is what love is all about, Helen—sacrificing yourself for the one you love. In a way it was a relief, being freed from the pain of her infidelities, but I soon found that life without her was nothing. Cold and frightening and lonely. It was years before I recovered from my depression. I thought about suicide many times and came quite close once. But each time I hesitated, perhaps with a faint hope that someday I might meet a woman worthy of my love." He turned, looked deep into her eyes. "A woman like you, Helen."

"Oh, Jo," she whispered, "you're so sweet."

"Well," he said briskly, jumping to his feet, "one more brandy, and we'll get back to work."

This time he used a 120 camera mounted on a metal tripod, the lens wiped with a thin coating of Vaseline. A small floodlight was placed on the floor behind Helen. The light was pointed upward and threw a radiant halo around her head and shoulders.

They spent a half hour shooting three rolls of film, twelve shots each. Then Jo Rhodes switched off the studio lights, turned on the air conditioner.

"Enough for one session," he declared, moving his equipment back against the wall. "I'll take these to the lab tomorrow, and we should have contacts by next week. I'll call you then, and we'll get together and decide what we want to print. How does that sound?"

"Fine. I hope you'll let me pay..."

"Nonsense, dear." He smiled, kissing her cheek. "That's why men were put on this earth—to buy gifts for women. If you offer to pay, they'll make you resign from the female sex. Now then, let's relax and cool off. What shall we have—more brandy? Wine? Liqueurs?"

"Maybe I better not," Helen said dubiously. "I feel a little woozy."

"It's just the heat from the lights. Perhaps a glass of chilled wine will revive you. I believe I shall have a small cognac. Now you just sit right there and let me serve you."

An hour later, after four of his small cognacs, he rose somewhat unsteadily to his feet and murmured, "Please excuse for moment. Slip into something more comfortable."

He was gone for so long that she became uneasy. But he finally exited from the bedroom, smiling serenely. He was wearing a long black silk robe, the back decorated with an embroidered crimson dragon couchant. Beneath the robe were bright-yellow silk pajamas. On his feet were Persian slippers, the toes coming to long points that curved backward. At the end of each point was a tiny silver bell that tinkled as he walked. About his throat was knotted a white silk scarf, Ascot fashion. His fez was tilted rakishly over one eye. He was smoking his Gauloise in a long, intricately carved ivory holder. The pince-nez was a poor substitute for a monocle.

He stood in front of her, weaving gently, and held his arms wide.

"Behold!" he said, grinning foolishly. "A vision of delight!"

Suddenly, without warning, his bones dissolved. He melted softly onto the floor into a puddle of black and yellow silk. His fez bounced off and rolled away. The bells on his toes tinkled merrily.

Helen rushed to him, knelt beside him. He was apparently unhurt. He was asleep, breathing heavily, still grinning. She shook her head in wonder.

She went into the bedroom, fetched a pillow and blanket. She straightened him out as best she could, slid the pillow beneath his head, tenderly tucked the blanket around him.

"You nut," she whispered affectionately.

When she came out on the street, her trench coat thrown over her shoulders, she heard a distant grumble of thunder. The air was thick; no stars showed.

The few cabs she saw were either occupied or showing their "Off Duty" lights. She began walking east, toward Third Avenue. Between Lexington and Third a long black car pulled up alongside her; a raucous voice shouted, "A lift for a lay!"

"Up your kazoo!" she yelled back. The car sped away with a chirp of tires.

Another roll of thunder sounded no closer; she decided to walk home, to walk up Third Avenue to Fifty-first Street and then east to her apartment house near Second.

She swung along, her good legs flashing, bemused by the evening, smiling occasionally, belching once, tripping twice on curbstones. She went into the first clean bar she came to, used the toilet, then continued her march uptown.

There was Jo Rhodes and Richard Faye, and even Harry Tennant and Charles Lefferts. Something would happen. She felt she might live forever. But she tried not to hope, lest she put a whammy on the future.

Then thunder cracked overhead. She was at Fiftieth Street when it began to rain. She ran the rest of the way home. By the time she dashed into the lobby she was drenched and shivering.

8

THE CLOCK-RADIO CAME on a few moments before 8 A.M., and
Helen Miley awoke to the final cannonade of *The 1812
Overture.*

"Jesus God!" she gasped. She sat bolt upright in bed,
convinced the Russians had landed at Battery Park and were
coming uptown via the Lexington Avenue subway.

The music ended, the announcer came on, and she reached
for her first cigarette of the day. She sat with her arms around
her knees, smoking, waiting for the news...

"Israeli officials reported today that four Arab guerrillas had
been killed in..."

"One Negro was killed, and three wounded in a night of
violence that left..."

"Rhodesian forces report killing more than fifty guerrillas in
an ambush near Salisbury..."

"A family of six was killed when their car..."

Remembering the movie *Gunga Din* she had seen on *The Late Show*, Helen Miley raised her arms heavenward and in a tremulous voice intoned, "Kill! Kill! Kill for Kali!"

Pleased by this, Rocco staggered to his feet. He yawned, tasted his tongue, and shuddered. He came padding over to the bed. Helen reached down to tweak his ears.

"Honey baby Rocco boy," she said. "Did you have a good night's sleep, dear?"

She bounced out of bed, naked, and trotted into the outside hallway. She peered out the peephole to make certain no one was in the corridor, then unchained and unlocked the door. She opened it just wide enough to whisk in the morning paper deposited on her mat.

She turned immediately to "Your Horoscope for the Day." She looked for the paragraph headed Aquarius.

"Socially very active with a dramatic climax possible by next weekend. Your friends will stir things up."

"Hot damn!" she exulted.

She gave Rocco some chopped chicken liver (with onion), then went over to the cage, took off the night cover. The bird stared back at her sullenly.

"Well?" she demanded.

Silence.

"Smart ass," she grumbled. "If there's anything I can't stand, it's a smart-ass parakeet."

She poured some seed into its dish, then went into the bathroom and pulled on her shower cap. It was really a dish cover but served admirably as a shower cap. While she soaped and rinsed, she sang two verses of "Sitting One Night in Murphy's Bar," a ribald ballad that Charlie had taught her.

Powdered and scented, she returned to the bedroom and dialed WE 6-1212 to find out what the weather would be like. "Cloudy in the morning, clearing toward noon. High in the low sixties. Precipitation probability forty percent. Tonight will be..."

She finally found two stockings that matched. She tugged them on, hitched them to a minikin garter belt she had bought in a Times Square shop called Stage Undies.

Her inflatable bra was just a wee bit soft; it took only one breath to restore its rigidity. Then she pulled on an ivory-silk chloë shirt, St. Laurent print peasant skirt, a blazer, and boots.

She looked at herself in the full-length mirror on the inside of the bedroom door.

"Killer," she said.

She ran a comb through her hair, then shook her head violently to give the short curls a go-to-hell look. She applied makeup swiftly, smacked her lips, and was ready for a fight or a frolic.

She lighted a cigarette, grabbed up purse, newspaper, trench coat, and scooted out the door.

"Bye, Rocco," she called. "Be a good boy."

"Morning, Miss Miley," the doorman said.

"Hi, Marv. What's good?"

"Sandestone in the third," he told her.

"Two on the nose," she said, fumbling in her purse. "And here's a buck. When you get a chance, take Rocco for a walk, will you? Just to the corner and back. Walk slow—he ain't the man he used to be."

"Who is?" the doorman asked.

She had breakfast in the luncheonette on the corner.

"Morning, Jer," she said. "How's the cold?"

"Better, sweetheart. You look ravishing this morning, and if there wasn't any other customers, I would."

"Keep trying, Jer," she advised. "A talent scout is certain to discover you someday."

"The usual, honey?"

She nodded, put on her glasses, unfolded the newspaper. She began reading the advertising column. When she reached out for the black coffee and toasted bagel, they were on the counter in front of her.

"Morning, Miss Miley," the elevator starter said. "Soon as this fog clears up it's going to be a beautiful day."

"Right on," Helen agreed, remembering her horoscope. She thought for a moment—thought of the four men currently in her life.

"Make it four-four-one, Joe," she said. "A dollar on four-four-one." She handed it over.

"Best of luck, Miss Miley," he said, taking out his little notebook.

Susie Carrar and Harry Tennant were both on phones when she entered. They looked up, returned her wave. She bounced into her own office, shrugged out of her trench coat, tossed it onto a littered drafting table.

She sat down at her desk, leaned far back in her swivel chair, put her feet up, lighted another cigarette, began to read "Ship Arrivals and Departures" in the morning paper, repeating the notices aloud:

"*Concordia Faro.* Kuwait, Manama and Basra. Sails from Hamilton Avenue, Brooklyn.

"*Export Challenger.* Haifa and Istanbul. Sails from Pier B, Brooklyn.

"*Lightning.* Havre and Felixstowe. Sails from Pier 13, Staten Island.

"*Rotterdam.* West Indies Cruise. Sails from West Houston Street.

"*Michelangelo.* Algeciras, Naples, Cannes and Genoa. Sails from West Fiftieth Street."

She was silent a moment, dreaming... then added, "And the good ship *Swanson and Feltzig* sailing to nowhere from East Forty-eighth Street."

Harry Tennant knocked once, then came stooping through the door. Helen took her feet off the desk, straightened up.

"Dammit," she grumbled, "I've got to quit putting my feet on the desk or start wearing pants—one or the other."

"Yes, indeedy." He smiled. "How do you feel this morning, Helen?"

"Full of beans. What's happening?"

"Those Concord releases didn't come in. I called Solly, and he said the machine broke down."

"Oh, sure," she said bitterly, reaching for the phone, "it always breaks down on our job when he's got a rush job for someone else for more dough...Solly?...This is Helen ...Don't dollink me, you miserable creep...Where the hell's my releases?...Solly, I swear I'm coming down there right now, and if you're working on someone else's stuff, I'm going to call your wife and tell her we're making it together and I want her to give you a divorce...Solly, I swear I will...I'll fix you good...all right...All right, Solly...Just as long as they're here by noon."

She hung up, winked at Tennant.

"I put the fear of God in him. He thinks I'm joking about his wife, but he's not sure."

"Are you joking?"

"Oh, sure. I wouldn't do that to any guy. The cheap bastard. He does about twenty thousand a year with us, and last

Christmas he gave me an umbrella from Korvette's. Laurel and Hardy each got a case of scotch, and I got an umbrella. The story of my life. What else have you got? Pull up a chair."

For more than an hour they went over releases, mailings, schedules, luncheons....

"Listen, Harry, I've got a twelve-thirty lunch date, but I should be back by two-thirty at the latest. When the releases come in, will you start putting the kits together? I'll tell Susie to help you if she doesn't have correspondence. Then when I come back, I'll pitch in, too. But I'm afraid we'll have to work late. There's almost five hundred of the damned things. Can you work late?"

"Sure."

"Thanks. You're a white man." She grinned at him, but he didn't smile.

"I'll have some food sent up about six or so. Do you want to eat Chink?"

"That's fine with me."

She leaned back in her chair, stared at him.

"Sorry you took the job?"

"Oh, no. I like it. I'm learning a lot. I'm on the other side of the fence now. When I was on the paper, I was flooded with releases and invitations and press kits. Most of them went into Deep Six. Now I'm trying to peddle them ... you know?"

"Sure. Listen, there may be a chance, just a chance, that we can keep you on. Abbott and Costello are making a pitch for the Everbright account. If we get that, we'll really need you full time."

"I'd like that."

"Well, don't buy any swimming pools. It's just a chance. Got a light?"

He leaned forward with a match. She leaned forward with her cigarette. Their heads were on the same level; quite unexpectedly their eyes locked.

He was, she saw, a remote, handsome man, closed up in himself, the fire banked. His eyes were brooding, wary, almost flinching.

"Helen," he said in a gravelly voice, "I was wondering...."

He was silent. He took a deep breath, turned away, stared at the sign on the wall. He cleared his throat.

"I was wondering," he said loudly, "if you would care to have lunch with me someday when you're free."

"Sure, baby. Love to. You just say when."

He turned back to look at her again.

"Did you ever go out with a black man before?" he asked softly. "I mean in public. To a restaurant, a theater . . . like that?"

"No, I never have."

"Well . . . you know, sometimes people talk. I mean, they see you and me together, and they'll say things, just loud enough so we can hear."

"Screw 'em," she said wrathfully.

"Well, Helen, you think about it. If you decide you'd rather not, I'll—"

"Goddammit, Harry, I did think about it, and I said yes, I'd like to have lunch with you. Why are you making such a big deal about it?"

He gathered up his papers, unfolded to his full height, looked down at her, smiling gently.

"Besides," she said, "there are only two races in this world—men and women. Correct?"

He considered that a moment, his head cocked to one side.

"You know," he said, "you just might be right."

She was late; it was raining lightly; she couldn't get a cab. Like an idiot, she had left her trench coat in the office; by the time she arrived at the restaurant the challis skirt clung to her like a wet shroud.

"Did you miss me?" she asked, and gave him a saucy smile.

Richard Faye lurched to his feet, upsetting a glass of water over the cloth. A waiter came rushing over to spread a dry napkin.

". . . of it," the waiter said, showing his teeth.

"Hi, there!" Faye said. "I wasn't—I didn't—I thought—"

"Dry Rob Roy," she said firmly, plunking down and moving her chair closer to his. She donned her horn-rimmed glasses and stared at him. "Good God," she said.

He had obviously gone to some pains to dress for their luncheon, and she was touched. Touched and dazzled.

A Lauren suit, with more buttons than she could count, gave him a waist.

"Very nice." She nodded. "Shit-brown is *your* color."

He laughed; they clinked glasses.

"I'm one up on you," he said.

"One?"

"Ah . . . two. I thought you were going to stand me up."

"That'll be the day." She put a hand over one of his. "How *are* you, baby?"

"Now I feel great." He withdrew his hand, knocked a spoon to the floor, bent to retrieve it, lost his napkin.

The waiter came rushing over, replaced the napkin, provided a clean spoon. "... of it," he said, looking at Faye with loathing. "Order now?"

"In a minute," Helen said. "This man just picked me up, and we're getting acquainted."

The waiter smiled his way backward until he bumped into the maître d'. "A couple of nuts," he muttered.

"All about me?" Faye said. "Well... where should I start?"

Really not too bad, she thought, staring at him. There was a face beneath that blotch, a body beneath that suet. I'll carve off thirty pounds, she vowed, and get rid of the fruity cologne. And every time he snaps his fingers at a waiter I'll slap his hand.

"A researcher," he was saying. "Not a writer. Just a researcher. Amerinews Syndicate. I get all the facts together and turn them over to one of our staff writers. He does a feature on it, and we send it to our clients here and abroad. Not a big outfit, but we have offices in London and Rome. We're doing a thing on space-age cooking—you know, microwave ovens and electronic appliances and things like that. Which explains what I was doing at your luncheon."

"Did you know," she said, "that when you talk, the tip of your nose goes up and down?"

They ordered melon, to be followed by soft-shell crabs with a salad, and a small bottle of white wine. Faye reached for his cigarette, discovered it had fallen off the edge of the ashtray and was charring the tablecloth.

"Oh, prunes." He frowned. "I don't know what's wrong with me today."

"... of it." The waiter sighed, spreading another napkin over the wound.

His eyes were good, she decided. Big and brown and pleading. A cocker spaniel's eyes.

"Here, boy," she said.

"What?" he asked.

But just then a spoonful of cantaloupe leaped from his spoon and hid in his lap. "Tch!" he said, dug into his crotch, and glared at her.

"Not a word," she vowed, raising one palm.

"So then," he said, nibbling on a crab claw, "I was an airline reservation clerk, sold magazine subscriptions on the phone, and demonstrated bathroom fixtures."

"You've bounced around," she said, gulping her wine.

"Bounced. Yes."

"But what do you really want to do?"

"Yes . . . that's it . . . "

"What's it?"

"What do I really want to do?"

He broke off a piece of French bread, buttered it, dropped it to the floor (butter side down, of course) and stared at it. The waiter stared at it.

"Well . . . " he said dolefully, "I really don't know. Something."

They sat back. He lighted her cigarette, then held the match under the wrong end of his. The filter began to glow.

"I'm nervous," he said.

"I never would have known," she assured him.

"I was working for another news syndicate. Not the one I'm working for now. I did the fillers. You know what they are? One-and two-liners. Newspapers call them boilerplate. They set them in type and use them to fill out columns. You know, things like: 'The African crocodile, ordinarily a ferocious beast, is helpless when turned onto his back.' And 'Every year in the British Isles an average of three children are born with rudimentary tails.' Things like that."

She ordered a small cognac, thinking of Jo Rhodes. Faye ordered a Gallianos with a slice of lime. He squeezed the lime, pinching it neatly over Helen's shoulder onto a nearby table. The waiter groaned.

"Anyway," he said, "I spent mornings at the library researching fillers in the encyclopedia and scientific books. Then, after lunch, I'd go back to the office and write them up. I had to turn out about twenty-five fillers a day. It was fun for a while. I learned all these odd facts about koala bears and how much the minerals in the human body would be worth if they were sold."

"How much am I worth?"

"About three dollars. One day I was really hung over and didn't get to the library. So after lunch I went to the office and wrote twenty-five fillers. I made them up. They sounded all right. 'One out of every fourteen eggs contains a double yolk.

The lemur is noted for its insatiable appetite for scallions. The first woman's corset containing whalebone was made in Waltham, Massachusetts, in 1816.' Things like that. I just made them up."

"What happened?"

"Nothing happened. The editor read them and passed them, mats were made, and they went out to all our clients. The papers printed them. No one complained. So I stopped going to the library every morning and started sleeping late. I'd get to the office after lunch and make up twenty-five fillers. They got wilder and wilder."

"No one caught on?"

"No one. Once I wrote, 'Scientists are puzzled by the complete absence of athlete's foot on Samoa.' The syndicate got a letter from a doctor who was doing a book on skin diseases. He asked for the source of the filler, and the editor bucked the letter to me and scribbled on it, 'Tell him your source.'"

"What did you do?"

"I got drunk. I thought it was the end. But then I figured, oh, shoot. So I wrote the doctor it was from a book called *Samoan Doctor* written by J. C. Whitten in 1937. I never heard any more about it. About a year later I saw the book the skin doctor had written. In a section on fungus infections he said, 'Scientists are puzzled by the complete absence of athlete's foot in Samoa.' In a footnote he credited J. C. Whitten's book *Samoan Doctor*. I had become immortal."

"Crazy. You must have laughed."

"At first. But then it bothered me. My lies were getting into print so easily that I began to doubt everything I read. What was real, and what was being made up by someone like me who wanted to sleep late? So I quit that job and got a job with a fishing magazine."

"Are you a fisherman?"

"Heavens, no. All I did was edit copy and read proofs—things like that. Well, we had one writer, a chap in Florida, who did stories on pike and trout and bass. Fish like that. His photographs were magnificent. He always had a lead photo of the fish leaping out of the water, dripping and glistening. One day I mentioned to an editor what great photos they were. The editor laughed. He said this writer would buy a stuffed fish from a taxidermist. Then a friend of the writer's would put on scuba diving gear and get into water about six or seven feet deep. He'd take the stuffed fish down with him. Then, standing on the bottom, he'd throw the stuffed fish upward, out of the water, and the writer would photograph it."

"Beautiful."

"Helen, why am I telling you all this?"

"Beats the hell out of me, baby."

His soft face drooped; he looked down.

"Oh," he said, "I know... It affected me. I mean the phony fillers I wrote and the phony fish coming out of the water. I began to think about what was phony and what was real. It bothered me. I haven't gotten over it yet."

She put a hand on his. This time he didn't shrug it off.

"I'm real," she said.

"Oh, my, yes." He smiled. "You're the realest person I've ever met in my whole life. But am I real?"

If there was an answer to that, she didn't know it.

"I mean," he faltered, "what I feel, the way I react to people. Is that real? Check, please."

He added the check carefully.

"It's a dollar too much," he told the waiter. "You made a mistake."

The waiter snatched the check back, added it again.

"It's correct, sir," he gritted, returning it.

"Helen, you add it."

She added it.

"It's right, Uck."

"If you say so."

He seemed bewildered, vulnerable.

They came out into the sunshine, the pavements still damp but the sky so blue it looked as if it had been washed, wrung out, hung up to dry.

"Will I see you again?" she asked.

But he was lost somewhere; she had to repeat her question. Then he was amazed.

"You want to?"

"Of course."

"Oh," he said. "Well... next week. How about Wednesday?"

"That's fine, Uck."

"We'll have lunch or dinner. I'll call you."

"Good. Thanks for the feed."

"I talked too much," he said, hanging his head. "I acted like a goof."

"You're not a goof."

"I'm not, you know. I guess I was a little nervy. You're the first woman I've been out with in—in some time. I've forgotten how to act."

"You did just fine."

"I'll improve." He smiled, throwing his shoulders back, straightening his spine. She heard the little crack.

She kissed him on the cheek; he cringed. They said good-bye. He put on a brown bowler at least two sizes too small for him, walked away from her. She watched him drift down the crowded sidewalk, the silly hat bobbing, his figure floating, helpless and unreal.

"All right," she said, hands on her hips, "let's get organized."

Harry Tennant had already pushed the drafting table next to her desk and had stacked neat piles of releases, spec sheets, photos and biographies of the executives of the company and the scientists who had developed the product. It was a spray-on deodorant for cats in heat.

The press kits were being assembled for a scheduled conference and luncheon on Monday. Standing behind the desk and table, Helen, Susie Carrar and Harry set up a little assembly line, tucking the printed material into a bright-orange cover decorated with a drawing of a little kitten sniffing its crotch.

They worked steadily, with little talk, and the pile of assembled kits grew rapidly. They knocked off at five thirty, and Susie called the Chinese restaurant downstairs for platters of shrimp with fried rice, chicken chow mein, sweet-and-sour pork, kumquats and pistachio ice cream. Also, a double Rob Roy for Helen, two scotch and sodas for Harry, a bottle of celery tonic for Susie.

They ate everything, finished their desserts, drained their drinks. Helen went into Mr. Swanson's office and brought back a bottle of bourbon from the office bar. They mixed it in paper cups with ice water from the office cooler.

Susie Carrar departed a few minutes after seven. Helen and Harry worked on for another hour, pausing only to mix fresh drinks. And then it was done, the completed kits piled on the floor in impressive stacks.

"Good job," Helen said with satisfaction. "We'll get a cab on Monday to get 'em over to the hotel."

"I could borrow a car," Harry Tennant offered. "I could drive down on Monday morning. It would be better. We might not be able to get a cab."

"Would you do that? That's great, Harry. It would be a big help. God, I'm dead."

She flopped back in her swivel chair, head lolling. Harry Tennant came around behind her, began slowly massaging the muscles of her neck and shoulders. His long, smooth fingers pinched gently, probed, soothed.

"Oh, oh, oh," she murmured in ecstasy, rolling like a broken doll. "What would you charge by the hour?"

He rubbed away at the ache and the stiffness. Then he stopped abruptly, walked to the other side of the office, lighted a cigarette, bent from the waist, peered out the window.

"Better be getting home," he said, voice muffled. "We're all finished here."

They turned off the lights, locked the outside door. They stood awkwardly on the sidewalk. There was something...

"I'm going to walk home," she said finally, her voice too loud. "It's not far from here. Fifty-first near Second. Walk me home?"

"Yes," he said. "Sure."

They ambled. The cool night air was a kiss. People stared at them.

"Don't get your ghetto complex in an uproar," she advised. "You're—what?—six-seven. I'm five-three. They probably think we're from the circus."

He smiled down at her. "No sweat."

Once he put his hand on her arm to halt her when a cab came ripping around a corner, but otherwise they walked without contact and without talk.

They stopped outside Helen's apartment house. The doorman on duty—Mike, the mean one—looked at them, expressionless.

"Come up for a nightcap, Harry?"

"No," he said definitely. "Thanks, but no."

"Look now," she said desperately, "it'll be all right. Goddammit, I live here. Who the hell cares what *he* thinks?"

Tennant looked at her.

"Oh, Jesus." She sighed. "Harry, there's a bar around the corner on Second. The Everest. I hang there. They know me there. It'll be all right."

There were three old men sitting at the bar of the Everest, watching the last home baseball game of the season on TV.

Thack was behind the stick, polishing glasses. He waved a bar towel at Helen when they came in. They took a booth in the back room. Clara slouched over, defiantly displayed a black eye to Helen.

"My God," Helen gasped. "Again? What a mouse! Clara, why don't you lose that guy?"

Clara shrugged, made a comic face. "I can't," she said. "He loves me too much."

They laughed, and Clara said, "Who's the boyfriend?"

"Clara, this is Harry. Harry, Clara."

They traded smiles. Clara took their order, shuffled toward the bar.

"She's got this guy," Helen explained. "Every once in a while he hangs one on her. But she keeps telling me, 'I deserve it, I deserve it!' Every time I tell her to leave him she says, 'Who else have I got?' I guess she loves him."

"Sure," Harry said. "They married?"

"I don't think so. But it doesn't seem to worry her."

Clara came back with their drinks and a basket of potato chips.

"Yell when you're ready." She yawned and returned to her morning paper at a rear table.

Helen twisted around. "Clara," she called, "what happened to Sandestone in the third?"

Clara ran a finger down the column of results. "Placed," she shouted. "Eight to one."

"Son of a bitch," Helen said. "Close—but no cigar."

Harry laughed. "You play a lot?"

"A few times a week. Nothing big. A couple of bucks. About a month ago I hit a long one for almost a hundred. I went right out and bought a wig, and I haven't worn the damned thing since."

"Good. I like your hair the way it is."

She grinned with pleasure and ran her fingers through her short curls. They just sat there, drinking, smiling, feeling good.

"You know," she said, making little faces in the dampness on the tabletop, "I really don't know much about you."

"Not much to know."

"I mean where you're from and where you grew up. Things like that."

"Oh . . . well. I was born in Georgia. A little town. Templeton. My folks came up to New York when I was about three, four—around then. Lived in Harlem. My father was a janitor, and my mother was a maid. I got a sister, two years younger than me, and a brother, four years younger. I live with him. Our folks put us all through college. Well . . . my brother dropped out after a year. We worked, too, you know, but we couldn't have done it without my parents."

"They still alive?"

"No. My father died about five years ago. My mother died just last year."

"My folks are gone, too. You live with your brother? What kind of a place have you got?"

"It's not bad. A railroad flat on a good block. Fourth-floor walk-up. Five rooms. All small, of course, but we have separate bedrooms. It's rent-controlled, so that makes it better. It's livable. It's where we all lived when everyone was alive. I grew up in there. Outside the kitchen window there's a kind of a little place. Not a terrace or anything like that, but the roof of a dormer window on the floor downstairs. It's like a little flat roof. My mother kept geranium plants out there. It was in the sun."

"What does your brother do?"

"My brother? He's in this organization. It's a city thing, but they get state and federal funds, too. They find summer jobs for kids and hold classes at night. My brother teaches a class in black history. He's very active in all these things. I keep telling him he should go back and finish his education and get his degree, but he say he's too busy."

"Sounds like he is."

"Oh, he's busy all right. Two years ago he got his head busted open in a riot. Right now he's out on bail."

"What for?"

"He bad-mouthed some cop during a demonstration."

"Is your sister in New York?"

"No. She married a doctor, and they moved out to Los Angeles. He opened an office in Watts."

"Watts? Can't make much money there."

"You're so right. But that's what they wanted to do. My sister works with him, like a nurse-receptionist. She took a course in nursing so she could help out."

"They got any kids?"

"Not yet. But she writes they're trying."

"Clara!" she yelled.

The drinks came with a bowl of salted peanuts. Harry

Tennant took a handful, stuffing them into his mouth. Helen watched him, smiling.

"When things are eating at you, you eat at things."

"Right on." He nodded.

"You ever been married, Harry?"

She felt she had touched him on his rusty hair with a magic Walt Disney wand that had little sparkles coming from the tip. He suddenly came alive, brave, eyes bright, teeth glistening, sadness vanquished.

"Jesus Christ," he said excitedly, hunching across the table toward her. "No, I never have been married. But I was engaged once. For six months. To Iris Kane. You know her?"

"The singer?"

"That's right. She's big now. You know—the Plaza and the Americana, Las Vegas, all the white clubs. And she's been on television. I hear she's getting her own show next year. And right now she's making a movie."

"She's beautiful."

"Beautiful? A Venus! Blacker than I am, but a Venus. You've got to meet her. She's something. Everybody says so. Oh, I do love her. So much."

He took a long swallow of his drink, but he couldn't calm down.

"Helen, what we had—well, babe, I just can't hardly tell it. We had our own world. I'd do a day's work and come home at night, and there she'd be. Jesus, we laughed. I can't tell you all. It got so I was part her and she was part me. You know? I mean, we'd fight just for the sake of making up. It was so sweet. She was my life . . . I could tell you things. Like picnics and birthdays. A wristwatch she bought for me—see? Here it is—and a little fur cape I bought for her. Talking about the neighbors and buying groceries and going to the Apollo and dancing. Getting drunk together and her singing for me. Just for me. Making love. Making love. Always loving . . ."

"You lived together?"

"For a while. Just for a little while . . ."

Then he was quiet again, his face slowly congealing. Clara came over with another round of drinks. "This one's on Thack."

"I just don't know what's going to happen," he said dully. "I try not to look ahead more than a day at a time. But I got to keep dreaming she'll come back to me. I got to. Because without her I'm just nothing at all."

"She'll come back," Helen said, comforting him.

He retreated on his bench seat, huddled in the corner of the booth, smiled at her. He began to move his glass around on the damp tabletop, the befuddled chess player.

"Babe, you do some funny things when you want something real bad. I don't really believe in God. Right? But I promised God I'd never touch another woman if she'd come back to me. I promised I'd never get drunk again or take any drugs or anything like that. I wouldn't go dancing. I wouldn't swear. Things like that."

She nodded miserably, thinking of all the times she had made similar vows in the hope of getting something she wanted very much. But God had never answered her prayers—unless the answer was no.

"How come you broke up? A fight?"

"Oh, no," he protested. "Nothing like that. We just drifted apart. We drifted ..."

He was silent a moment, looking at her strangely.

"You see ... there is something you should know about me."

"What's that, Harry?"

"I think I'm a white man."

"What?"

"Yes. I think that's what it is. I know it is. My folks were hardworking and brought me up the same way. I been working since I can remember—selling newspapers and delivering groceries. Things like that. I always had good food and a warm bed. I went to school regular. I got my college degree. I got a good job in a white business—marketing and advertising and public relations. Sure, I got put down. We all do. But after I got into college, I kept thinking it was just bad manners. My folks taught me to be polite. Speak softly. Then, after I started working, it hardly happened at all. I was just like every young white guy I'd meet at press conferences and luncheons and things like that. We had the same hang-ups, the same worries. Get a better job, make more money, meet a woman. All alike. When this racial stuff started—I mean when it really began to boil—I could understand it in my mind, but I couldn't feel it. Shit, I know there's starvation and repression and keeping us down. I *know* it, but for some reason I can't *feel* it. I just can't feel it. I'm a tar-baby Babbitt. You ever read that?"

"*Tar-baby Babbitt?*"

"No, just *Babbitt*. It's a novel by Sinclair Lewis."

"No, I never read it."

"Well...what I'm saying is that I can't be against the establishment. I just want to be part of it."

"That doesn't sound so bad."

"My brother thinks so. My sister thinks so. And Iris Kane thought so."

"That's why you broke up?"

"Yes. She was active in all these causes. Still is. Singing for free at meetings. Giving all her money away. Freedom marches. Demonstrations. Stuff like that. I couldn't do it. I tried to do it for her, but she knew. It just wasn't in me. Isn't in me. I look in the mirror, and I don't see a black man. I see a white man with maybe dark skin. I know my job. I'm really good at my job."

"I know you are, baby."

"But I can't belong. Something's missing in me. I just can't belong. I mean, to my people. I've got this—this thing, that I'm not really black at all."

"Wow."

"Well," he said, looking around the room, "that's the sad story of my life. You asked for it. It's pretty nutty, wouldn't you say?"

"Yes. Pretty nutty."

He looked at the wristwatch Iris Kane had given him. Helen nodded, finished her drink quickly.

He walked her back to her apartment house. They exchanged a fast good-night. It was still early, but she wasn't in the mood to take Rocco for a walk. She undressed slowly, washed her face, took a sleeping pill, got into bed.

She stared at the walls and thought of the cruel city, the women who wanted, the men who weren't. She wondered if she should cut loose, go someplace new, start a new life, everything new.

Except for her. She'd be the same old her.

"What's wrong with me?" she asked aloud.

But the sleeping pill took effect before she could think of an answer. And when she awoke in the morning, she had forgotten the question.

9

THE PHONE WAS ringing as she came through the door. She made a dash for the living room, hopped over Rocco, grabbed it up.

"Hello, ducks," Peggy Palmer said. "I've been—"

"Darling, I just got in this minute," Helen said. "Let me take my shoes off, mix a drink, and I'll call you right back. Okay? I've got a lot to tell you. Call you in three minutes."

She hung up without waiting for Peggy's reply. She rushed into the bathroom. When she flushed the toilet, Rocco put his paws up, began to lap the fresh water.

"Disgusting," she said. "Filthy, dirty, disgusting Rocco boy."

She undressed in the bedroom, letting her clothes drop onto the stained shag rug. She had vulcanized the leak in her bra, but the patch had worked loose. When she dropped the bra to the floor, the remaining air in the left pouch expired with a long, thoughtful sigh.

She poured scotch over two cubes of ice, carried the glass into the living room. She curled up naked in the corner of the couch. Rocco padded in to lick her toes.

"Charles," she said. "Honey baby Charles boy."

"Hello, ducks," Peggy said. "How did you make out?"

"Terrific," Helen said, sipping her drink. "Just sensational. It's all set for tonight. His place. He said cocktails at about nine—but you know what that means."

"No dinner?" Peggy wanted to know.

"Baby, if I have dinner once more with that man, it's going to be the strangest love triangle in history—me, him and Howard Johnson. That's all we've been doing—going to lunch or dinner or a movie. Finally I said, 'Listen, Uck, what's with this food routine? You don't have to feed me every night or take me to the movies or whatever. Can't we be alone for once, for Chrissakes?'"

"And what did he say?"

"He said oh, sure, he wanted to be alone but—you know, Peggy, how unhip I told you he was. Honest to God, he's the hardest man to know I've ever met. I've never been up to his place, and he's never been up here. I've known him for two or three weeks, but I don't really, honey, know a damned thing about him. Or nothing important anyway. He could be hung like a yo-yo for all I know."

"You should be so lucky," Peggy muttered.

"Well, finally I laid it right on the line. 'Look, buster,' I said, 'let's just get together at your place or mine and *talk*. That's all we have to do—*just talk*. I'm not going to rape you, Uck,' I said."

"You think maybe he's afraid of sex?"

"Peg, I don't know what the hell's with him. So finally he said, 'Well, all right, come over late tonight, about nine, and we'll have some drinks and talk.' So it's all set for tonight, baby, and naturally I'm keyed up very high."

"Well, I want to wish you the best of luck and all," Peggy said, her voice forlorn. "Do you think you'll sleep over?"

"Listen, dear, I'm going prepared to spend the weekend. I'm taking my big bag—you know, the canvas one I got for thirty-six ninety-eight just because the catch was tarnished a little—and I'm going to pack everything in it. Baby, I hate to ask you this, but if I stop over at your place on the way, could you meet me in the lobby and lend me your fox?"

"Of course, Helen. Just ring the bell three times, and I'll know it's you and bring it right down."

"You really are a dear, Peg. I wouldn't ask, but I want to make a good appearance, you know, it's not like we were going pub-crawling or anything like that and I might spill something on it. I'll just wear it up to his place and make this grand entrance and then it'll be inside all night. Listen, any time you want to borrow my pearl string you just say the word, you know that. Did the Camel call?"

"Well, he did and he didn't," Peggy said. "He could only talk for a minute but said he'd call right back, which he has not done hence. He's still trying to get a hotel reservation for tomorrow. I think it's silly. I mean getting a hotel room right here in New York instead of going someplace nice like the Catskills or something. But who knows how a man figures?"

"I sure as hell don't," Helen admitted. "Look at my guy—four lunches, three dinners, God knows how many movies, and he hasn't even kissed me yet. Every time I touch him you'd think I had running sores or something, for Chrissakes. Well, listen . . . you're going to make it with him then?"

"I guess I might as well," Peggy said judiciously. "It's like you said: I better find out the worst before I even think of marriage."

"That's smart," Helen agreed. "I've got to dash now, doll. I want to bubble-bath and get dressed to the balls. I'll stop by your place about eight thirty."

"What are you going to wear?"

"The black jersey, I think. That stupid bra of mine sprung a leak again. I might try patching it with a Band-Aid, but if that doesn't work, I'll just leave it off. After all, I won't be wearing it long anyway."

"Listen, ducks, be sure and call me Sunday morning. I should be home by then, and I'll want to know how it came out."

Helen made a suitable rejoinder to this, and the two women hung up, chuckling.

She looked in the mirror in his apartment house lobby, was pleased with what she saw. The black jersey seemed sprayed on her. Peggy Palmer's fox chubby and the canvas bag gave her an aloof smartness, she decided. Her tight curls were still damp from the bath. They clung to her skull like a blond helmet.

In the big handbag were horn-rimmed glasses, cigarettes,

matches, lighter, rouge, lipgloss, mascara, extra panties, a joint, a mascara brush, tweezers, comb, fourteen dollars in bills and sixty-seven cents in change, a paperbound copy of *Nana*, two subway tokens, an ad for a Macy's white sale, a St. Christopher medal, two ticket stubs for a performance of *Twentieth Century*, a plastic shower cap, a fingernail file, a dried champagne cork, a folding toothbrush, a ball-point pen, a sealed pack of facial tissues and three loose ones, a small jar of cold cream, five bobby pins, two three-cent stamps, two orange boards, a photograph of Walter Pidgeon clipped from a newspaper, an empty aspirin tin, a full aspirin bottle, three Enovids, two Darvan, four Valium, four Empirin, two Dexamyls, two twin-packs of Alka-Seltzer, a folding douche bag, a bill from Lord & Taylor, six Indian head pennies, a silver dollar, two Kennedy half dollars, a vial of Ciara, and a small, soiled photograph of a woman having relations with a horse.

She took the self-service elevator to the sixth floor, found 6-B, drew herself erect. She took a deep breath, lifted her chin, rang the bell. She heard approaching footsteps. The door opened.

"Hello there." The elderly woman smiled. "I'm Edith Faye, Richard's mother. You must be Helen Miley. Do come in. Dickie's down buying some ginger ale, but he'll be right back."

"Thank you." Helen smiled. "Uck-uh, Uck-uh, Dick didn't mention you. I thought—"

"I think Dickie wanted it to be a surprise." Mrs. Faye smiled. "Let me take your things. Such a pretty fur."

"Such a pretty apartment." Helen smiled. "I suppose you—"

"Really too big for just the two of us." Mrs. Faye smiled. "And call me Edith. Dickie and all his friends do. Yes, since Mr. Faye died, Dickie and I have often talked of moving into something smaller and more modern—but of course you know what rents are like in these new apartment houses. Now you sit right there, Helen—I may call you Helen, may I not?—and we'll just have a nice little chat until Dickie gets back. I'm so happy you could drop by. I was saying to Dickie just the other day, 'Dickie,' I said, 'why don't you have your friends over more often? It's not right that I should just sit here day in and day out, night in and night out.' Not that I'm really lonely, of course. Dickie is such a comfort to me."

"Yes, Mrs. Faye." Helen smiled. "I'm sure—"

"Edith." She smiled. "Do call me Edith. I had a spell of illness last year—my heart, you know—and I couldn't ask for a better nurse. I tell you Dickie waited on me hand and foot. I always say a good child is a blessing from heaven. Especially when one reads every day of children slaughtering their parents with hatchets and things like that. Are your parents living, Helen?"

"No. They're both dead."

"What a shame they've passed away. But you must believe, my dear, that the soul hasn't died but is living in a different, happier form."

"Yes," Helen said.

"Do you live with relatives, dear? Or friends?"

"No. I live alone."

"Oh, my, such a danger. I was reading just the other day of a young woman who lived alone, and this monster followed her home from work one evening and in her hallway—well, of course, the paper didn't go into details—they never do, you know—especially the *Times*, which is the only paper Mr. Faye ever allowed in this house—all the others are simply trash, he would say—and the poor girl will never be the same, I'm sure. To what church do you belong, Helen?"

"Well..." Helen coughed. "I haven't—"

"The old things are best—don't you agree, my dear? Church and love of country and a few old friends. I was saying—"

He came in loaded down with grocery sacks. He had the decency to blush.

"Well," he said with a smile as slight as the crease in a tweed suit, "I see you two have met. Well."

"Really, that's much too heavy for you to carry," his mother said severely. "You should have made them deliver it. Goodness knows we spend enough with them. Men just don't know the first thing about shopping—don't you agree, my dear? Mr. Faye was exactly the same way. Send him out for a head of lettuce, and he'd come back with a roast of beef. Just putty in the hands of anyone with something to sell. Now take the packages into the kitchen, dear. Put the butter in the refrigerator and the eggs on the shelf. The canned things go in the right-hand cupboard, and you can stack the ginger ale under the sink."

"Yes, Edith. Would you like a drink?" he asked Helen.

"Yes, Dickie."

"Just a small glass of port for me, dear. You know what the

doctor said. My heart," she explained to Helen. "I have to be so careful. Fresh greens and broiled meat are all I'm allowed, and just one small glass of port on very special occasions. What a pretty frock. My, things are form-fitting this year, aren't they?"

"Well, not quite like this, Edith," Helen said. "I have this wonderful tailor, and after I buy a sheath, I take it in to him and try it on. Then I take a deep breath, and he just stitches it on me like a second skin. Of course, if I ever swallowed an olive, I'd look preggy, but it does fit well, doesn't it?"

"This weather," Mrs. Faye said mournfully. "We seem to be having so much rain lately. We really don't have autumns anymore—don't you agree, dear? Why I remember taking long walks with Mr. Faye in October when the nights were so balmy one needed only a thin scarf. Oh, Dickie, you used the hobnails. Well...never mind. It's just that they were a wedding gift, Helen, and there are only four glasses left, and I'm so afraid something might happen to them."

"Edith," he said morosely.

"I'll be careful," Helen promised. "Thanks, Uck-uh, Uck-uh, Dickie. Well, over the river and through the woods."

"My," Edith said, "I do admire a witty woman."

They sipped their drinks, looked up, smiled, sipped their drinks, looked up, smiled.

"Well," Edith said, her eyes as hard and shiny as licked stones, "isn't this nice?"

"How are things at the office?" he asked hoarsely. "How's business?"

"Okay," she said. "Loeb and—"

"Helen works for a public relations firm, Edith," he said hastily. "They publicize new products and things like that."

"How *interesting*," Edith said. "Oh, don't set your glass down there, dear; I'm afraid it will leave a ring. Dickie, do get those coasters I crocheted for you. You never want to use them. They're on the top shelf of the linen closet, next to the lace doilies. Men are so awkward around the home—don't you agree, dear? Mr. Faye was the same way. That man was always knocking over vases and kicking the legs of tables. I said to him, 'Mr. Faye,' I said, 'you may be a really fine sassafras broker, but you are the clumsiest man God ever created.' And do you know what he said?"

"No. What did Mr. Faye say?"

"He said, 'Well, my dear, you promised to take me for better or worse, and I'm afraid this is part of the worse!'"

"My," Helen said, "I do admire a witty man. Oh, thank you, Dickie. What a lovely little coaster. And crocheted out of grocery store string. That *is* clever, Edith."

"Thank you, dear. Do you think you might like to have half a dozen for your home?"

"Oh, I couldn't—"

"They don't take me long at all, and I have plenty of string. I've made them for all my friends, and I must say they do come in handy. I'll get started on yours tomorrow. Would you like them in that leaf pattern, Helen?"

"Yes, that would—"

"Or perhaps you'd prefer a checkerboard design?"

"Well, either will—"

"But I always say the checkerboard is so masculine. I think the leaf pattern would be nicer for a young lady's home."

"Could I have another scotch, Dickie?" Helen asked.

"My," Mrs. Faye said, smiling, "someone was thirsty. Dickie, why don't you put some of those little cheese crackers on a tray and bring them in? And I made some watercress sandwiches. The crackers are in a tin on the top shelf, and the sandwiches are on the bottom shelf of the refrigerator. Use the wooden tray—the one Aunt Evelyn sent from Hawaii."

"I know, Edith," his voice came faintly. "I know."

She was a blunt, neckless woman with blue hair elaborately set. Swollen veins made a bulging network under her elastic stockings.

"Well." She smiled at Helen. "Isn't this nice?"

"Do you have any other children?" Helen asked desperately.

"No." She frowned, sitting impaled on a vertical spit. "Dickie is my only baby. There was a little girl, but we don't speak of her."

"Oh," Helen said, "I'm sorry..."

"She would be a year older than Dickie, but as far as this family is concerned, she is dead. It is harsh, perhaps, but it is fair. We never discuss her."

"I'm sorry. I didn't mean—"

"She has chosen her path," Mrs. Faye said, smoothing the pleats of her blue silk dress, "and now she must walk alone. We did what we could, but she decided to reject our love and our advice. And now she must suffer. I'm sure she is suffering. Please don't feel we are cruel, my dear, but what will be, will be. I prefer not to talk about it."

"Of course."

"She had so much to give." Edith sighed. "So much. And she threw it away, simply *threw* it with both hands. A tragedy, my dear. A genuine tragedy. Someday, perhaps, I'll tell you the whole story, and you'll understand. But it's too painful to—"

"Here we are," he said. "Another drink and something to eat. Edith, how about another port?"

"Not right now, dear. You know what the doctor said. Now why don't you sit down, and we'll just chat. You've hardly said a dozen words."

"I've been busy," he protested. "I've been making—"

"Dickie has so few women friends," Mrs. Faye said to Helen. "I really do feel a boy his age should socialize more. But of course, it's so *difficult*. There are no more classes as there were when I came out, and one really can't be *sure*, can one?"

"No," Helen said. "One can't."

"Of course, he has many men friends, and they frequently visit. My, we have some high old times. Do you play Hearts, my dear?"

"No."

"But I do feel a woman is a *softening* influence on a man. Mr. Faye was such a great old bear of a thing when I married him. He was always puffing his pipe and burning holes in his coat pockets and throwing things around just every which way. I'm sure I had a softening influence on him. 'Edith,' he said to me once, 'God made me a man, but you've made me a gentleman.' I've never forgotten that."

"Do you mind if I smoke?" Helen asked.

"Of course not, my dear. I don't indulge, but I know how the habit—Dickie, get an ashtray for Helen. The blue one with the ridged edge. Light it for her, Dickie. Where are your manners? My, you've dropped a photograph from your purse, my dear. Your parents? I'd love to see it."

"Oh, no," Helen gulped. "No, it's nothing. Not my parents. A friend. Just a friend. Goodness, these are delicious watercress sandwiches. How do you make them?"

"Why," Edith said, puzzled, "you merely cut up your watercress and put it on your bread. Make sure you have plenty of butter on your bread. Really quite simple, my dear."

"I must remember." Helen nodded. "They're very delicious. Well, this has been nice, really nice. But now I'm afraid I must run along."

"So soon?" he said, his baggy face drooping. "You've only been here a moment."

"Surely you can stay longer, Helen?"

"No," she said firmly. "I really must go. I'm going out of town tomorrow. Friends in Philadelphia. A christening. Early train. I must get a good night's sleep. So sorry, Edith. Thank you for having me. I've enjoyed every minute of it."

"Well . . . if you must run. I do hope you'll come back. Dickie has spoken of you so often I felt I had to meet you. You've made quite an impression on this baby of mine, Helen."

"That's nice." Helen smiled. "Well, thanks again for everything."

"Perhaps the next time you visit I'll have your coasters ready," Mrs. Faye said, examining the liver spots on the backs of her hands.

"Wonderful. I'm looking forward. Good night, Edith. So nice. Good night, Dickie. No, don't come down. I can find my way. I'll grab a cab."

She carried the fur, smiling resolutely until the door of the elevator shut them from view. Then she looked in the polished brass, scowling at her reflection.

"I should have smashed her frigging hobnails," she said wrathfully.

10

CHARLES LEFFERTS MADE a noise like ripped silk. He moved convulsively in the darkness.

"My God," he gasped, "you *are* in a mood."

"I'll kill you," she said.

"Helen...."

"Shut up," she muttered. "Tonight you die like a dog."

His hollow laugh fluttered, turned into a meek little scream. "Your teeth." He giggled. "Take it easy."

"I won't take it easy. Here—that's my leaf pattern. And here—that's my checkerboard design."

"What the hell are you talking about?" he wondered, then yelped again, trying to wrench away.

"God made you a man," she growled. "I'm making you a gentleman."

He writhed, twisted, snorting, groaning.

"For better or for worse," she murmured. "This is part of the better. The lace doilies are in the linen closet."

"Are you drunk?" he demanded. "Oh, God, baby."

"Fresh greens and broiled meat," she said, "and one glass of port on very special occasions. Except in October when only a thin scarf is necessary."

"You're insane," he decided.

"Socialize," she whispered. "Socialize, you bastard."

"Take that," he said, entering into the festive spirit. "And that."

"Yes," she breathed, "the old things are best."

"Also that," he added.

"I'm putty in the hands of anyone with something to sell," she told him. "Send me for a head of lettuce, and I come back with a roast of beef. Be careful, buster. It was a wedding gift, and I wouldn't like to break it. The top shelf, darling. The crackers are on the top shelf."

"Goodish. Oh, oh, oh."

"I do feel a woman is a softening influence on a man."

Her voice died away.

They stopped talking.

He leaped out of bed, took a quick shower, powdered his armpits, lighted a cigar, crawled back beside her. The cigar glowed in the darkness. He held it out to her. She took a deep drag.

"Jesus," she said, "I felt that in my toes."

They handed the cigar back and forth, slowly filling the room with heavy smoke.

"My people never make war on your people," she grunted. "It is good. We will dwell in peace in the land of many pines."

"You were lucky you called when you did," he said. "I was just going out the door when I heard the phone ring."

"Yeah," she said sourly, "I sure am lucky."

"What's *with* you?" he demanded. "You in one of your all-men-should-drop-dead moods? My God, don't you ever cut your toenails?"

"I really despise your guts," she said thoughtfully. "I wish to hell I had known you were habit-forming."

"Come on—tell Uncle Charlie. Who lit the fuse on your Tampax?"

She drew a big mouthful of smoke, blew a perfect ring up into the darkness. She set the cigar butt carefully in the ashtray on the floor. She turned on her side, wriggled close to him, stroked his hair.

"You're getting bald," she said.

"You go to hell!" he shouted, and she laughed softly at the terror in his voice.

She traced his body with her fingertips as she told him all about Richard Faye and her visit to the Faye apartment. He listened silently, moving a bit when she pried a cool finger into his navel, tugged gently at the hairs on his thighs.

"And so that's the end of that," she concluded.

"No," he said seriously, "I don't think so. I think Dickie will be after you stronger than ever. He's Edith's boy, sure, but now he's met someone Edith's afraid of. He's going to prove his manhood by seeing you—and screw Edith. Also, Dickie realizes you don't like Edith, and he likes you for that, too."

"Thank you, Dr. Freud," she said. "Open your mouth and close your eyes, and I will give you a big surprise."

He did and she did.

He put his feet high up on the wall, squirming around until he was lying on the back of his neck. He looked at her, upside down, lips gaping in his forehead, eyes blinking in a huge chin.

"You say he's about forty? Poor bastard. I think you should marry him, baby."

"So you can get rid of me?"

"What difference would that make? No, just to let him live it up a little away from Edith. He's got a good job? Sounds like a perfect Frank. And you can be a perfect Shirley."

She cradled her head in the hollow of his neck and shoulder.

"You're sweet," she said. "I didn't think you could be so sweet. But what the hell, honey—I'm looking for a man; he's looking for a mother. It wouldn't work out. I've got a better idea."

He laughed quietly, his stomach bobbing up and down.

"No, thanks," he said.

"Aren't you ever going to get married?"

"Nope."

"Why not?"

"Why should I? What's the percentage? Give me one fat reason."

"You're going to end up a smelly old man in a furnished room, pinching the behinds of little girls in the park for kicks."

"Everyone tells me that." He sighed. "Why can't I end up a

fragrant old man living at the Waldorf and pinching a young model now and then?"

"Don't you want a son to carry on your reputation as a stud, you son of a bitch? Don't you want a family?"

"Hell, no. If they kept all kids in dark closets till the age of eighteen, I couldn't be happier."

"Aren't you ever lonely?"

"Sure. Occasionally. Who isn't? The loneliest woman I know has a wealthy husband, three children, and a lovely home. What does that prove?"

"You taste nice—you know that, doll? You smell a little like cedar, and your skin tastes sweet. I might just eat you up."

"Do," he said.

"You like me, don't you?"

"Sure."

"In your own dirty, crabby, twisty way I think you love me."

"Do you?"

"You wouldn't rub the bacon with me if you didn't."

"It's a game," he said. "You're a good player."

"How long did it take you to learn all the wrong things to say?"

"Are we going to fight again?"

"Why the hell not?" she demanded angrily.

"The payola. The big payola."

"Now what the hell is that supposed to mean?"

"Women shack up with me of their own free will. But they've got to convince themselves it's a big love affair and not just the old twitch. So when I refuse to join in the con, they get sore at me. I'm a filthy seducer, and I should be castrated by law. I've robbed them of that which is more precious than life itself. Then they've got to cry and carry on and call me dirty names to get their self-respect back."

"You know everything there is to know about women, don't you, buster?"

"Very little," he admitted unexpectedly, "but about a hundred times more than the average husband. Just don't try to hype me, baby. You like the brangle-buttock game as much as I do."

"More," she said.

"All right—more. So why bug me when it's over? You gave and I gave. You got and I got. We're even. And that's as far as it goes."

"Ahh ... shit," she muttered and put her legs up on the wall alongside his.

He turned on his side, propped himself on his elbow, peered down at her body. She was as loose and flowing as a silk ribbon.

"I bet if I had bigger tits, you'd marry me," she said.

"Nah. You're just right for this weather. Come late November or December I get out my overcoat and switch to heavier suits. I stop drinking gin and tonic and start on bourbon. Then I'll give you up and find a meatier pig. But right now you're perfect. Fall weight—know what I mean?"

She tried to be angry but couldn't.

"I just can't take you seriously, baby." She laughed.

He found the spot low on her naked ribs, flicked it with his practiced tongue; she leaped two feet off the bed, straight up.

"Nobody does." He sighed.

11

"NOTHING MUCH, KIDDO," Helen murmured, propping the telephone between chin and shoulder while she fumbled for a cigarette. "I counted the walls twice and changed the laces in my suede shoes. Otherwise, it's been a very dull evening. So tell me—how did you make out with the Camel?"

Peggy Palmer giggled nervously. "Ducks, get set for the biggest surprise of your life."

"He's got two dongs?"

"Better than that—I'm going to be married."

"Peggy. My God. Peggy Palmer. Peggy, tell me about it! Tell me every single thing! What in God's name happened?"

"Well, listen, darling, I'm calling from a phone booth so I'll have to cut it short. But I just couldn't wait to get home; I had to tell you about it right away."

"So *tell* me!"

"Well, we checked into this hotel last night like I told you.

There's nothing cheap about him, I must say, Helen. He had the bellboy bring up a bottle of champagne. A small one. You should have seen the bellboy, ducks. The cutest little thing with curly black hair and buttons all over."

"The hell with the bellboy," Helen growled. "What *happened*?"

"Well, we had a glass of champagne, and he laughed sort of and said he guessed I knew what we were there for, and I said yes, and he said he'd go into the bathroom and give me a chance to get settled."

"Settled?"

"That's what he said. My God, Helen, he must have been in there an hour. I thought he had fallen in, for Chrissakes."

"Men kill me, baby. They really do. What were you wearing?"

"I had my new shorty pajamas—the blue ones I got in that sale at Bloomingdale's—you know, the chiffon with white lace trim—and finally he came out naked as a needle—boy, is he ever fat—and switched off all the lights."

"And?"

Peggy sighed.

"A rabbit," she said softly. "A goddamned rabbit. Fast? An Olympic champ. And the grunts! I was worried, ducks. I mean I thought he had sprung a hernia or something. Well, then we were just lying there without saying a word, and I was thinking how silly it was to spend twenty dollars for the room for such a short time—but of course, we had it for twenty-four hours and didn't have to rush out or anything. It was a beautiful room with twin beds and a dresser that—"

"Oh, screw the room!" Helen exploded. "What about the proposal?"

"Well, as we were just laying there and not saying anything, he began to whistle."

"Whistle?"

"Yes, he just whistled through his teeth. I felt it was quite out of place and told him so, but he said he liked to whistle in bed and I better get used to it because I was going to hear a lot of it. Well, I didn't understand him at first and said don't count your chickens before they are hatched, my boy, and one summer doesn't make a swan, and how did he know I was going to hear him whistle in bed again? And he said he heard that a husband and wife spend a lot of time in bed together, and I tell you,

Helen, my heart just stopped. It just *stopped*."

"I can believe," Helen said eagerly. "Then what happened?"

"Well, naturally I wanted to pin him down, and I asked him right out if that was a proposal, and he said—"

"I'm sorry, your time is up," a voice said. "Deposit a dime for the next three minutes, please."

"Listen, operator," Peggy said desperately, "I don't have any more change, and this is important."

"I'm sorry," the operator said. "Your time is up."

"Oh, isn't she mean!" Helen said.

"I am not mean," the operator said. "But after all, we have certain rules and regulations by which we have to abide by them."

"This girl just happens to have become engaged," Helen said wrathfully, "and you broke in just when she was telling me about it."

"Well, I certainly want to wish her the best and all," the operator said, "but still . . . I tell you, miss, why don't you give your friend the number of the phone you're calling from, and then she can call you back."

"That's a good idea, Peg," Helen said. "What's your number?"

Peggy told her.

"Stay right there," Helen said. "Hang up, and I'll dial you right back. Thank you very much, operator."

"My name is Francine," the operator said wistfully. "You're very welcome. And I want to wish you the best of everything, Peggy."

"Likewise," Peggy said. "Call me right back, Helen."

"Then what happened?" Helen asked breathlessly after she had dialed Peggy's number. "You were just pinning him down when Francine interrupted."

"Wasn't she sweet?" Peggy said. "I wish I knew her address so I could send her a card or something. Well, like I was saying, I asked him right out if he was proposing, and he said yes, he was. Then he asked me if he could kiss me, and I said okay but that was *all* because I don't believe in engaged couples having sex before they are married, and he said he agreed completely and all he wanted to do was kiss me. So then he kissed me and rolled over, and he was asleep real soon, but of course, I was too excited to sleep. I was going to sneak out and call you, but then I thought I better not in case he woke up and I wasn't there and what would he think? This morning we just got up late and checked out and went and got something to eat. Then we saw a double feature on Forty-second Street—*Deep Throat* and *Hot Shot. Hot Shot* wasn't much, but don't miss *Deep Throat.* It's got a scene in it—honest, ducks, I don't know how they let them show it. So that's all there was to it, and now I'm engaged to be married, just like that."

"Darling, I want to wish you the best of everything," Helen Miley said warmly. "When is it going to be?"

"We didn't talk definite dates. I mean, I thought he had done plenty for one night, and I shouldn't push him. He mentioned something about long engagements, but I'll have to talk to him about that. I don't believe in long engagements—do you?"

"Hell, no. Grab him fast, baby."

"I fully intend to," Peggy said primly, and already Helen could detect the superior tone of a woman with a man all her own. "Well, listen, I better sign off now and get on home. How about lunch tomorrow? I want to hear all about your date with Uck and how it came out."

"Not much to tell, kiddo, but lunch is fine. I'll call you tomorrow morning. And best wishes again, Peggy. I hope you'll be very happy."

"Thank you very much. My only wish, Helen, is that you should find a fellow, too. Wouldn't it be wonderful if we could have a double wedding?"

"Grand," Helen said, without spirit. "Good night, doll, and thanks for calling."

She put the telephone slowly back in the cradle. She looked down at Rocco, coiled sleepily at the end of the couch.

"Peggy's getting married, Rocco," she said.

He lifted his head, yawned.

"Honey baby Rocco boy," Helen murmured. "Do you love me, honey baby Rocco boy?"

She rose wearily to her feet, stood motionless a moment. The apartment was suddenly enormous, empty, frightening. She moved about slowly, locking doors and windows, snapping off lights.

When she stood in front of the parakeet cage, night cover in hand, the bird hopped to the front perch, stared at her bravely.

"Focku," the bird chirped. "Fockufockufocku."

"Thank you very much," she said bitterly. "Proud of yourself, you little bastard?"

She went into the bedroom, took off her robe, sat down at the dresser. She put her hair up in curlers, buttered her face with night cream, slung a No-Chin strap over her ears and down under her jaw. She stared at her image in the mirror.

"Darth Vader," she said hollowly.

Rocco glanced at her, growled in alarm, then slunk to his blanket, curled up in a ball.

"Good night, honey baby Rocco boy," she called.

She clicked off the light, opened the bedroom window wide, climbed into bed. She felt bone-weary. She lay there, vowing not to take a pill, hoping for sleep, trying to remember the name of that boy in high school who had been expelled for drilling a hole in the wall of the girl's locker room. William, she decided. William Jamieson.

After a while she dozed off, lying on her back, naked and uncovered. At first she thought the buzzing was part of a vague dream she was having—William Jamieson was drilling a hole in her bedroom wall. Then she awakened, realized it was the front-door buzzer. She got up, stumbled in the darkness, cursed, flicked on the bedside lamp, struggled into slippers, went flapping into the hallway. She stood close to the door.

"Who is it?" she demanded.

"Uck. Uck Faye."

The No-Chin strap kept her jaw from falling.

"It's late," she whispered. "Go away."

"It isn't late," he said. "I want to talk to you, Helen."

"I don't want to talk to you. Go on—cop a walk."

"Please, Helen..."

She suddenly remembered the curlers, night cream, chin strap.

"Jesus," she said aloud. Then, "All right. I'm going to unlock the door. But you give me a minute to get into the bedroom. I'm bare-ass naked. Then you come in, lock the door and put the chain on, and go into the living room."

"Thank you, Helen," he said humbly.

"That's quite all right, Dickie," she said stiffly. She unlocked the door, darted back to her bedroom.

When she came out ten minutes later, she was wearing yellow silk pants and a man's shirt knotted in front. Her belly button showed. Her hair was combed out, her face free of makeup. She was smoking a cigarette in a giddy holder.

He rose from the living room couch when she entered, didn't

sit down again until she was curled up in a soft chair. Rocco stalked out, inspected them sleepily, went back into the bedroom.

Faye hung his head, massaged his hands.

"Well?" she said sharply.

"I didn't plan it that way," he started. "I swear I didn't. I tried to get her out of the house. I thought I could. But she's shrewd, Helen. She's sharp. She finally got it out of me that you were coming over, and then I couldn't have budged her with a peavey. That's a long-handled hook used to move logs. I rushed down for ginger ale, figuring I could call you and head you off, but you'd already left."

She was silent.

"It's happened before," he said miserably. "She always wants to be there."

Helen looked at him steadily. "All right," she said finally, "I'll buy that. You didn't plan it. But if she acts that way all the time, for Chrissakes, why didn't you suggest meeting me here, instead of at your place?"

He wouldn't look at her. He couldn't look at her.

"I don't know," he said, so low she could hardly hear him. "I guess I was frightened."

"Frightened? Of what?"

"Of you."

She snorted. "You're a big boy, buster. You outweigh, outreach, and outmuscle me. What's to be frightened?"

He looked up at her then. "You outlove me."

She sat a moment, puzzling, then went into the kitchen, mixed two scotch and waters. She brought them back into the living room, handed him one.

"Here," she said. "Set it anywhere you like."

"Helen." He winced. "Please, don't. You've got to understand her."

"Oh, I understand her," Helen said angrily, gulping her drink. "She's a lonely, bitchy old woman. She's got more drive and balls than you'll ever have. She's got her claws into you deep, and she won't give up until you pry them loose. That's the way it is, isn't it?"

"Yes. But she thinks it's for my own good. She really thinks she's doing it for me."

"The old craperoo," Helen sneered.

"Sure," he agreed. "All right . . . what shall I do? Leave her? She's my mother. I'm all she's got. So do I walk out on her? You tell me."

"I shouldn't have to tell you anything. What kind of a man are you anyway?"

"What kind of a man?" he asked, surprised. "I don't know. That's God's honest truth. I don't know what kind of a man I am."

She looked at him narrowly. "Ever sleep with a woman, Uck?"

He stared at the floor. "A few times. Whores. It was no good."

"You want to stay here tonight?"

"I don't know."

"I don't know, I don't know," she mimicked. "There's a hell of a lot you don't know."

"Helen," he pleaded, "I'm trying. I'm really trying. I'm just beginning to discover what's happening to me. I see it happening, and it's terrible. I don't want it to happen, but I don't know how to stop it."

"What's happening?"

"Things," he muttered. "I'm getting mushy. I was always too soft, but now I'm getting mushy. My body and what I am, inside. Custard. The strength is going out of me. I can't be the kind of man I want to be. I'm becoming someone else, someone I don't like. The next few years—God, I'm afraid to think of it. Helen. Helen . . ."

Then, suddenly, he was across the room, down on his knees, clutching her legs, his face in her lap, all ready for a session of growling in the busby.

"Helen," he murmured, "Helen . . ."

"Get on your goddamned feet," she snapped furiously, pushing at him. "I'm no Edith, buster. Get over there on the couch. Go on, *get*."

He dragged himself upright, slunk back to the couch, sat down again, stared.

"You hate me," he said.

"No, I don't hate you." She sighed. "I just don't like to see a man crawl, that's all. Listen, son, I'm the kind of a woman who's been through the mill twice. I've done a lot and lived a lot. And I know there's nothing you can't change if you really want to. You can be any kind of a man you want to be if you want bad enough. But do you?"

He was silent.

"I meet a lot of men like you. More every day. No balls. That's not for me. I want a *man*. You understand? I'd rather have a guy who kicks my tail or slams me in the chops now and then than a guy who puts his head in my lap and cries. That's my bit. What the hell's happening to men anyway?"

He didn't say anything.

"You're not on the chew, are you, Uck?"

He raised his head. "What?"

"Fag?"

He stared at her. "No."

"Uck."

"Once."

"Uck."

"Or twice."

"When?"

"Long time ago."

"When?"

"Years. Years ago."

"Who?"

"A guy. A friend."

"Still see him?"

"Yes. But it's all over."

"Uck."

"I swear it is, Helen. I swear to God."

"Edith know?"

"Of course not. She doesn't even guess at these things."

"I'll bet. He one of those guys you play Hearts with?"

"Yes."

"Swish or rough trade?"

"He's a weight lifter."

"Oh."

"I swear it's all over, Helen. I never think about it anymore. Why are you doing this to me?"

"Doing what?"

"Asking me these things. Making me say these things."

"I don't know you," she said wonderingly. "I've been seeing you for weeks, and I actually don't know you. I want to find out, that's all."

"It's one of the things," he said. "One of the mushy things. I'm afraid. You're the first woman I've met I can talk to. You've got the guts I wish I had. You never pity yourself, do you?"

"Sure. Sometimes."

"But not always. Not like I do."

"I take it as it comes. I get through each day."

"God," he said hoarsely, drooping.

"What?"

"I'm so miserable."

"You don't have to be."

"I can't do it myself."

"What do you want from me?"

"You're hard."

"Oh, sure."

"I want to learn that. I want to be hard."

"And shiny and ride with the punch."

"And shiny and ride with the punch," he repeated.

"You really want to, Uck?"

"Yes."

"Really?"

"Yes. *Yes.*"

"You can do it."

"How?" he begged. "Tell me how."

"Do it, that's all. You're too fat. You eat too much, and you drink too much. Cut down. Get rid of your cats. No more games of Hearts. Tell the Muscle to get lost. Tell Edith. Don't ask her—*tell* her."

"My God."

"Not all at once. Little by little."

"My God . . . you think I can?"

She shrugged. "Do you want to?"

"I swear I do. I *do.*"

"I'll help."

"Oh, Helen, that'll be divine."

She cursed.

"I'm sorry," he said hastily. "No more 'divine.'"

She nodded. "It's a good place to start."

"Can I stay?"

"Tonight?"

"Yes."

She thought it over. "No. I don't think so. Next weekend maybe."

"All right."

"All right," she mimicked again. "'Helen, may I stay the night? No? All right.' That's what I mean. You've got a lot to learn, kiddo."

"Yes," he said angrily, "I'll learn."

She softened. "You'll do okay, Uck. I'll see you once during the week for lunch. Then you come over Friday night. Tell Edith you're coming."

"I will."

"Eat a lot of seafood."

"All right."

"And chili."

He laughed.

"Plenty of graphite in the old Eversharp," she explained. "Rare steaks—things like that. I'll teach you a lot."

"Yes," he said happily. "Oh, yes."

"But promise—the weight lifter goes."

"I'll tell him tomorrow."

"*Call* him. Don't see him."

"Thank you, Helen."

"For what? Let's wait and see. God, I'm dead. Shove off, Uck."

He rose, straightened his spine, squared his shoulders, sucked in his belly, lifted his chin.

"What a sack of suet." She smiled. "That can! But that's okay, baby. You can't drive a spike with a tack hammer. Good night, sweet."

He strode across the room, yanked her to her feet, kissed her hard.

"Wow," she said.

"Teacher," he said.

"Knock me another."

He kissed her again.

"Double-wow," she said.

"Helen, I love you."

"Mmm. Again."

"I love you."

"Backwards."

"You love I."

"Both ways from the middle."

"Love I you. Love you I."

Laughing, holding hands, they walked toward the door.

"Friday," she said.

"I'll bring your coasters," he teased.

She said two words to him. They weren't "Happy Birthday."

12

Her radio-alarm clicked on, and, she was to remember later, she awoke to "Every Day Is Ladies' Day with Me" from *The Red Mill*. She lolled a few minutes, feeling the cool outside air, the sweet warmth beneath the covers.

She turned her head and looked at Rocco curled up on his blanket.

"Honey baby Rocco boy," she called, dangling a hand over the side of the bed.

But he didn't come over or even lift his head. He seemed to be brooding.

"Sleepy?" Helen asked him. "Go ahead—cork off. Live a little."

She swung out of bed. She sat there, yawning and stretching, scrubbing her scalp, licking her lips. She stumbled over to the window to slam it shut, let the Venetian blind rattle down.

She stood in front of the full-length mirror fastened to the inside of her bedroom door. Breasts sagging a bit? Waist bulging a little? Ass sinking a trifle? She raised her hands high over her head, clasped them, began moving her upper torso side to side, bending from the waist, wuffing.

Ten side bends. Then ten deep knee bends, while hanging onto the knob of the closet door. Then pulling in her stomach muscles until they trembled from the strain, while she counted six. Then bending over to touch the floor, trying to keep her shaking knees locked and straight. Count of ten.

Then she gasped, "Jesus!" sat down on the edge of the bed, and smoked a cigarette while the radio played "In Old New York." Rocco's eyes were open. They had followed her exercises, but he wasn't moving. She went over and knelt by him, her naked body a question mark on its side.

She put a hand on his forehead, felt his button nose. He seemed feverish.

"What's the matter, baby?" she asked. "Aches and pains?"

His tail moved faintly. Suddenly, he began to catch his breath in great asthmatic sobs—"Ah-hunh, ah-hunh, ah-hunh"—his mouth wide open, his eyes squeezed shut.

"You stop that," she said, suddenly frightened. "Now stop it."

She put a hand lightly on his chest. After a few minutes, he began to breathe in his usual wheezing gasps.

"I'll bring you some milk," she promised him. "I'll bring it right in here to you. You won't even have to move."

She went into the kitchen, poured some milk into his feeding dish, added some warm water, stirred in a raw egg, and, at the last minute, decided to add a few drops of brandy. She took it into the bedroom. He was lying on the floor, head between his paws. He looked up at her. She didn't like the sound of his breathing. Something was catching in there.

She put the dish down near his nose, but he wouldn't even sniff at it.

She smoothed the scraggly hair on top of his head. "Honey baby Rocco boy," she said. "I'm sorry you're not feeling well."

She took a quick shower, swallowed the Pill, came back into the bedroom. He was still there, his head still down. His eyes were moving about the room. He was looking at everything. He hadn't touched his breakfast.

"Better?" she asked him hopefully. "Feeling better?"

She dressed quickly. She was knotting her belt when his

racking, pained breathing started again. He couldn't stop. His whole body shook as he tried to gulp some air.

Beginning to feel panicky, she knelt again by his side, put a hand lightly on his cheek, tried to speak soothingly.

"Come on, baby," she whispered. "Come *on*."

Now his whole body was shaking, quivering, his back legs jerking and twitching. She pulled his Black Watch tartan blanket over him, tucked it around his neck. But the trembling didn't stop. Now his mouth was stretched wide open. Some kind of a glaucous liquid was oozing out.

"Oh, my God," she said, biting at her thumb knuckle.

She grabbed the directory, looked up the number of her vet—the one on Fifty-third Street. She dialed, but there was no answer. It was just a few minutes after nine.

She sat there, the dead phone in her hand, thinking. Now the thing to do is think. I must think how to handle this. She thought and decided to give her vet another five minutes. Then, if his office didn't answer, she'd call the ASPCA. She'd take Rocco over to them. How? He was too heavy to carry in her arms. She didn't have a carrier. The doorman could get him down to a cab. How? Maybe she could get a box, a carton. She could line it with his blanket. The doorman could...She dialed Swanson & Feltzig. Susie Carrar answered brightly.

"Hi, sweetie," Helen Miley said. "Is Harry in yet?"

"Morning, babe," his calm voice came on. "How you feeling this morning?"

"Harry," she said lightly, "something silly has happened." She looked at Rocco. His black tongue was lolling. She could see his chest heaving under the blanket. "Rocco—he's my dog; I told you about him—he doesn't look so good. I think maybe he's dying or something. He can't breathe. I've got to get him to the vet or maybe the ASPCA. But I don't know how to handle him. I don't think he can walk. I was wondering..."

He didn't hesitate a second.

"I'll be right over," he said. "No sweat. Ten minutes at the most. Hang on."

"Oh, yes," she said, her eyes filling...

Harry Tennant was there, down on his knees alongside Rocco, stroking his head, wiping his lips with a soaked cloth, when Helen finally got through to her vet.

"Is this an emergency case?" he asked, the compleat surgeon, water dripping from his elbows. Gown! Gloves! Mask!

"Yes, it is. He can't breathe. He's not moving. He seems—"

"Bring him over right away. A Dalmatian, you say?"

"A sort of a spaniel," she said faintly.

She couldn't have managed without Harry. He went downstairs, got a big empty carton from the liquor store on the corner. It said "H&L: The Scotch of Pleasant Memories" on the side. They lined it with newspapers, then with Rocco's blanket. They laid him tenderly inside. Harry carried it down to the street. Marv was on duty and practically threw himself under a cab to stop it. They got Rocco over to the vet.

There was one old woman in the outer office. She held a tiny kitten on her lap. The kitten mewed.

"You shut your mouth," the woman said.

They waited five minutes. Harry was about ready to break down the inner door when the nurse strolled out, starched and smiling.

"Doctor will see you now," she said to Helen.

"I was here first," the biddy snapped.

"This is an emergency." The nurse smiled. "Please be patient."

The kitten wailed.

"You shut up," the old woman said.

Harry carried the whiskey carton with Rocco inside into the inner office, deposited it gently on the stainless steel table. He touched Helen on the shoulder, smiled at her, then went back to the outer office, closing the door behind him.

"Now then," the vet said, "what have we here?"

"Doctor, he can't breathe, and he's trembling. He wouldn't eat anything this morning, and he gets these fits of—"

"Yes, yes," he said. "Yes, yes."

God, how he glistened. Steel-gray hair, skin that looked as if it had been scrubbed and rubbed with sandpaper. Huge hands with fingers that had been squeezed from tubes. And spotless whites. A halo about his head and in the background, faintly, a diapason and a mixed choral group going, "Oooh-aah-eee-aah-ooh-aah. Hallelujah!"

He lifted the stethoscope off Rocco's heaving chest and faced Helen.

"A moment," he said. "Let us check his medical history."

It was beautiful—the cards on a revolving file, each card with an identifying serial number. Then punch the number into the master file, and out pops Rocco—worms, infected eyes, diarrhea, asthma, seven teeth extracted, etc. There's Rocco in the master file.

"Rocco," he said. "Yes. Twelve, is he? Or thirteen?"

"Going on thirteen."

"Yes. well we're afraid he won't make it."

"Won't make it?"

"He's in very bad shape, Miss Miley. We can't do a thing about the breathing. That ulcerated tumor on the stomach never healed. His mouth is a mess. And look at this..."

He lifted one of Rocco's back legs, let it drop with a plunk.

"Don't do that," Helen said angrily.

"No feeling. We think we've got paralysis there."

"Paralysis? From what?"

"Miss Miley, he's old. For his breed, he's just an old dog. He's falling apart. We can't put him back together again. Now he's in pain. He can hardly breathe."

"Isn't there anything you can do?"

"No."

She put a hand on Rocco's face. He got his tongue out to give her fingers one lick.

"Nothing?" she asked.

"No," the splendid fellow said. "Nothing."

A fire engine went by outside. She could hear the siren.

"How do you do it?"

"What? Pardon? We didn't hear you."

"How do you do it?"

"Oh. With a needle. A shot. Absolutely no pain. He just goes to sleep. You can hold him if you like. We assure you, he'll feel less pain than he's feeling now."

"And after?"

"After?"

"You don't—you know—you don't chop him up, do you?"

"Chop him up?" he cried indignantly. "Certainly not. We take care of everything. Leave everything to us. Well?"

"You're sure you can't do anything?"

"Positive. He's a terminal case. Well?"

"Yes. All right."

He whisked a form from a file drawer.

"Sign here, please," he said.

She went back to the outer office. Harry was waiting, smoking a cigarette.

"You shut your mouth," the old woman said to her kitten.

"Listen, Harry," Helen said, "you might as well go back to the office. There's nothing you can do here. I'll be in later. This afternoon maybe. Thanks for everything. You were great. I couldn't have managed without you."

"How is he?"

"Rocco? Well... not so good. They're going to put him down. The doctor said he should be put down."

"Oh?" he said. "Ah," he said. "Well, maybe I'll just wait around. I'll just sit out here and wait. Whenever you're ready to go."

"No," she said, putting a hand on his arm, smiling up at him. "Thanks anyway, but I can handle this. You go back to the office. I'll be along later. Okay?"

"Sure, babe," he said, reaching down to pat her cheek. "Take care now."

He turned, went out the door.

There was a small inner room off the main consulting room. She sat there in a silly chair of steel tubing and black plastic webbing, and she waited. She waited thirty minutes, but perhaps it was five. The shining doctor came in carrying Rocco on a disposable paper mat—the maître d': "And here we have the whole roast suckling pig garnished with...." He started to put Rocco on the floor, but Helen took mat and dog onto her lap.

"We estimate twenty minutes at most." He smiled.

She looked at him with hatred. "Thanks," she said.

Rocco seemed very calm, very quiet. He just lay there, breathing easier now, staring straight ahead. Helen began stroking him.

"Laugh and the world laughs with you," she told him. "Cry and you cry alone."

His eyes rolled sideways to look up at her. His tail gave one feeble twitch.

"The man worthwhile is the man who can smile when everything goes dead wrong."

Rocco liked that one. He raised his head slightly, and she bent her head to kiss him, smelling that beloved stench.

"So, you dirty bastard," she said, "you're leaving me alone, are you? You're leaving me by myself?"

But mostly she didn't talk. She just sat there, holding him on her lap on the disposable paper mat, touching him.

"Stupid dog," she said once.

He was very good. His eyes rolled sideways to look at her.

Finally, his old lips curled back to reveal his horrendous gums and teeth, and he began to pant slightly, black tongue hanging. She stroked him mechanically, her hand moving from muzzle to neck to body to tail—long strokes. After a while she began to scratch gently around his tail, which he dearly loved.

He was going, going... Eyes closing. Breathing stilled. She leaned close.

"Listen, sweetie," she whispered, "before you go there's something I've got to tell you. Something I've never told you before..."

Rocco tried to lift his head but couldn't make it.

"You're not really my son," she whispered. "You're adopted. But I wanted you. I wanted *you*."

After a while the shining man came in.

"Well," he said briskly, "are we finished?"

"Yes," Helen Miley said, "we are finished."

She came out into the sunlight, and there was lank, black Harry Tennant, leaning against the building, smoking a cigarette, watching the world go by.

He looked at her. "Okay?"

She nodded.

He took her arm; they began to amble.

"Home?" he asked. "Or back to the office?"

"Maybe I'll just take the day off."

He didn't say anything. Just walking along beside her. Just there.

"God, what a beautiful day," she said.

"Look at that sky," she said.

"I love days like this," she said. "You get maybe a few good weeks in May and maybe a few good weeks in October. You know? Sky clear. Air you can breathe."

"I really love this day," she said.

He let her run off at the mouth like that, occasionally looking down at her, smiling his distant smile. Then they were on the sidewalk outside Helen's apartment house.

"I better get back to the office," Harry said.

She looked at him.

"All right," he said. "For a few minutes..."

He sat on the couch in the living room, hunched over, forearms on his knees, his long basketball player's hands dangling. Helen made coffee and also served some powdered doughnuts. She took one bite out of her doughnut, then ran into the bathroom, slamming the door behind her.

He sat there patiently, looking down at his hands, thinking what strange things hands are, really, when you stare at them long enough. That squarish piece of meat and bone with crazy lines on it. Those five long things coming out of it. There didn't seem to be any design to it. It looked as if it had been put together by a demented carpenter or maybe by a kid who takes a roller skate apart, nails the parts on the front and back of a two-by-four, adds an orange crate and pieces of sawed-off broomstick for handles, and he's got a Cadillac. Right? That's what a hand looks like.

After a while Helen came out of the bathroom. She had washed her face with cold water and was feeling a little better.

"I'm going to have a slam," she announced. "You want one?"

"I'll join you." He nodded.

She had a bottle of scotch and brought it out with some glasses, a soup plate full of ice cubes, a pitcher of tap water. She took hers with water, but Harry drank his warm, sipping it.

"How long did you have him?" he asked.

"All his life. One Christmas I got a bonus—fifty dollars. He was in a window up on Lexington, with a bunch of others who looked like his brothers and sisters. I mean they all looked like the same litter. They were chasing each other around on the torn newspaper and biting each other and rolling around and making wee-wee. You know. But he was just sitting there, very solemn, staring out the window. He looked so lonely. Like nobody loved him. I learned later it was an act. The kid was an actor. They should have made him join Equity. He knew exactly how to get bought. You sit there and stare out the window, your eyes wide open. Your eyes glisten. Maybe you squeeze out a tear. And after a while some jelly-hearted slob comes along and buys you and takes you home to a warm place where you have a soft bed, and they love you and feed you. The little bastard. He had it all figured out."

Harry chuckled. "I guess he did."

"Well... what the hell. He was only a dog."

Harry nodded. "Better get another one."

"Maybe. Someday. Not right now." She looked over at the parakeet cage. The bird was preening himself. "You think he knows? The bird?"

Harry shrugged. "Could be."

"I really don't like that bird. I guess I shouldn't say that, but it's the truth. I just don't like him. There's nothing between us."

"Why did you buy him?"

"He was on sale at Gimbel's. I thought he'd be, you know, like company for Rocco while I was gone all day. But Rocco didn't like him either. I think I'll get rid of him. You want him?"

"No," Harry said. "Thanks."

"I suppose you think I'm some nutty dame, getting all upset about a dog."

"No, babe, I don't think that."

"He had papers, you know. He was someone. His grandfather was a champion. Some kennel out in Nebraska. I could show you his papers."

"No, that's all right."

"Well, anyway, I loved him."

"Nothing wrong with that."

"I guess not. Stinky little bastard..."

She poured herself another drink hastily, took a big gulp.

"We've all got troubles," she said.

"Sure. That's what life is all about."

They just sat there quietly, nibbling on their drinks, the whiskey getting to them.

"Do you think there's a heaven for dogs?" she asked suddenly.

"Sure. Why not? All living things. Dogs and all animals and cockroaches and bugs of all types. Why should it only be for people?"

"Yes," she said wonderingly. "That's right."

So....

She came over, sat beside him on the couch. She put an arm around his neck. She kissed him.

"I feel so," she said. "I feel so."

"I know, babe," he murmured. "I know."

He shouldn't have said the word "babe" right then because it shattered her. She really let loose and came apart. He had his hands full, holding her, stroking her, comforting her, saying things until her weeping dried, until she calmed down and stopped trembling.

"Jesus, I'm sorry," she gasped. "I'm really sorry. I didn't think that would happen. I really thought I could handle it."

She couldn't understand what he was saying. He was just saying things in a low voice, whispering, kind of, stroking her hair. He took out his breast-pocket handkerchief—it was silk in a nice yellow and red paisley pattern—and wiped her tears away. He was doing everything right, holding her, very serious.

He held her until she was all right again. She took three deep breaths, then pulled away, got up, began walking around the room. She picked things up. She put things down.

"So... what have we got?" she asked. "The mailing on the Cantabile account will go out this week—right?"

"Yes, that's right."

"Let's see... the letters to the Parking Association?"

"I checked with Solly this morning. He's working on them. We'll have a rough proof tomorrow."

"Yes. Good." She stared out the window. "I'm going to be all right now, Harry."

She called Susie Carrar. All was quiet at the office. The Bobbsey Twins hadn't come in, and there was no crisis. So Helen and Harry had another scotch.

"This is nice," she said. "I really like this. It's nice to play hooky. Ever play hooky?"

"Oh, sure, babe. A couple of times. It *is* nice."

He pulled his tie open, unbuttoned the neck of his shirt. He opened the laces of his shoes. Then he sprawled out, flopped way down on the couch so his body formed almost a straight line from the back of his neck to his heels.

"I'm making myself at home," he informed her.

She nodded happily.

"I guess you think I'm pretty fresh, Boss?"

"I like fresh men," she declared. "I like men to come on strong. I like to flirt with men in restaurants. You know—sort of look at them. I like it when men wink at me on the street or when truck drivers whistle and say dirty things. Once they were digging up Forty-sixth Street, and for a week I walked two blocks out of my way so these guys digging this ditch would whistle at me. They waited for me every morning. It was a great way to start the day."

"Wooo-ee," he breathed. "I haven't had so much to drink before lunch for years and years."

"Harry, are you hungry?" she asked anxiously. "I could make you something. Like a sandwich. Or I could call the deli."

"No. That's all right. Thank you, babe."

"Listen," she said, suddenly serious, "I don't want to make trouble for you."

"Trouble?"

"Well. You know. I mean about those things you said. You said you wouldn't touch another woman if Iris Kane would come back to you. You promised God. That's what you told me."

"Right on." He sighed, eyes closed. "That's what I said. I promised God."

"God," she scoffed. "I don't think He's so great. I saw a little kid on the street the other day all crippled up. And I saw a beautiful young girl, and she was blind. And earthquakes and floods and all that. All those people die. Little babies. I think He's doing a lousy job. I could do a better job than that."

"Maybe you should be God."

"I still say He's, you know, like inefficient."

He opened his eyes, looked at her solemnly. "Well, you know how hard it is to get good help these days."

Then they broke up. Before they knew it, she was in his arms; they were rolling around on the couch, muzzling each other. But it didn't feel right, just yet. Helen kicked off her shoes.

"The thing to do," she said, "the thing to do. . . ."

"The thing to do?"

"Yes. The thing to do—is to have another drink?"

He thought that over. "Yes," he finally agreed, "that's the thing to do."

She brought more ice from the kitchen, slopped more scotch into their glasses, spilling some on the cocktail table.

"We think we've got paralysis there," she said.

"What?"

"Harry, it may take some time. I mean to get adjusted to each other. People get married, and they spend weeks. Months. You know?"

"I guess you're right."

They were silent. Drinking. They didn't have the need to talk right then. They sat in quiet for almost fifteen minutes. But then it picked right up again. . . .

"I figure about three minutes for us," she said.

He considered. "Maybe two."

She took him by the hand, her little white thing gripping that great clump of overripe bananas, and she led him into the bedroom. They stood side by side, staring at their reflection in the big mirror on the inside of the bedroom door.

"Great God above," Harry said in an awed voice, "if we're not the damnedest."

They were, too. The mirror couldn't even catch the top of his head. And she barely came to his wishbone. They stood there, hand in hand, staring at their image, trying to make some sense out of what they saw and what was happening—him so tall, black, skinny; her so short, blond, white, the good body on her.

"I could tuck you in my vest pocket," he told her.

"You do that." She nodded. "You do just that."

She was a fast woman out of her clothes. Dress over her head, panty hose peeled off her legs—and that was that: bing bing bing.

"Leave your wristwatch on," she said to him.

"My wristwatch? Boy, that's freaky. Helen, that's really freaky. I've known some people they like freaky things—but my *wristwatch*? Babe, you've got to admit that's really freaky."

"That's not freaky." She yawned, a great jawbreaker of a yawn. "I just want you to wear it. Good-bye."

She whisked into the other room. By the time she came back with the scotch, the soup plate of ice cubes and some new water, he was in bed. The sheet was pulled up, tucked around his chin. But his feet were sticking out—long, shiny, prehensile feet that looked like antique musical instruments. Fugue in A-Sharp Minor Written for Harry's Feet.

She slipped beneath the sheet, snuggled close. She kissed him.

"I give you this," she said.

"And I give you that," he said.

"And I give you this."

"And I give you that."

"And I tickle you here."

"And I tickle *you* here."

"And this for you."

"And *this* for you."

It went on and on, interrupted occasionally to splash some whiskey.

"And now I give you this."

"And now I give you that."

They lay back, panting. Wondering what the hell all this was leading to. Knowing.

"Now look," he said finally. "Let's be sensible about this."

"Sensible."

"Let's be smart and logical."

"Smart and logical."

"You know..." he said. Long pause. "You know because

you're so short and I'm so tall . . . well, you know I get on top of you and you're going to be breathing into my chest hair and your feet will be scrabbling at my knees."

She thought about that. It seemed reasonable.

"That's true," she acknowledged. "So?"

"So then I won't be able to kiss you. And I want to kiss you, babe."

She punched him in the ribs. "Harry."

"Well, I do."

"All right," she said. "Now just let me figure a minute."

She figured a minute.

"You could lay on your back," she suggested, "and I could sit on top of you. Sport? How about that?"

"No good." He wagged his head. "Too far away. I want to *kiss* you, babe."

"I could lay on my—no, that won't work. Maybe if we—no. Listen, Harry, what about the cocktail table in the living room?"

"What about it?"

"No, it's too low. Now take that dining table I've got. It's the right height. But you'd have to stand up."

"Shit," he said. "Back of the bus. It would be all right, babe, but when I bent forward to kiss you, my ass would shoot out. And then where would we be?"

"The toilet seat?" she suggested.

"The laundry hamper?" he offered.

"Out the window?" she said. "Hanging by our heels?"

"Upside down on the—" he started, but then they both were laughing so much, crying, that he couldn't finish. All they could do was splutter, and she forgot Rocco.

What they did finally, was that he sat on the edge of the bed, flat feet on the floor. She sat astraddle. He held her, his big hands pressing. Her feet were on the bed on each side of him. They were comfortable. And they could kiss. They kissed.

"You know, babe," he said. "I don't feel anything at all."

"Thanks a whole bunch."

"No, I don't mean it that way. You know I don't. I love to be close to you, my hands on your sweet little ass. It's all right with us, babe. It's just fine. But what I meant was that I don't feel what all those books say I should feel."

"All what books?"

He put one hand between her shoulder blades. He slid the other arm and hand under her sweet little ass. And suddenly he rose to his feet, effortlessly. She clasped her arms about his neck. She linked her ankles about his hips.

He stalked about the room. There she was, impaled on his lean shaft. He carted her all over, a little white heating pad he cuddled to his heart.

"Oh..." he said. "You know." His black face was pocked with sorrow. "I've read all these books by blackies and whiteys. According to them, I should be pronging you because I want to strike back at whiteys or because I'm breaking the taboo or because I'm ashamed to take a black woman to bed. Like I said, I don't feel anything like that at all."

"What are you talking about, sport?" she asked anxiously. "Is it something I should know?"

"No. Just let me talk."

He walked about, smiling at her. Once he gave a little jump. He went deeper into her; she groaned with delight.

"I should be feeling guilty. Or maybe taking revenge. Or wanting to hurt you. Like the books say. But you know what I feel?"

She rubbed her cheek against his.

"I hope you feel as good as I feel."

"I do, babe, I do. No guilt. No pain. All that stuff they write about—what crap that all is!"

"Sure, Harry. Give a little jump again."

He gave a little jump. She giggled.

"Oh, boy!"

He strode around the room a few moments more, holding her tight. Then he deposited her gently onto the bed, rolling. They lay on their sides. He was still inside her. As he had predicted, her face was in his chest, her feet scrabbled at his knees.

They clasped hands. Both stared sideways at the wrinkled ceiling with the paint peeling away in one corner.

"Put your arm around me," she murmured. "Hold me."

He put his long arm around her, held her close. Then his eyes shut so tightly his eyelids were all squinched up.

"Harry?" she asked. "Are you falling asleep?"

No, he was not falling asleep.

"What was that all about? What you were talking about when we went for a stroll?"

"Oh," he said. "That."

"Yes, that. What was it about?"

He opened his eyes, looked at her with wonder. "You're something, you are."

"I guess I'm not very intelligent. I guess I'm dumb."

"You're smart," he assured her. "You are one smart babe. You're like a new woman. It doesn't mean a thing to you, does it?"

"What? What are you talking about?"

"Me a black. You don't even think about it."

"Why should I think about it?"

"Oh, Helen, Helen." He laughed, hugging her close. "I swear."

"Listen, sport," she said, "don't you think we've talked enough?"

He agreed.

He traced her spine with his fingertips, moving the skin gently over each little bump. He probed slowly with his hands, rolling her over, opening her wide, straining to her.

He scratched with fingernails on the insides of her arms, on the insides of her thighs. She began to move. Her whippy arms floated up into the air like the feelers of a butterfly. Then her legs began to move, began to curl around him, soft ropes.

A hum came out of her. Almost a song.

She touched him, stroked him, with hands and feet, threading the needle into her hand and through her, right up through her. She moved languidly, floating under him, a cloud.

"Oh," he said, with wonder.

Expertly she performed all the little household chores: slid a pillow under her buttocks, kicked their legs free of the blankets, bunched a pillow beneath her head. She sighed, ready. Never once did she close her eyes.

She was so silky, so soft. His own smooth skin seemed to slide around on her, finding no friction. But her waving arms went about him, searching legs linked and clamped. He put his hands beneath her. His hands were so big (and she so slender) that his fingertips touched.

They moved, they moved, whispering things. They were so slow, so deliberate, in punishment and delight. She pulled his weight to her and hung on, monkey on a stick. Bit his nipples. Scratched his back.

They found a syncopation they liked, an iambic rhythm that was not elegant but served them well. They strung out their song as long as they could. Helen flaunting her skill. Harry showing his strength.

Until, finally, their brains began to float free. Eyes glazed, bodies skimmed with a sweet sweat. Her fevered face pressed against the thumping of his heart. His fingers pressed into her.

"Please," she said.

"Please," he said.

And away they went, horse and rider. Trot. Canter. Gallop. And over the fence.

It was, they agreed later, something.

13

SHE SCAMPERED THROUGH the door, only a few minutes late. But when she looked around the restaurant, she saw no Jo Rhodes. Several tables were occupied, all by men. Heads turned quickly, slowly, slyly, to stare at her legs, the way the silk sheath clung to her fanetta.

Eat your hearts out, she thought happily.

The man who came from behind the bar looked like Jean Gabin of 1948, his face seamed with a hundred unhappy love affairs. He wore a chunky gray flannel suit. His hair, cut *en brosse*, was white. He gave her a stare that lasted one ten-thousandth of a second and in that time comprehended the size of her breasts, the firmness of her thighs, the fact that she was unmarried and had no objection to leaving the lights on.

"May I help you?"

"Does Mr. Rhodes have a table?"

His face crinkled up like Reynolds Wrap.

"Jo? But of course! He has not yet arrived. Allow me..."

He conducted her to a corner table for four, tucked her away gently. A waitress came running with breadsticks, butter, a dish of ice-cold radishes and celery hearts.

"Perhaps something?" the owner asked.

"A very dry Rob Roy, please."

"Excellent." He smiled and moved away.

Boy, could I go for you! she thought.

A party of four men arrived, then a young couple, then two middle-aged women, one of whom the owner greeted with an enthusiastic *embrazo*. He led them to a table in the rear. Helen stared as they walked past. The woman embraced was tall, stately, coldly handsome. Helen stopped the owner as he went back to the bar.

"The woman in the tweed suit," she whispered. "She looks so familiar. I know I've seen her before."

"But of course. A very great lady and a very great actress. Anise—"

"McLean," she finished excitedly. "My God, I saw her in *Six Bottles for Paddy*. She was wonderful."

"Yes. Now she is starring in *Kippers in Marakeech*. Every Wednesday, before her matinee, she comes here for luncheon."

Helen turned to stare again. "What a beauty!" she said enviously. "She's like a queen."

"Yes." He smiled. "That is true. Regal."

Jo Rhodes came bouncing through the door, pince-nez askew, Gauloise dribbling from his lips. He was wearing a plaid deerstalker cap, carried a cardboard portfolio under one arm; a gray cashmere suit, in his buttonhole was a single ripe daisy. He hurried toward Helen, a miniaturized boulevardier, and she thought his long woolen underwear might have slopped down onto his shoes until she realized he was wearing spats.

He stopped alongside the table, cocked his head to one side, gazed dreamily.

"'Helen,'" he said, "'thy beauty is to me like those Nicaean barks of yore that gently o'er the perfumed sea the weary, wayworn wanderer bore to his own native shore.'"

"Son of a bitch," she said delightedly. "That's beautiful. Did you write that?"

"A long time ago," he murmured modestly, handing his cap to the owner. "Thank you, Irving. I'll keep the package. You know what I'd like."

"Is his name really Irving?" Helen asked, her heart going down for the third time as the owner moved away.

"Of course not. It is Henry—or really Enrique. But I call him Irving. It is a private joke that amuses both of us. You see, one day he—"

"Jo Rhodes!" a marvelous contralto voice trumpeted alongside their table, and there was the famous actress Anise McLean, arms outspread, eyes agleam.

"Bless my soul!" he spouted, sprang to his feet, embraced her as best he could, losing his pince-nez down the front of her jacket. She retrieved it for him, then clasped his sere cheeks, kissed the peak of his skull.

"You villain!" she sang, and the walls shook. "Why haven't you called? I've been languishing for you— *languishing*!"

"Well—ah—you know... Anise, Helen Miley. Helen, my dear, this is Anise McLean, a very dear friend of—"

"Friend, hell," the McLean shouted. "Deprived lover and spurned mistress would be more like it." Unexpectedly, she ran her fingers through Helen's tight blond curls. "You little boy," she said. "Just charming. Terrifico. *Magnifico*." She took Jo Rhodes' mustache in her fingertips and shook it back and forth. His head wagged wildly. "Be careful of this wretch," she said to Helen. "The most dangerous man in New York. Never believe a word he says."

"I won't," Helen breathed.

Then she was gone back to her own table; the water goblets stopped ringing.

"My God," Helen said, marveling, "do you know *everyone*?"

"Well, ah—you know... I photographed her years ago for a defunct magazine called *Flair*. I am sure you don't remember it. But it was Anise's first starring role, ingenue in *Sex Comes a Cropper*. I posed her with a snake coiled about her bare bosom. It was a sensation."

"I can believe it."

"She was touchingly grateful. She offered—"

"Did you have an affair with her?" Helen asked, truly interested.

He tossed his head back and hugged himself. A vagrant tear squeezed out the corner of his left eye, wandered down his cheek.

"Oh, oh, oh," he gasped. "No, my very dear. I did not have an affair with her. But we have remained good friends. Occasionally a luncheon, occasionally a dinner. A crazy gift at

Christmastime. Like that, Aha! Here is my cassis. Thank you, luv."

The waitress smiled, left them menus, slid away. They clinked glasses, sipped, then Jo bent to the side, unfastened his portfolio, and, one by one, displayed three 11 by 14 blowups of the soft portraits he had taken of Helen.

Happiness caught in her throat.

"My God." She sighed. "I'm so beautiful!"

"But of course."

"Do I really look like this?"

"To me you do. This is how I see you."

He had caught the innocence. It was there in black and white. The innocence. She stared hungrily.

"Thank you, Jo."

He raised her hand to his lips, nibbled her fingertips.

"Now then...I will order. A very simple luncheon. Scampi dynamited with butter and garlic. *Endives braisées*. A bottle of chilled Muscadet. *Café filtré*. Small, short, to the point. How does that sound?"

She nodded, still staring at her portraits. There she was, The Stranger staring back at her, a distorting mirror. Her lips seemed fuller, jaw softer, eyes younger. She gleamed, ripe with hope.

I'm going to make it, she thought suddenly.

They ate, laughed, chatted, exchanged one garlicky kiss. She had a single glass of wine, but the bottle was almost empty when he took off his pince-nez, stared at a spot six inches over her head. His eyes glazed over.

"Excellent food," he said throatily. "The best *endives braisées* in New York. Perhaps the best in the world—except for a certain bistro in Les Grenouilles."

"Les Grenouilles?"

"It's in the south of France. On the sea. Very close to the Spanish border. I don't believe I've ever mentioned it to you, but I own a place there. A small villa. Quite charming."

"You own a house in France? Jo, that's wonderful! Tell me about it. Why don't you live there?"

He brought his gaze down, looked into her eyes, not quite focusing. He shrugged.

"Really, it isn't much. Les Grenouilles is a small, sleepy village. As you drive along the coast road toward Spain, it is on a turnoff toward the sea. Time has passed it by. Dogs sleeping in the middle of the main street. Old men smoking their long-stemmed clay pipes. Women picking lilac petals off the plants, gathering them in the laps of their black dresses. Lilacs are the village's largest cash crop. The petals are sent off to Paris. For perfume, you know. All the women wear black. They say it's an ancient custom to commemorate the time the men of the village went off to the Crusades and never came back."

"And the village hasn't been discovered?"

"You mean by tourists? Oh, no. Not yet. A few motorists lose their way and wander into Les Grenouilles, but there is nothing much there. One outdoor café. One bistro with a slate-topped bar. Once a year there is a week of bullfighting in a small arena—we're very close to the Spanish border. But the bull is never killed. French law, you know. But if the matador is able to touch the bull's testicles with what is called a coup stick—in the local patois it's called *le cucumber*— he is considered the victor."

"Jo, that's incredible."

"Oh, yes. But it's a quiet place. Most people would think it dull. I never found it so. Of course, I only go there early in spring or late in October. In summer a fierce, hot, dry wind blows in from the Bay of Biscay. It's known as *La Sonora*. It causes a disease called déjà vu."

"What's that?"

"Something like scabies. So you can understand why the village is not advertised in travel folders. But we who know it, love it. There it is, drowsing in the hot Mediterranean sun. Hardly a sound except for the occasional bark of a dog or the cries of the sellers of lottery tickets. Sometimes bands of gypsies come across the border from Spain and set up their tents. They do wild dances and sell snails fried in ghee and fresh fennel."

"Oh, Jo, it sounds marvy."

"It is marvy. Les Grenouilles. How I long for it. The tin Pernod signs swinging in the breeze. The painted donkey carts. The fishing boats."

"What do they fish for?"

"Anchovies. They go out for weeks at a time, most of the men and older boys of the village. Then, about the time they're due back, the cry goes through the village (in French, of course): 'The anchovy boats are coming! The anchovy boats are coming!' And all the black-clad women hurry down to the beach to welcome their men home and see if there was a good catch."

"How wonderful."

"Yes. It is lovely to see. There are so many things you'd like. The native boys diving off the cliffs by torchlight to prove their manhood. The wine of the region. They don't make enough to export; the vineyards are quite small. The wine is called *blanc de blanc de blanc*. An exquisite white. Very dry. The sand beaches. From a ventriculated lava flow that's been pounded by the sea and sun-bleached for centuries. The sand is fine as sugar."

"Oh, Jo, I'd give anything to have you writing copy for us. You're making me *see* it!"

"Yes. Perhaps once or twice during the year a cruise ship may pull into the lovely little harbor, and boats will bring tourists ashore. They wander down the main street—really the *only* street—and buy shark's-tooth necklaces and carved peach pits. If they are fortunate, they arrive during the annual mushroom festival. Mushrooms are Les Grenouilles' largest cash crop."

"I thought you said it was lilacs."

"Mushrooms are the largest cash *food* crop. They are gathered, hung in racks to dry, then packaged and sent all over the world. During the harvest the mushroom festival is held. Booths open up around the village square. You can buy wine, little bits of fried dough stuffed with blueberries and ground chestnuts, and hunks of wild pig roasted with asparagus and pickled eggplant. At night all the young men and women dance *la mignonette*. They form two circles, the girls revolving clockwise inside, and the boys revolving counterclockwise in the outer circle. When the music stops, they grab the partner nearest them, and if acceptable, they disappear into the shadows with dirndl skirts flashing and laughter echoing. How gay it all is!"

"Oh, God, Jo. I'd love to see it. What kind of a place do you have?"

"My place? Well, it's more than two hundred years old. Used to be a mill. In fact, the moss-covered wheel is still there. Doesn't work now, of course. A main building made of stone. Damned cold in the winter, which is why I go only in spring and fall. I've had modern plumbing put in—well, relatively modern judging by the rest of Les Grenouilles. But we still cook on wood-burning stoves."

"Is it closed when you're not there?"

"Oh, no. An old couple live there and take care of it for me. I 'et them have it rent-free. Pierre and Marie. He was a poilu in World War One. Lost an arm at Verdun. She's just as old, has a face like a dried apple. Delightful people. Both of them smoke clay pipes. They had one daughter who became a star of the Folies Bergère and later married an English lord. But they never hear from her. In fact, she—"

But Helen's attention had veered. At the table next to theirs a young mother, smile frozen, was having lunch with her retarded son. He was perhaps twelve, perhaps eighteen; it was difficult to judge. He had a small tonsure, like a skin yarmulke.

Helen had been vaguely aware of the mother cutting the boy's veal into small squares and then watching anxiously as, with a turned, distorted hand, he forked it bit by bit into his mouth, grinning and chewing. He managed his rice and string beans, got the glass of milk to his lips, mother wiping off his chin each time.

Then the meal was finished. Dishes were cleared away. Mother leaned forward, put a hand on son's arm. He listened, grinning, nodding. She rose, took a few steps, looked back, smiled at him, went hurriedly toward the ladies' room.

The moment she was out of sight, son rose, shambled over to their table where Jo Rhodes was saying, "Naked if you like. The beach is completely deserted at dawn, and if—"

He became aware of the boy standing at his elbow. Jo looked up and knew at once. He bounced to his feet.

"Hello." He smiled. "Won't you join us?"

He pulled a chair out. The boy sat down, grinning.

"My name is Jo," Rhodes said, "and here is Helen. What is your name?"

"Name?" the boy said.

"Yes. What is your name?"

The owner loomed up, but Jo waved him away. Waitresses hovered.

"Bobby," the boy said, looking around the room, smiling now, happy.

"Good name—Bobby." Jo nodded. "Did you enjoy your lunch?"

The boy looked at him.

"Did you have a good lunch?"

Bobby nodded, smiling. A thin line of milk-white spittle came from the corner of his mouth. Jo took his napkin, leaned forward gravely, wiped it away.

"Ah, yes," he said, "the food here is excellent. We had a good lunch, too. What are you going to do after lunch, Bobby?"

The boy's face twisted. His hands clenched into crippled claws; he looked down, stared at them.

"Polar bear," he said finally.

"Bless my soul!" Jo shouted. "The polar bear. You're going to the Central Park Zoo to see the polar bear. Isn't that right? You're going to see the polar bear and the elephant, too."

Bobby laughed, a laugh of triumph. "Elephant, too." He nodded.

"And the monkey." Jo laughed. "And the lion."

"The monkey." Bobby laughed. "The lion."

Helen was trying very hard, very hard. But her napkin was to her eyes, and she couldn't stop.

Mother came back, saw what was happening. Her face shattered. She grasped Bobby under the arm, raised him to his feet.

"I'm sorry," she gasped to Jo. "I'm really sorry."

"What for?" Jo smiled at the boy. "Bobby and I are friends. Isn't that right, Bobby?"

"Friends." The boy smiled, his beautiful eyes burning.

Jo Rhodes put out his hand. The boy looked down at it, puzzled. Then slowly, tentatively, his soft, clawed hand went out. Jo reached for it, shook it enthusiastically.

"Have a good time at the zoo, Bobby." He smiled.

"Polar bear," Bobby said, and let his mother draw him away. Then he looked back. "Friends," he said.

Helen took Jo's hand in hers, kissed it, rubbed her wet cheek against it.

"You were so great," she said, sniffing, "so great."

"Nonsense," he said angrily. "What the devil are you talking about?"

The owner brought them each a cognac.

"Permit me," he said.

"So, what I've been trying to tell you," Jo Rhodes said finally, a Gauloise cemented to his lower lip, "is that I have this delightful villa in the south of France. I am twice your age. But I have money. What I would like... what I would like... is for you to come to France with me. For as short or as long a visit as you like. A day, a month, a year, forever. No conditions. No demands. Just a new life. I will make any arrangements you desire. Naturally, I will pay for everything. I do not fool myself. I know I do not have much time left. I think we might find some happiness—for a day, a month, a year, forever. Whatever you wish. Please, no answer now. But will you think about it? Will you promise me you will think about it?"

Helen looked at him wonderingly.

"I will think about it, Jo. And I thank you. And I love you."

He lighted a fresh Gauloise with a wax match.

"Now then," he said briskly, "you must get back to work, and I must see a new exhibit at the Goldenstein Gallery. These prints I will save for you; I cannot ask you to carry this package. And also, it will serve as a lure to bring you back to me. Am I correct?"

"You are correct."

He scrawled his initials on the check while Helen was moving toward the door. The owner drifted over, whispered in Jo's ear, "Charming, Jo. A good one, this."

Jo Rhodes looked toward the door where Helen was waiting, the solid fanetta under the silk, the sassy bazooms there, the jaw, leg and horn-rimmed glasses.

"The innocence," he murmured. "The innocence!"

14

"E.F. or F.F.?"

"Let's eat first," Richard Faye said. "We'll have a red steak, green salad and black coffee. Is that the Italian flag?"

"Who cares? It's our flag."

Later they pushed back from the table, trading small belches. Helen came around behind him, put her head down, nuzzled his neck.

"The dishes," he said.

"How about a kissy first?"

"A kissy? Oh, my God."

He tried to give her a kissy on the cheek, but she clamped her open mouth to his. He pulled away slowly, eyes blinking. He tried to smile, his soft face spreading.

"Have you reached the Age of Consent?" he asked.

"Christ," she muttered, "I've passed the Age of Request."

They left the dishes to soak. They went into the bedroom slowly.

"The Last Mile," Helen said solemnly. "Listen, Uck, you look terrific. I swear your can is down two inches."

"Lost five pounds." He nodded nervously. "Took a notch in my belt. I think I could lick my weight in wildcats."

"You'll get your chance," she promised. "How's Edith?"

"Very well, thank you."

"What did she say when you told her you were staying the night here?"

"She objected. In fact, she made a scene."

"It figured. And the Muscle?"

"A lot of ugly things were said. I don't want to talk about it."

They were silent, standing by her bed.

"How do you feel?" she asked him.

"Frightened—but I'm glad I'm here. I'm going to be all right."

"Of course," she said. "But don't be frightened, baby. We'll do fine."

She sat down on the bed. He put his hands in his pockets, kicked at a cigarette burn in the rug.

"Maybe we should nap a few hours," she suggested, looking at him shrewdly.

"If that's what you want."

"Maybe we should." She nodded. "Just for a few hours. I'm sleepy."

They undressed swiftly. He didn't look at her. They slid swiftly beneath the sheet and single blanket.

"Edith should see me now." He giggled. "She'd die."

He turned on his side, away from her. He felt her fingers on his arm, stroking. The fingers stroked, paused, stroked. Gradually, the stroking slowed. Then her fingers were motionless on his arm.

"Helen?" he whispered to the darkness. There was no answer. He wasn't sure she was asleep. But it made it easier...

"I can't understand how I made such a mess of it," he murmured. "It was probably a lot of little things. It was no big one thing... I was a fat child and never played the rough games. And I was too close to Edith. I had long curls until I was seven... Then, when I was eleven or twelve, we had a maid who slept in. A skinny girl with dirty heels. She'd do things to me and make me do things to her. Helen, I was so young, and she smelled of mothballs. She'd sneak into my bedroom almost every night. She said if I ever told Mother what we were doing, she'd cut it off, and I'd be a little girl. Then she got a job somewhere else and moved away. I missed her. I missed having her sneak into my room every night and doing those things. I found out where she was working and called her. But a man answered, and I was too scared to ask for her ... Dear, are you asleep? When I was in high school, an older girl wanted me to go all the way with her. In the basement. I told Edith about it, and she called the girl's mother. The girl was sent away to a very strict boarding school. I'm more ashamed of that than of anything I've ever done in my life ... It was all so dry. My sister couldn't stand it. She ran away with a musician when she was eighteen. Daddy and Edith never tried to get her back. They wouldn't even answer her letters. They said she was dead as far as they were concerned. I don't know where she is now. Down South somewhere, I think ... Dear God, what a family ... When I was at Duke a few of us went to a whorehouse. They had the bottom halves of the beds covered with heavy black cloth because most of the customers kept their shoes on. That's the kind of place it was. I picked an older woman. She was all wrinkled and flabby and worn. A thing. She just lay there and closed her eyes. I could have killed her. Why didn't she stop me? I offered her an extra dollar if she'd cut off a strand of her long gray hair for me. She cut it off. I carried it around in my pocket for a long time, but finally it got very matted and dirty, and I threw it away. I used to do all kinds of frightful things with it. I was lonely, Helen. It's just that I was lonely ... Are you asleep? .... Who knows what goes on in people's minds? If we all had to stand up in public one day and tell our most secret thoughts and dreams and desires, everyone would commit suicide, it would be so horrible. We're all so foul ... After Daddy died, Edith and I lived together. I was working then, and I'd bring girls home to meet Edith. But none of them was good enough for me, Edith said. That one used poor English, that one had sloppy table manners, that one smelled, that one didn't wear gloves ... I picked up a woman on the street one night, and we went to her room. When we started, she called in a man from the next room. Her pimp, I suppose. He hit me and called me a queer. I told Edith that muggers had beaten and robbed me. I had all I could do to keep her from going to the police. Oh, God, what it means to be alive ... Then, late in the war, I was drafted into the Navy. I was stationed at Norfolk.

That's in Virginia. You can't imagine what it was like. It was going on all over—in cars, in parks, in hotels, even in alleys. A young blond boy from Texas—well, he and I would go on liberty together. That's how I got started, Helen. He was younger than me, but he taught me. He was lonely, too. That was the trouble with us: We were just lonely. I kept swearing I'd never do it again—but I did. I wasn't happy. It wasn't giving me pleasure. But I couldn't stop. Then the war ended. The blond boy went back to Texas. He said he'd write, but he never did. I didn't care. I had convinced myself that nothing had ever happened between us, that I had never known such a boy... I've always been able to do that—pretend I've never done the things I've done... Then I dated women for a while. I made myself go out with them even when I didn't like them. It was the same thing all over again. Edith told me none of them were good enough for me. Finally, I stopped going out... A few men I meet in bars or at work visit a couple of nights a week to play Hearts with Edith and me. None of us are fags... exactly. Not swishes, I mean. But we're all lonely. Someone brought along this weight-lifter one night and I got involved with him... He's a big man, very strong. Not an ounce of fat on him. All muscles and tanned skin. Very black, shiny hair. And ruthless. He doesn't care. He just doesn't care. He takes what he wants and doesn't care what he's doing to you or what you feel. A very strong, aggressive man. Edith likes him. I wonder if she knows about us? Maybe... I don't know. I told you two or three times, Helen, but it lasted almost two years. It wasn't anything dramatic. I didn't feel deeply one way or another—but every time he'd call I'd go. I gave him money. It broke up about a year ago. It just stopped, even though he keeps coming over for Hearts. I think he found someone with more money. I don't care. A little maybe, but I'm really glad... Helen, are you asleep?... You know, I don't understand it. I just can't figure out how I became what I am. Do you think it's all ordained before we're born? I'm Cancer the Crab. I keep feeling I never did all the things I did, but someone else was doing them through me—was making me do them. Because I didn't want to live like that. I wanted my life to be different. But I couldn't manage. I'm almost forty now. Maybe I have twenty or thirty years left. I don't understand it. It's all been wrong, and I can't for the life of me think how or why it happened. And blah-blah-blah. Why couldn't I have been the kind of man I wanted to be? Why couldn't I have married and been a god—I mean, a *good* husband and father? I like children. I'm very good with them. But worst of all is the thought that I didn't have the choice, that it was all done to me, and I couldn't control it . . . I was ready to give up. I was ready to let go and drink and drift along and not care anymore. Helen, that's why meeting you has been such an enormous thing. You've got enough strength for both of us. You said I could change if I really wanted to. That's what you said—isn't it, dear? Maybe, finally, it's going to be different for me. Maybe I'm finally going to be the kind of man I want to be . . . Helen? Are you asleep?"

The stroking began again, fingers sliding up and down his arm. Then she stroked his fatty back, his plump hip, his legs. He began to tremble. He turned slowly to face her. She came into his arms, twisting a little to get close to him.

"Baby," she breathed, "oh, baby."

He touched her timidly. He almost cried out. She flowed against him, bending to him, pressing to him. He shut his eyes tightly. He was holding his dream-self. He choked with the strangeness of it, touching his own slender beauty, feeling his own smooth softness, stroking his own silky coolness.

"What?" he said.

She lay motionless. "Knocking," she repeated. "Someone's banging at the front door."

Then he heard the noise. He heard the knocking and the mad bird screaming, "Fockufockufocku."

"Maybe they'll go away," Faye said nervously. "Who could it be?"

"I don't know." She swung her legs out of bed. "I'll get rid of them. God damn it. God damn it to hell."

She pulled on her robe. She went into the hall.

"Who is it?" she demanded.

"Is Dick Faye there?" a man's voice asked. "I've got to see him. His mother's had an attack—a heart attack."

Helen unlocked the door, leaving the chain on.

He was huge, tall and broad, with padded shoulders making him seem even wider. His black hair, shiny, was brushed back in a duck's-ass. She could smell the cologne. He looked amused, his lips pulled up in a pucker at one corner.

"The Muscle," she said.

"Bitch," he said pleasantly. "You tell Dickie his mother's had a very serious heart attack. Dr. Franklin thinks Dickie should be there. If you let me in, I'll tell him myself."

"I'll tell him," Helen said. She stared at him through the crack, their eyes linked through the chain. "Why don't you let him alone?" she asked.

"Why don't you go shag yourself?" He laughed. "Just run along now like a nice little scut and tell Dickie. Maybe, if you behave yourself, I'll come back later and let you go—"

She closed the door softly. She stood a moment, her forehead pressed against the door. I could kill him, she thought wildly. I could get the bread knife from the kitchen (the long one with the serrated edge), pull the door open suddenly, and stab him right in the kishkas. After a while she stopped shaking. She went back into the bedroom, told Faye about his mother. He rose at once, with no change of expression. He began to dress.

"I'll bet it's a fake," Helen said miserably. "I'll bet she had that attack on purpose. I mean, I bet it's a complete phony."

"It may be." He nodded sadly. "But I have to go. By the time I get home it'll be pretty late. I don't think I better come back tonight, Helen."

"Whatever you say."

"I'll call you just as soon as I know."

"You do that."

He came over to her, took her face between his hands, smiled weakly.

"It was close, wasn't it?"

"Yes," she said. "Close."

"I'm sorry, dear. But there'll be other times."

"Oh, sure."

"I better go now."

"All right."

"I'll call you from home."

"All right."

His waxy face sagged farther. She thought he was going to cry.

"Good night, Helen. Thank you for the—thank you for everything."

She unlatched the chain to let him out into the corridor. The weight lifter was leaning against the wall, smoking a cigarette. She closed the door quickly and locked it.

She washed the dishes, put them away, straightened the living room, swallowed a Librium. She sat on the edge of the bed, stared at the shaded window. Finally, she reached for the phone, dialed Charles Lefferts. She counted the rings. It rang fourteen times before he picked up the phone.

"Hello?" he said cautiously.

"Charles? This is Helen Miley. I was wondering if I—"

"Bob!" he roared. "Bob Cranshaw! How are you, old man?"

Softly she hung up the phone.

15

"Of course it was phony," Helen said wrathfully. "As phony as a square grape. She knew Uck wanted to spend the night here, and she pulled this fake heart attack. She's a shrewd bitch. She knew it was the one thing that would bring him running, the poor darling. He called me the next morning, just sick about it. The things he told me!"

"Tell us," Peggy said eagerly.

"Not ever. They were told to me in strictest confidence. Not that he made me promise never to repeat them or anything like that. But I just wouldn't *want* to, honey. You understand?"

"Oh, sure, ducks," Peggy said, disappointed. "It's just a shame he has to run every time she cracks her little finger."

"Men are no damned good," Carrie Edwards said darkly. She was a plump little wren, a childless widow who worked in Peggy Palmer's office. Her dyed hair lay in carefully marceled waves from ear to ear. Her legs were luscious, and she was generous enough to sometimes wear satin jogging shorts and share her good fortune with the world.

The surprise wedding shower was over; most of the guests had departed. The room had been straightened, glasses stacked in the sink, ashtrays emptied. Peggy's gifts were tied in a neat bundle so she could carry them home. Peggy and Carrie had lingered for a final cup of coffee.

"See that," Helen said, pointing to a windowsill. "That's where Rocco used to look out. He'd put his paws up and stare out the window for hours. In the last days of his life he became a Peeping Tom. There's this new French poodle in the apartment across the air shaft, and he kept watching for her. The old fart. He couldn't *do* anything, but he had this dream."

"My late husband was just like that." Carrie nodded. "He bought this little telescope, and every summer night he'd go up on the roof. To look at the stars, he said. Stars my ass, I said, and if the cops catch you, it'll serve you right. Not that he was a sex fiend or anything like that, you understand. He just liked to look."

"Men," Helen said philosophically.

"So what about Uck?" Peggy asked her. "Are you going to try again?"

"Next Friday," Helen said. "And this time nothing is going to spoil it, I swear. Uck was really sore at Edith. That boy is really coming along. Like he said, the Mother Inferior has been pulling this stuff all her life and getting away with it. Well, I'm just as tough as she is."

"Tougher," Peggy said admiringly.

"Damned right." Helen nodded. "I like the big dope, and I'm not going to let him go without a fight. The coffee should be perked by now. I'll bring it out here."

"I had the same problem with my late husband," Carrie told Peggy while Helen went into the kitchen. "His mother just wouldn't let him go. She wanted him to wait. Wait for what? I asked him. Wait till I'm older, he said. You're twenty-four now, I told him, and old enough to make up your own mind."

"So he proposed?" Peggy asked.

"Not right then," Carrie admitted, patting her waves. "But I started letting him love me up in the back of one of my father's hearses. He was an undertaker, you know. I'd let Fred go so far and no farther. It went on for weeks. His face got all broke out, and he said it was so bad that every time he saw a funeral he got a hard-on. Finally, one night, he asked me. We were married seventeen years before his gallbladder burst, God rest his soul. It just blew up and exploded like a balloon. The doctor said he never saw the like. There was a piece about it in a doctors' magazine. He was famous, Fred was—only, of course, he wasn't here to see it. Please, Helen, no more cake. I couldn't eat a bite."

"Just a little," Helen urged. "You'll diet tomorrow. Well, Peg, how does it feel? Just think—a month or so from now and you'll be an old married woman."

Peggy shivered. "I shouldn't say this, but I hardly know the man. I mean, here we are getting married and all, and it's like he was a stranger. There's so much I don't know about him."

"And plenty he doesn't know about you," Helen winked. "But don't worry, sweet—my lips are sealed."

"That's the way it should be," Carrie said stoutly. "What he don't know won't hurt him. I went all the way twice with the fellow next door before I got married. I was going to tell Fred, but then I never did, and I'm glad. He died believing he had married a virgin, God rest his soul."

"Couldn't he tell?" Peggy asked nervously. "I mean the sheets and all?"

Carrie Edwards looked at the other two women narrowly. "I'll tell you something I've never told a living soul before. Promise you'll never repeat it?"

"I promise," Peggy said.

"I promise," Helen said.

"Well . . . after Fred went to sleep on our wedding night, I got up and stuck my thumb with a pin and smeared it on the sheet."

"My God," said Helen.

"My God," said Peggy.

"Of course, in those days it was more important to be a virgin when you got married. Men don't seem to care so much today. Things are more easygoing like. Live and let live. It was different then. For instance, Fred wanted to sleep in the raw, but I wouldn't let him. 'I'm not one of your fancy women, Fred,' I told him, 'and you dress when you go to bed with me like a Christian should.'"

"I wouldn't care if my husband slept in the raw," Helen said.

"It's brutal in hot weather," Carrie told her. "You stick together and wake up all wrinkled. Peggy, I think you should make him wear something in bed."

"Gee, I don't know," Peggy said worriedly. "I never thought

of that. I guess there are a lot of things which will come up in married life."

"If you're lucky," Helen said.

"I mean problems," Peggy added hastily. "Like what should I do about the bathroom? I mean, supposing he's shaving or something, and I want to use the bathroom. Should I go in there while he's in there?"

The younger women looked at Carrie expectantly.

"It depends," she said judiciously. "Maybe at first you better not. But after you've been married awhile and it's like, you know, an emergency, it just doesn't make any difference. You just don't think of it."

"You mean—right in front of each other?" Peggy asked, awed.

"Well, you won't stare. He'll be in the shower or shaving, and if it's an emergency, why you just go right ahead. He's a human being, after all."

"I suppose so," Peggy said nervously. "There's certainly more to it than I thought. I mean it's not easy. Like what about sex? What if he wants to and I don't or vice versa?"

"You should put your foot down right from the start," Carrie advised. "Don't let him get the idea that you're available any minute of the day or night. Like when he's drunk or you're all dressed ready to go out or maybe you just don't feel like it. Be smart about it. Like if he's done something wrong or you want to buy something. You know what I mean."

Helen protested. "I don't think a wife should use sex as a punishment or like a bribe when she wants her husband to buy her something. What the hell's the point of being married if you can't jump in the hay any minute you feel like it?"

"You have never been married," Carrie Edwards said stiffly. "You know not whereof you speak."

"I thought we could have maybe like signals," Peggy mused. "You know, something cute like throwing his hat on the bed or something like that."

"Or throwing you on the bed." Helen nodded. "Something cute like that."

"No, I'm serious, ducks. I mean, how will I know if he wants to, and how will he know if I want to?"

"Signals are very good," Carrie said approvingly. "However, you will find that after you've been married awhile, it becomes a regular thing. Like every Friday night Fred would bring home his pay and then take a hot bath. We'd have wieners and sauerkraut and a quart of beer. Then we'd go to bed. That way there was no question."

"What if he wanted to on Tuesday or Thursday night?" Helen asked.

"He just didn't. We had this regular schedule, and we stuck to it."

"Wieners and sauerkraut," Peggy repeated. "Friday night."

"Another thing," Carrie said. "Sometimes, after men have been married awhile, they think they can do all kinds of things. You know—fancy things. One night, after we had been married a year or so, Fred wanted me to—well, I won't tell you what it was."

"What was it?" Peggy and Helen asked together.

"Well—" Carrie looked down thoughtfully at her tiny feet and wiggled her toes. "Well—no, I better not tell you. It might give you ideas. I told him, 'Fred,' I said, 'you can get one of your fancy women to do anything you want, but don't expect me to do anything but what is required by law because that is *all* I am going to do.'"

"What did he say?"

"My, he was mad. He stomped out of the house and didn't come home till midnight, drunk as a lord and smelling of some cheap perfume. It was weeks before I let him come near me, and then he had to buy me a new coat. A gray tweed it was, with a rabbit collar. He never tried any foreign things again, I can tell you."

"Well, Carrie"—Helen shrugged—"like you said, times have changed. People do a lot of things today maybe they didn't do years ago. Who knows—maybe Peg likes some of the fancy things. Do you, Peg?"

"Well," Peggy said, inspecting her engagement ring closely, "I don't—he could—well, you know. . . . It depends. First of all, he's really not a very fancy kind of man. I mean, he's so quiet and all. That's another thing that worries me—what are we going to talk about? Lots of times now when we have a date, we just sit there. But every night? I mean, won't it be embarrassing just sitting there night after night, week after week, year after year?"

"You'll find plenty to talk about," Carrie assured her. "He'll come home and tell you what happened at the office, and you'll tell him about your fight with the butcher. And then there'll be things that come up—bills and the neighbors and the children, if you have them. I was never blessed, you know. And of course, there's radio and TV and going to the movies. Don't worry—there'll be plenty to do."

"I guess so," Peggy said forlornly. She looked up at Helen, her eyes misting over. "Well, ducks, I guess our good times are all over. No more cruising the bars for me."

"That's right." Helen smiled.

"It's like my life is ending in a way." Peggy sighed, punching at her eyes with a tissue. "I feel sad. I mean it's like all the fun is over."

"You *want* to get married, don't you?" Carrie asked.

"Oh, sure. But it's like you want something all your life and then when you get it, it doesn't seem so much. I guess he's a nice fellow and all, and I suppose we'll be happy, but I don't know..."

Helen went over to the couch, put her arm around Peggy's shoulder, kissed her cheek.

"Don't worry, baby," she whispered. "It's going to be all right. It's going to be just great, just what you wanted. You got a man and a home all your own. I wish I was in your shoes. You'll wake up every morning, and you won't be alone. You'll have your very own husband in bed with you, every morning."

"But make him wear something," Carrie cried.

16

THEY SLEPT LATE on Saturday morning. Then a shaft of sunlight, mote-flecked and bright, struck through the window, flashed in Harry Tennant's eyes. He roused, rolled, blinked, turned his head. The lemon sunlight of October was flooding the room. Light poured through the wide window, spilled across the floor, drowned the furniture, engulfed the bed.

Sunlight glinted off the reddish hairs on Harry's chest. He looked down, saw how the tarnished sunlight of October plated his skin, smoothing it. He purred with pleasure.

He turned onto his stomach, lifted himself onto his elbows, looked at Helen. She was sleeping on her back, hands clasped between her legs. She was wearing a pair of men's pajamas. The long sleeves came to her fingertips. Only her pink fingernails peeked out beyond the blue cuffs. There was a fancy monogram, MG, embroidered on the pocket.

Harry reached into his pillow, pulled a short feather out of the tick. He stroked Helen's neck with the little feather, drawing it back and forth in the soft hollow of her throat. She stirred, her neck muscles moved. She moaned a bit, turned uneasily. Harry started tickling her chin, her nose, her ear.

She opened her eyes, stared a moment at the ceiling. Then she turned her head, looked at him suspiciously. But Harry had closed his eyes, was lying on his stomach, breathing deeply and naturally.

Helen shut her eyes again, then opened them suddenly. She caught him about to tickle her lips with the feather. Her outraged expression sent him into chugs of laughter. He took her in his arms, hugged her tightly.

"Helen, Helen, Helen." He laughed. "Oh, my very own babe!"

"You dog," she shouted. "You dirty dog—waking me that way."

She pulled him to her breast, dug her face down into his neck and shoulder. She nipped his shoulder. He felt the sting of her teeth on his flesh.

"What a dream I was having!" she said, marveling. "Man, what a dream that was. But this is all right, too. This is really fine, honey."

She ran her fingernails up and down Harry's naked back. He shivered, moved closer to her. She scraped his skin with her fingernails, looking up at his face, smiling at him.

"That's hard to take, isn't it? That's really awful, I know."

She bent away from him, tried to take off the blue pajamas. She got all mixed up in the pajamas, all tangled. Harry didn't help. Harry didn't help at all.

"Now stop it," she told him. "Give me a minute, will you? Stop it, honey. Damn you anyway."

She got the pajamas off, rolled them into a tight ball.

"See that?" she said, pointing to a coat tree in the corner of the bedroom. "Now watch this..."

She sat up in bed, threw the bundled pajamas across the room. They sailed through the air, unfolding as they sailed. They ended up hooked neatly over the coat tree.

"You couldn't do that again in a million years," he scoffed.

She snuggled back into his arms, giggling. "I don't know, kiddo. I've had a lot of practice."

"Who's MG?" Harry asked casually. "The initials on the pajamas?"

"MG?" she murmured. "I can't remember. It's been a long, long time."

She put her lips to his neck, to his shoulders, to the soft, tight skin stretched across his ribs. She nibbled on his ear.

"Oh, baby, baby, this is fine. You know what I wanted last night?"

"What did you want?"

"I wanted it just like it was. I wanted us to smoke a cigarette, talk awhile, and then go to sleep. Maybe we'd sleep for an hour or two, or maybe we'd sleep till morning."

"Well, we slept till almost noon." Harry yawned. "We went out like lights."

"I knew how it'd be. I'd wake up thinking, oh, Christ, here I am alone again. But then I'd roll over, and there you'd be, and here it is Saturday, and we don't have to go to work, and we can mess around as long as we like, can't we? Oh, it's just so wonderful having someone in the morning."

"Yes." He nodded. "I know what you mean."

"It's just that I'm alone so much. You know? It's not good for me to be alone so much. It does something bad to me. It gets me all wound up inside. But when I have someone with me, I want every minute to count."

"But you fell asleep first, babe," he chided her. "My God, one minute you were talking to me, and then the next minute you were asleep."

"I know. I guess I was tired. It was a fine sleep. I feel great. I'm hungry."

"All right," Harry said. "Let's see—we bought some milk and eggs and cheese and mushrooms and some bologna and a crumb cake from Horn and Hardart. I'll get up and make us some breakfast."

"In a while," she whispered. "Don't get up now."

He snared his fingers in her short blond curls. He pulled, tilting her head back. He kissed her lips. He kissed her hard, his lips hard against hers. He strained close to her.

"Harry," she gasped. "Honest to God, honey..."

He felt her springy body with his fingers. He ran his long fingers over her body, pinching the chirpy breasts, pressing the sturdy shoulders, gripping the tight thighs. He put his hands upon her.

They made love then. They made love with much laughter, much rolling about, biting of flesh, tasting of flesh. It was flooded with the tarnished sunlight. It was all with reverence.

Then they lay quiet, panting softly. Then they were still, warm and weary.

"Helen," he murmured. "Darling, darling..."

She rubbed her cheek against his shoulder. She moved her palm in circles around the small of his back, not touching the flesh, but close, feeling the short hairs, feeling the heat of him.

She pulled away a little, laughed up at him.

"Think it'll last?" she asked. "Think it's here to stay?"

"Nah." He shook his head. "It'll never last. It's just a fad."

"Think it'll ever replace basketball?"

"Well"—he considered gravely—"you need five men—"

But she closed his lips with hers. She savaged him with her mouth. Then they unclasped their arms. They lay silent on their backs. Helen lighted a cigarette; they watched the white smoke curl up into the sunlight.

A new kind of cigarette, he thought suddenly. With black smoke.

"Honey," Helen asked anxiously, "have I been good for you?"

He turned over, pressed his lips against her hair. He put one arm across her breasts. He felt her breathe. He timed his breathing so they breathed together, their chests expanding together.

"You've been wonderful for me," he said.

"Oh, you bring me." She sighed. "You really do. You never drag me down."

"You're way ahead of me," he told her. "I never can catch up with you, babe. You're giving and I'm taking. All the time."

"Honey," she said, laughing, rubbing her fingers through his crazy hair, "don't talk nutty. Honest to God, man, you do me good. Just being with you. You're so sweet and dumb, and you try to be cool, and you don't really, honey, know what the hell it's all about. What a flat you are! What a square!"

"That's me all right."

"No, you're not. You're not a flat. When I'm with you, I start sharp and I stay hard. That's how you make me feel. So don't worry about it."

"You give too much," he muttered. "You just give and give. One of these days you'll give all of you away, and there won't be nothing left."

"Oh, my," Helen mocked, stubbing out her cigarette. "You

must understand, my dear Harry, that I am just a poor, uneducated Ohio schlumph, and I cannot rightly understand just what the hell you are talking about, my dear."

He laughed, grabbed her about her naked waist. They rolled on the creaking bed, laughing and kissing. Then they stopped and kissed. They kissed. They kissed.

"I love you, babe."

"Say it again."

"I love you, babe," Harry Tennant said.

She sighed with delight, moved closer to him. She put an arm across his shoulders.

"That sounds so nice. That sounds so good and true."

"It is good, Helen, and it is true."

She was quiet a moment. Then she sat up in bed. She took his face between her hands, looked deep into his bewildered eyes. She came so close to him their noses were almost touching; he could feel her breath warm upon his lips.

"Listen," she said, "about those pajamas... I really don't remember who MG was. Does it bother you?"

"No," he said, surprised that it didn't. "It doesn't bother me at all. I don't care what you did, ever, before I met you."

She sighed, released him, fell back onto the bed.

"Well, there haven't been a lot of men, and there haven't been a few. But that was all yesterday, and I never give yesterday a tumble."

"Yeah." He nodded. "I'm in favor of today myself."

"It's tomorrow I love," Helen said softly.

"What do you want from tomorrow?" he asked, his voice muffled in the pillow.

"Want?" She made it sound like a vice. "What do I want?" She pressed back into the bed, yawned, stretched her arms wide. He watched her brisk little breasts point up. "I don't want much. I guess what I want most of all is mornings like this—waking up and seeing beside me the guy I went to bed with the night before... and knowing his name."

She rolled over, put her lips against his knobbly spine, tasted him, stretched out her arms. She could touch from the back of his neck the backs of his knees, a luscious octave. She could hold almost all of him within the span of her arms. She put her cheek upon his back. Her head went up and down as he breathed.

"Oh, man, man, this is fine." She sighed. "It's no good sleeping alone; it's no good a-tall. But listen, honey—you've got

to love the one you're sleeping with, even if it's only for a night. If
you love him, it's all right. If it's just for kicks, why. that's the
worst thing you can do. Or drunk or hopped up. It's dirty bad
then. Darling, darling. It's too precious."

"I love you, Helen."

"Sure, baby, sure. You know what I like about it? It gives me
the idea that I'm needed, that the guy wants me and needs me.
It's the only thing that counts for me. Everything else in this
world is just shit."

"I want you," he muttered, turning to kiss her fingers. "I need
you."

"That's nice, honey. I like to hear that. Knock me a kiss."

He twisted his head around; she kissed his lips. Then she
returned to lying over him with her face pressed against the small
of his back.

"Well, let me up, babe," he said. "I'll make us some
breakfast."

"No," she said drowsily, "I'm not going to let you up."

"I'll bring you breakfast in bed," he offered. "We'll have
scrambled eggs. Maybe I'll make an omelet. We got mushrooms.
Or cheese."

"I won't let you up," she refused, pressing his body down into
the bed. "I'm going to keep you prisoner."

"I'll make some strong coffee," he pleaded. "And we'll have
some crumb cake from Horn and Hardart also."

"I don't want you to get up," she insisted. "I won't let you up.
I won't."

"I always forget how strong men are," she said, watching him
move about the room, gathering his clothes. "I always think I'm
pretty strong until a man really uses his strength, and then I find
out I'm not as strong as I thought. You're really strong, honey."

"I sure am." He winked at her. "Strong back, weak mind."

"You got enough brains for me," she told him. "You do all
right. Listen, Harry, are you sure you know how to make an
omelet?"

"You just leave everything to me," he assured her. "This will
be like no other omelet you've ever tasted. You'll love this
omelet."

He went into the bathroom, showered quickly. There were
three towels hanging on racks. Two were flowered. One was
white with a blue stripe that had U.S. NAVY printed on it. He dried
himself on the NAVY towel. He used one of her two toothbrushes.

He couldn't find a comb, did the best he could with his fingers. He looked a long time at his reflection in the medicine cabinet mirror. He bent close until his nose was touching the glass.

"White man in black face," he whispered. "What are you doing?"

The omelet was messed up a little, with mushrooms spilling out both ends. But it was good; they ate it all. The coffee was strong and hot. Helen had two cups. The crumb cake from Horn & Hardart was also good.

Helen didn't eat it in bed. She got up, pulled on her robe, and they ate at the little table in the kitchen. They didn't talk much while they ate breakfast. They had a cigarette with their coffee. Harry put two cigarettes in his mouth, lighting both from the same match.

"I saw Humphrey Bogart do it in a movie," he told her.

Helen watched him, smiling a little. He went around behind her, kissed her hair. She raised her face, rubbed her cheek along his lips.

"I'm so happy, honey," she whispered. "It's been fine. It's really been a fine morning."

He hesitated a moment, then said, "You told me I don't know what the hell it's all about. So tell me. What's it all about?"

"You and me, baby," she murmured. "You and me."

17

SHE FELT DREAMY.

"I feel dreamy," Helen Miley said to Richard Faye.

"I feel dreamy," Richard Faye said to Helen Miley.

They were snorting coke, and that's the way their conversation was going. They weren't very good at it—snorting. But they were trying...

"Listen," he said, beginning to bloom, "I read these books with the sex scenes. And they're always so wonderful."

"What's so wonderful? The books?"

"No. The sex scenes. And the woman always gasps—that's what it says: 'She *gasped*...' and she gasps, 'Now. Now. Now.' How come you never gasp, 'Now. Now. Now'?"

"Now. Now. Now," she gasped.

"No," he said sadly, "it just doesn't work."

"Son of a bitch," she said sadly.

So they laughed, hugged each other, smoked their cigarettes, still trying...

"Uck, you know what bugs me?"

"Me?"

"Well... sometimes. But what really bugs me is taking in my laundry."

"Laundry?"

"Well... you know. I throw my dirty stuff in that wall hamper in the bathroom. And every week I stuff it all in a pillowcase and take it to the Chink around the corner on Second Avenue. He's got a little—Susan is her name—and she sits on the counter and laughs. Boy, is she ever sweet. I could eat that kid up. I bring her candy sometimes. Every Christmas he gives me a calendar and a box of lichee nuts. Isn't that nice? Anyway, there I am every week bringing in my dirty laundry. And then I take my dry cleaning to another place down the block."

"So?"

"Well... I got this marvelous dentist on Fifty-seventh Street. He hardly hurts at all. I go maybe once or twice a year to get my teeth cleaned and a checkup. You know?"

"Sure."

"And this doctor I have. I get in the stirrups, and he looks in there. He says I have very strong abdominal muscles, and I'm in very good condition. You know I try to do these exercises every morning."

"Yes."

"Well, then, I also have some life insurance and the beneficiary is... the beneficiary is... I think some of my nephews and nieces. Anyway, I have life insurance. And last year I took out this thing—this policy—so that if I keep paying on it, when I'm sixty-five, I get a hundred dollars a month. That's wise—don't you think?"

"Yes. Wise."

"And... let's see. My shoes don't last long, but sometimes I get them resoled or have lifts put on. I take my Pill and use the cosmetics the ads say. I went to St. Patrick's last Christmas. The show was beautiful. And I do everything right—I mean I keep clean and all that. Do I have bad breath?"

"Oh, no. No."

She burst into tears.

"Then why am I so fucking miserable?" She sobbed.

"Miserable." He nodded. "Miserable."

He didn't know how to comfort her, so he turned on the radio. It was a little table model in a cracked plastic case because Rocco (may his soul rest in peace) had once knocked it over. A station came on; they were playing that long dance thing from *Donna Summer*. So immediately Helen Miley and Richard Faye stood, linked arms, began to dance sideways, very elegant, very formal. To the left, to the right, doing all the dips.

The music ended, they sat down again, lighted their cigarettes, which had unaccountably gone out.

"My problem," he said.

"Your problem?"

"My problem," he said, "is that I get this feeling that I'm a different person to everyone I meet. You know? I'm a person to my mother, and a person to you, and a person to my boss, and ..."

And then they were clapping hands in rhythm, a great spiritual, chanting, "And a person to my boss, and a person to my sauce, and a person to my loss, and a person to my moss ..."

But finally they stopped. He said, "Well ... you know."

"So?"

"So, who am I?"

"Aha!" she shouted. "Let's get at that steak."

It was an inch-thick slice of sirloin, bone and fat included.

"Got a good knife?" he asked.

"Not really. I've got this one. But I have a funny little thing with metal disks, and you sharpen the edge in that. You know how, Uck?"

He looked at her haughtily.

So he sharpened the knife, drawing it carefully through the intertwined disks. He didn't cut himself once, even when he tested the edge on his thumb. Helen watched him with a beamy smile.

"Gee," she said, "you really know how to sharpen a knife."

He wiped the blade slowly, then trimmed off a tiny bit of fat.

"Now take this into the living room and give it to your bird," he instructed her.

"No. Screw him."

"Take it to him, Helen. He's entitled."

"Oh ... shit," she grumbled—but she took the little piece of fat and came back in a minute. "He's pecking at it!"

"Of course." He nodded. "Who wouldn't?"

He did a very good job, slicing out the bone, trimming the fat, making a beautiful circle of raw meat that was tendered and marbled.

"I am going to slice off a piece of this steak," he said, "and I am going to eat it raw."

He looked at her.

"You are also going to slice off a piece of that steak for me," she told him, "and I am going to eat it raw."

So he sliced off two thin slices. It was aged beef, flavorful. You could have cut it with a ping-pong paddle. They ate their slices. He looked at her. She nodded. He cut the remaining meat in chewable chunks, and they took the plate into the living room with them.

"I have potatoes," she said faintly. "Salad. Frozen spinach. A big tomato. Stuff like that. And some pastry."

He didn't even look at her. They just munched their raw beef. Boy, was it good!

"I'll have diarrhea in the morning." She sighed.

He nodded happily.

She looked at the cigarette she was smoking. "It went out again. Where do you get these things?"

"A little girl where I work. A sweet young thing. Face right out of Botticelli. That's Sam Botticelli. He owns a deli in Ho-Ho-Kus. One day she had the whole office turned on."

"Hey," she said excitedly, "watch this!"

She leaped to her feet, tossed a seat cushion into a corner. Before you could say "Ivan Skavinsky-Skavar," she was standing on her head, on the cushion, her feet propped up in the corner of the walls, her skirt flopping down around her head. He caught a frightening glimpse of yummy thighs and blue bikini panties, with little pink rosebuds along the seams.

"Oh, my God," he groaned—genuine anguish.

And then she was on her feet again, face flushed.

"How about that?" she demanded.

He applauded politely.

"Yoga," she explained. "It's all self-discipline."

They went back to eating their raw steak.

"Do you think..." she asked, "do you think...do you think...if we had a nice tall scotch and soda that it would, in any way, interfere...I'm thirsty."

"Well...."

She bounced into the kitchen, brought back nice tall scotch

and sodas, and now they were really busy—with the drinks, the raw steak, the powder.

"It's all coming together," someone said.

Richard Faye, Boy Derelict, who thought too much for his own good, sat there on the edge of his chair, leaning forward. He had lost weight all right, just as he had vowed. Now he seemed to float inside his clothes—a little boy playing house inside his father's suit. Some time, somehow, during the evening, he had unbuttoned his brown tweed vest and buttoned it up again. But he had missed by one. There was an extra button top right and an extra buttonhole bottom left.

The little bags were there, still swinging under his eyes, and he seemed to be resting his belly on his thighs. But undeniably he was thinner.

He asked, "You know what the saddest thing was I ever saw?"

"What was the saddest thing you ever saw?"

"Last year, at Thanksgiving, I saw a Puerto Rican restaurant, and they had a sign in the window that said, 'Thanksgiving Dinner Special. Turky and All the Tremens.' That's how they spelled it—Tremens—T-R-E-M-E-N-S. I wanted to cry."

"Listen," she said, "did I ever tell you I could touch the tip of my nose with my tongue?"

"Yes, you told me that and proved to me that you can do it."

"I don't care," she said, "I'm going to do it again." And she did.

He rose to his feet, cigarette elegantly clasped between thumb and forefinger, highball clasped in the other hand, brain barely clasped inside a pulsating skull.

"We are now going to make a movie," he declaimed.

Helen Miley jerked to her feet and saluted. "Sir! Do I get to take off all my clothes?"

"It is not, my dear, that kind of a film."

"What kind is it?"

"This is a love story."

"Oh, yes," she said delightedly, slapping her hands together. "I love love stories. What part do I play?"

"You are the wife, and I am the husband."

"It's a marvelous movie. I like it already. What must I do?"

He took a puff, took a sip, took a puff, took a sip.

"This movie," he said, "this movie takes place in 1925. We are living in a small suburb just outside Philadelphia, Pennsylvania.

I work for a large, prosperous corporation that makes the round cork liners that go inside the caps that go on bottles of Moxie."

"Moxie?"

"Moxie. A delicious soft drink with no artificial sweeteners. Chocolate-flavored. I am a—I am the production manager who makes certain all those cork linings come off the assembly line on time."

"And who am I? What do I do?"

"You are my Loving Wife. In this movie. We live in this suburban home. It is painted white."

"With green shutters?"

"With green shutters"—he nodded—"and also there are roses on the south side."

"Rambler roses," Helen said happily. "I like this movie. Do we have children?"

"Yes, we do. We have two children. Fondue is our oldest child. He is ten and very precocious. Last week he sold fourteen subscriptions to *Liberty Magazine* and won a bicycle. The little girl is named Tusk, and she is very sweet. She lisps."

"And she wears a hair ribbon?"

"Right," he said approvingly. "Pink."

"And she's very pretty and is always getting into mischief, and yesterday she fell down and hurt her knee, and I had to kiss it and make it well."

He looked at her gloomily. "You've seen this movie before."

"No, Uck, I swear I haven't."

"Well...yes, she fell down and hurt her knee, and you had to kiss it and make it well. Anyway, when the picture starts, I am coming home Friday night from the cork-cap-Moxie factory. I am on the interurban and—"

"Interurban?"

"I did some research on them last week. They were like trolley cars that ran from the cities out to the country. I saw some wonderful photos. They ran through meadows and through farms. Electric. Single cars. God, it was so beautiful. Anyway, I am coming home on this interurban, and my seat partner asks me if we are going to the country club dance that night."

"We belong to a country club?"

"Oh, yes. We are very well-to-do. All those cork liners, you know. And I say yes, we are going to the dance, and our Faithful

Family Retainer will stay with the children. So then, we get to this station way out in a meadow somewhere and—"

"And I'm waiting for you!"

"That's exactly right! You are waiting for me with the children, having driven over from our cottage in our 1922 John O'Hara, or something like that, and the kids shout, 'Daddy! Daddy!' and throw themselves into my arms. And I kiss them. I kiss Fondue, and he tells me about the subscriptions to *Liberty Magazine* and how he won a bicycle, and I kiss Tusk, and she tells me about how she fell down and hurt her knee and you had to kiss it to make it well. And then I kiss you."

"Oh, Uck! This is the part I like."

"All right. So now this is our first big scene in this movie, and we've got to establish right away what kind of a relationship we have. Okay? Now let's go. You speak first."

HELEN: Hello, Oh, my darling. Did you have a hard day in the orifice?

RICHARD: Yes, my very own sweetheart, I had a hard day in the orifice, turning out all those cork things that go inside the caps that go on bottles of Moxie, all over the civilized world. However, what sustained me was the thought of returning home to my very own wife and children in my very own little cottage with roses on the south side. And how was your day, Oh, my wife?

HELEN: The butcher overcharged me two cents a pound on pork chops.

"Yes"—he nodded approvingly—"that's very good, and I think it will be an excellent fade-out line for that scene. I don't mean to be critical, Helen, but I think you could, perhaps, deliver your lines with a little more feeling. I mean, that line about the pork chops has great significance, and if you *felt* it just a little more deeply..."

"I'll try," she said humbly.

They took a moment off to eat their raw beef, smoke their cigarettes, mix a fresh drink.

"Now then," he said briskly, "we've established a mood of mutual love and understanding. Right?"

"Right, chief."

"Now we are inside our little cottage. We have eaten the pork chops. You and I are upstairs in the master bedroom, dressing for the Friday night dance at the country club."

"That's great! What a scene! The critics will love me in this scene. I'm going to wear my white lace with that crazy hem with the points."

"And you're wearing a chemmy."

"A chemmy?"

"A chemise. That's what women wore in those days. It's like a bra and slip and panties all in one."

"Oh, I know. I've seen those. They button under the old crotcheroonie."

"Yes, that's right. Well, now the scene starts. I speak first...."

RICHARD: I'm through in the bathroom now, my very own darling, in case you wish to enter.

HELEN: No, Oh, my love, I am quite finished with my ablutions. I will merely sit at this dressing table which has a large mirror in front and two smaller mirrors on the sides, working on hinges so they may be adjusted, and I will complete my toilet.

RICHARD: Toilette.

HELEN: I will complete my toilette. You smell very lovely this evening, my husband.

RICHARD: Yes, my wife. I have used as an after-shave lotion a small bit of alcohol to which a modicum of wintergreen has been added. Do you find it offensive?

HELEN: *Au contraire,* light of my life, *au contraire.*

RICHARD: The Friday evening dance at the country club does not begin until nine o'clock, so there is no need for us to rush.

HELEN (*smugly*): No. There is no need for us to rush.

RICHARD: You're looking very lovely in this damned moonlight, Amanda.

"What?" she asked, puzzled. "What did you say?"

"Sorry. A bit of plagiarism in there. But I'll edit it out of the final version. Now then...I say:"

RICHARD: So there is no need to rush. Must you dress immediately, my wife?

HELEN: Oh, no, my very own man, there is no need for me to dress immediately. And the children are in their rooms, watched over by our Faithful Family Retainer. We have at least an hour.

RICHARD: In which we may disport?

HELEN: Yea and verily.

RICHARD: How beautiful you are, sitting there in your marquisette dressing gown on that little bench before the large mirror in front and the two small mirrors on the sides, working on hinges so they may be adjusted. Have I told you today that I love you?

HELEN: You have told me three times, which hardly seems enough. First, when you departed for the orifice in the morning. Second, when you gave me a ting-a-ling after returning from lunch at the You-Betcha Diner, and thirdly, on our trip home from the station. However, my man, I never tire of hearing those words.

RICHARD: Those three little words?

HELEN: Those three little words.

RICHARD: I love you.

"Jesus!" she said.

RICHARD: Because here we are in our own little cottage, on the outskirts of Philadelphia, Pennsylvania, with roses on the south side, and I have you and our two little people, and this is what gives meaning to the Moxie bottle caps. Do you understand?

HELEN: I think—

RICHARD: Loving you and the family, and it's 1925, and no one is at war, and everyone is rich and getting richer and drinking Moxie. Those radishes in your vegetable garden are doing well, and Fondue is going to grow up to be a bicycle tycoon, and Tusk will marry the son of a rear admiral. I just know it. Oh, God, my darling, I love you so much...

HELEN: And I have my very own man of my own. I wake up every morning, and there you are. And my own son and my own daughter. My house with the roses. My radishes...

"Now I walk over to you," he directed, "and you rise and we embrace. We look like that guy with the violin and the woman at the piano in the perfume ad—except that I'm wearing my one-piece BVD underwear with the slit seat and the legs that come to my knees. Now..."

RICHARD: Madam, are you aware that one of your mammary appendages is protruding through an aperture in your peignoir?

HELEN: You mean my tit's showing?

RICHARD: Madam, have you no fucking couth?

HELEN: None whatsoever.

"Now I begin to lead you over to the bed because we've got a whole hour to disport before the country club dance. And here comes your big moment—really the most dramatic moment in the movie. Because here is where you say—"

"I know, I know," she shouted gleefully, clapping her hands. "This is where I get to gasp, 'Now. Now. Now.'"

"That's exactly right. Think you can do it?"

HELEN (*gasping*): Now. Now. Now.

"Beautiful," he said, moving toward the bedroom. "You're a veritable Duse."

"A Duse? A doozy?"

"A deece. A dice. Will you be a sweet little outskirts-of-Philadelphia housewife and scamper into the kitchen to construct for us another drink? And meanwhile, I shall light our one remaining cigarette, which we shall share, and I shall also divest myself of my raiment."

"Yes, Oh, my husband," she muttered dutifully.

When she returned with the drinks, the door to the bedroom was half-closed. The lights were out. The shades were drawn. But enough pale light seeped in from the living room for her to see that he was naked. Naked and standing bedore the full-length mirror fastened to the inside of the bedroom door. She remembered Harry Tennant doing the same thing and had a moment of panic—all her men trying to see themselves, searching the reflections.

But, because God had given her a merry heart, a marvelous gift, she put such dark thoughts away from her, slipped out of her dress and skivvies. In a moment she was standing naked directly in front of him. His hands rested lightly on her shoulders. They stared at their dim image, seeming all silvery and poetic.

"It is midnight," he said, something catching in his throat. "And I now turn into a pumpkin."

He stared above her head, through the halo of her blond curls. He could see his face. Him. Richard Faye. Undeniably.

But from the neck down ... from the neck down flowed this limpid flesh, as graceful and fascinating as a moving column of water. He touched her shoulders, moved his hands gently down her arms. She shivered at his touch, murmuring...

And there he was, caressing himself. His hands slid smoothly over his saucy breasts and down the hollow of his waist, followed the flare of his hips, touched the living thighs. Happiness flowered in him. His brain went floating off somewhere.

They stood there a long time, one sad animal, watching those clumpy, hungry hands moving over their body. Delirium washed over them in welcome waves, and they made strange sounds. She reached behind them to pull him closer, her mind a mush, and he began to eat her hair.

And that is what they did.

18

It was a Sunday morning, as crisp and crunchy as a good apple, and *Charles Lefferts called her!* Beautiful. For one brief moment she was tempted to tell him she was busy. Very brief.

But then there he was, double-parked in front of the canopy in his fire-engine-red MG-A. He brought a wicker hamper of food, bottles, a Polaroid camera—all tucked behind the seats. She brought herself, smashing in her seventy-five-dollar French jeans.

He moved the car downtown, heading toward the tunnel to Brooklyn. They were going to Jacob Riis Beach, out on the Island.

"It will be deserted this time of year," he told her. "The idiots stop going after Labor Day. The idiots don't go before Memorial Day. They think you can only go to the beach from June to September. The idiots."

She turned sideways in the bucket seat so she could look at

him. He was wearing a frantic cap in pop-art houndstooth. His soft leather driving gloves had stitched holes where the knuckles came through. Oh, yes—and a marvelous chronometer that did everything but tell time.

He was a *bruuum, bruuum, bruuuum* driver, gunning the engine at red lights, lots of down-shifting on a turn, then revving—Mario Andretti—swinging the wheel ferociously without moving his hands on it, pole position in the Manhattan Grand Prix, eyes steely, nerves an amalgam of titanium and some secret ceramic, doing, oh, maybe thirty-five miles an hour when he caught the light, his Steinberg profile (pointed with a cold cigar) piercing the wind. It was living.

She scooted down in her seat as they went hurtling into the white-tiled tunnel.

"Whee!" he cried, and she smiled at him.

"The longest men's room in the world," she murmured, but he didn't hear her.

Then they were out in the sunlight again, a blue sky stretching to Pluto, and he was hysterical, long wool scarf (Princeton colors) whipping back in the wind, knuckles showing white through those holes in his gloves as he worked the stick, feet heavy on the pedals, sharp wind lashing tears from his eyes. She huddled down, a fringed carblanket about her shoulders, and she was happy for his glee, happy he had this—something, anything—in his plotless existence.

And eventually, they were on the beach. Miles and miles of sand still clotted with garbage from the Labor Day weekend, with hunks of tarred driftwood, decaying fish, a few bleached timbers, a few chunks of concrete broken from a wharf or dock somewhere and waved ashore.

But still, clean and washed—the way the sun and sea will do. Even the litter seemed clean—smelling of salt and brightness. In the scrubbed sky a gang of gulls, trailing their crazy pipe-cleaner legs and feet behind them. On the beach, dignified gulls pecking at empty bags of Fritos, and sandpipers goosing each other near the water.

A few people, not many, couples and families, bundled up, most of them huddled in the lee of the boardwalk, but some down near the sea—with barbecue fires going and a windshield of sharp-colored plastic on poles thrust into the sand.

It was not a mean picnic lunch he had prepared. There were joints of fried chicken, wrapped in aluminum foil and warm.

There were slices of cold roast beef, hard-boiled eggs, celery, a tin of brisling sardines. Chunks of garlic bread, plum tomatoes, sticks of cucumber. He had not forgotten salt, pepper, a key for the sardine tin, a corkscrew for the two bottles of chilled rosé he had brought. There was also a thermos of black coffee. Crystal wineglasses and paper napkins, the sweet.

They both wore heavy horn-rimmed sunglasses, sat with their backs against the crumbling concrete side of the boardwalk. Out of the wind it was loverly warm—hot. He peeled off cap, scarf, jacket, sweater, T-shirt. She removed blanket, jacket, sweater . . . and let the world applaud her little inflated bra. The sunshine was a blessing; they lolled in it, twisting, turning on the big beach towel he had spread.

Occasionally, they glanced blank-eyed at each other—two blind. But mostly they turned faces and pale torsos to that raunchy sun. He opened one of the bottles; they clinked glasses, sipped. They stared at the sky, peered at the light, watched those nutty gulls, grunted with contentment. It wasn't bad.

"Did you know," he said lazily, "did you know that I am the greatest lover in New York?"

"No kidding?" she said, just as lazily. "Where was the contest held—Yankee Stadium?"

He showed his teeth.

"Well . . . it's like manhood."

"Manhood?"

"Sure. Helen, you wouldn't believe how many fags there are in New York. And how many guys there are who aren't really fags but who just aren't interested in sex. And how many husbands there are who wear themselves out trying to make a buck and are just too tired to hack it. You wouldn't believe."

"I'd believe." She sighed.

"That's what I mean. All those guys who can't make you climb walls. That's where I come in. Manhood. Hey! Let's eat!"

They opened all his little foil and waxed paper packages. They began to chew, nibble, gulp. It always tastes better on a hard, clear, chilly October day—and so it did, so it did.

"Y'see," he explained, gnawing away at a drumstick, "it's a question of supply and demand."

She took a deep swallow of wine. Then both sat up straight, looked behind them as they heard a deep rumbling of the planks on the boardwalk. It was a police patrol car, coming down slowly, then turning off at the end of the beach.

"Supply and demand," he repeated, chunking away at a cucumber stick. "I've got something I can supply that is in great demand. You know?"

She looked at him in wonderment but didn't stop the job she was doing on a slice of rare roast beef.

"It's like a profession," he said, voice muffled with food. "I figure I'm a professional. You know—like a foot doctor."

"A foot doctor." She nodded.

"Y'see, every year more and more single women come to New York. Right? They get good jobs and make a lot of loot. But they're away from home. You understand? Home is Kansas or South Dakota or Indiana. Some place like that. They share good apartments, buy a lot of clothes, put money in the bank. But they got no one to talk to. You understand. All those fags and semifags and dirty old men. Right?"

"Right."

"You know how many go to shrinks? Hundreds. Thousands. Millions. Not because they need a shrink, but it's worth one-fifty a week just to have someone to talk to. Talk? This is living? You know what they really want? A wee bit of the old narsty."

She bit into a chilled plum tomato. Good. She sprinkled on some salt. Better.

"So," he said, "that's where I come in."

"Exactly."

"Yes. Like I told you—a profession. Is that so awful?"

"No. I guess not."

"I'm a man, a member of a disappearing breed."

"You mean you can get it up?"

"Well . . . yes."

"And women pay you for this, Charles?"

"Oh, not in *money*. I never take money from women. But you know—*things*. Like my car. This Polaroid camera. My African masks and jars of spices. Hi-fi. Things like that."

She looked at him speculatively. "And what would you like from me, Charles?"

"Oh, my dear!" He leaned forward, put a hand on her bare arm. He thrust his blah face close to hers; she could see the chicken fat on his lips. "My God, Helen, you've got the wrong idea—but completely. I'm not asking you for anything. Not a thing. You're one of the few women—one of the *very few*—I just like to be with. I'm not asking you for a thing. I just thought it would interest you. I thought it would amuse you if I told you these things. Jesus, I don't want anything from you. Just being with you is enough for me. You know that."

"Sure," she said. "Have a hard-boiled egg."

They ate awhile in silence while another police car rumbled by on the boardwalk over their heads.

"Tell me," Helen said, nibbling delicately on the Pope's Nose, which she dearly loved, "how do you account for this ability of yours to satisfy so many women?"

"Oh," he said, looking down modestly, wiping his fingers on a paper napkin, "it's just a knack, I guess."

"A *knack?*"

"Well . . . you know, I happen to be hung like a yak. And I've never had any complaints. You've never complained."

"That's true. You're very good at your profession."

"Sure. Well, you know, I don't have any other job. I have this small trust fund but—let's face it—women are really how I make my living."

She nodded wisely. By this time they were on the second bottle of wine, and she had the strangest feeling that she was watching an obscene television channel—a channel no one knew about but her. And there they were—Helen and Charles— starring in this soap opera, fascinating and utterly forgettable.

"But, Charles," she said, reaching for a stalk of celery, determined to play this out until the commercial came on, "Charles, what's going to happen to you? You can't expect this knack of yours to last forever. What happens to you when you get old? The manhood? I mean when you can't get it up thirty-seven times a day?"

"I've thought of that," he cried triumphantly. "I've been working on that. A widow. Or maybe a divorcée. Lots of loot. A home in California. The beach. Sun. Suntan oil. White linen evening jacket. The whole bit. You know? Goodish!"

"Oh, sure. Lots of parties. Maybe an Alfa Romeo. And maybe two or three times a week with her. Plenty. Right?"

"Right!" he sang joyously, gulping the wine and the breeze. "Two or three times a week. Jesus, what a sell! That's my fate. Does that sound so bad? Really, Helen, does that sound so bad?"

"No. Not so bad."

"But meanwhile, until I hit it big, I've got to keep hacking away at it, taking these things from all these women. You understand?"

"For your manhood?"

"Exactly! Just like I said—supply and demand. It's a profession."

"And you've got the knack?"

"Righto! I've got the knack. More?"

"Oh, God, no. I couldn't eat another thing."

"Then it's picture-taking time! Let me clean up first."

He was so neat. Bones, scraps and paper napkins bundled and tossed into a nearby litter can. Empty bottles discarded. Beach towel shaken out and folded. Very neat and lawful.

Then he opened his camera...

There is something unnerving about it. Familiarity doesn't breed contempt; it breeds fright. You may feel yourself and find to your satisfaction that you are a three-dimensional being. You are damp and have substance. Somewhere, hidden in that thin airmail envelope of skin, is a wild pump that goes on and on; the juices flow. Poke flesh with a finger, and flesh pokes back. The substance is you, unique. O God, you are alive.

So she posed, at Charles' request, in her French jeans and sweet little brassiere. But a few seconds later there she was—two-dimensional, in color a little much. She held herself in her hands, this little bit of cardboard, tried to understand but couldn't. Image. Reflection. Squinting in the sunlight. This unholy. immortality. The cardboard chilling. In a nonstop sequence her memory flashed: baby held in mother's arms, group photo of fourth grade at Theodore Roosevelt Public School, standing under the apple tree, bathing suit at the lake, on the porch with Eddie Chase, with John Smith when that nightclub girl came around, others, others, and the portraits by Jo Rhodes. And now...this. But if you can be captured on cardboard...if you can be reduced to chilly, two-dimensional paper, no pump going, then...then...

"Now I'll take some of you," she said brightly.

He couldn't have been less loath. Profile somber. Full face smiling. Imitation muscleman with biceps flexed. Peering over one shoulder, coy. And an additional roll of etc.'s. He tucked the finished prints into his wallet. She had never heard a man chortle before. He chortled.

"Hey," he said, "let's take a walk down to the shore. We'll walk along the beach and then come back and go home. Okay?"

"Okay," she said happily.

They dressed and tidied up—everything packed away in the wicker hamper, and hamper and camera covered with the beach towel. She slung the fringed car blanket around her shoulders because the wind punished. Hand-in-hand, they started down toward the sea, tripping, skipping, laughing at those gulls, nudging toes at a big crab shell, waving at people clamped around their barbecue fires.

They carefully avoided clumps of tar that had been washed ashore, zigzagged down until the sand darkened and began to sink beneath their feet. They turned, meandered along the beach.

She stopped him for a moment, looked up at the sky, the weakening sun drooping down. Someone had poured a very, very dry martini (twist of lemon peel) over the entire world.

"Charles," she said, squeezing his hand.

The sea was tinged with the late-afternoon light, some small whitecaps spilling there as the tide came in. Ozone. Fishermen in heavy boots swinging big rigs, casting far out. Wives sitting up on the sand near little fires, sipping hot coffee and dreaming. Sometimes the shrill yells of kids dashing bare-legged into the freezing surf and dashing out again. There is a life. There is a life for all of us.

They wandered down to an almost deserted section of beach. It was in front of the big boardwalk restaurant (closed) built of red brick, whitewashed. The sun and wind had eaten at it. There was that warm, white-flecked surface, so good to look at that you wanted to kiss it.

Anyway, most of the people at the beach had wallowed down through the sand and gone left or right, away from the main building. So Helen Miley and Charles Lefferts stood there a moment, alone, looking at the sea, not wanting anything to end.

"Look," she said, pointing, "I wonder what that is..."

He looked where she pointed. It was a thing. Dark and white. Rolling on the waves. A big piece of driftwood. A big dead fish. Something. Maybe...

"Well, let's go back," he said. "I'm getting cold. My feet are really getting cold."

"Wait a minute," she said.

It rolled in the sea, a lump. It was coming ashore—no doubt about that. It was coming to join them. It would disappear, the waves would wash it under, and then it would bob to the surface again. Something...

"Come on," he demanded, "I'm really cold. We'll pick up the basket and hop in the car. We'll go to my place. Nice and warm.

We'll have—you know—like a great meal. We'll have a steak and baked potato and a bottle of wine. How does that grab you?"

She stared, split, her mouth slowly opening.

Each wave brought it closer to shore. She stared as it bobbed, swirled, went under, came to the surface, did a funny little dance, disappeared, and then floated free again, turning its face to the lost sun.

"Look," she commanded him, "look..."

He took one brief glance, then looked away. "What's wrong with you?" he shouted. "Are you coming with me, or aren't you?"

She turned to see him, put out one hand to touch his arm, but he pulled away. He stumbled away from her. He went running away through the sand. He looked funny—not funny haha but funny strange. He was running hard, spurts of sand coming up with each strained stride. Once he fell to his knees, clawing at the air.

She watched him, befuddled, as he became smaller and smaller, running, stumbling, clawing, a curious creature flopping about like a madman. And there, above him, against the darkening sky, three tough-guy gulls, swooping and clawing, one of them bombing the beach, living it up.

She turned back toward the sea. It was still there, rolling, bobbing. A soft, white thing came out of the water and waved at her. That was nice.

She took a deep breath, vowed she would not be sick. She pulled the blanket tighter around her shoulders, began trudging back to the boardwalk. "I think that I shall never see," she recited aloud, "a poem lovely as a tree." That seemed to help; she kept reciting it until she was at the cement stairs leading up to the boardwalk. The stairs were mostly sanded over, but she got up there, leaned against the railing, breathing deeply. In comes the good air, out goes the bad air...

She was there, oh, maybe five minutes or so, when along came a police car, slowly, the boards rumbling softly under the tires. She stepped in front of it and waved her arms, grabbing the blanket just before it fell off. She walked around to the side of the stopped car.

The driver was fifteen years old (what was happening to her when the cops looked so young?), but his partner had been sent over from Central Casting. He was big, porky, Irish, rare-faced, the top button of his choker collar open. He was prying in his ear with a toothpick.

"Yes, missy?" he asked.

"Listen," she said, a little desperate, "there's something down there in the water. Near the shore. It's floating. I think ... I think ..."

God, was he good, He didn't sneer at her or anything. He just flicked his toothpick away and got out of the car. He smiled, put an arm around her shoulders, said, "Let's go take a look."

They started toward the shore. He stopped, yelled back to the car. "Bobby," he yelled, "if we need the launch, I'll raise my arm."

The fifteen-year-old boy nodded.

So there they were, plowing through the sand down to the rolling sea.

"You here alone?" he asked.

"No. I came with a man."

"And where is he now?"

"He went back."

The old cop nodded wisely, then put a hand on her arm.

"Just point out to me where you saw it. No sense your coming down all the way."

"That's all right," she said stoutly. "I won't get sick."

"You won't? We get two or three a year. I been in this precinct for twenty years. That's maybe fifty-sixty floaters. I crack my cookies every time. But I've learned how to do it. Now I don't splatter my shoes."

He looked sideways at her, but she was staring out to sea, her teeth clenched.

Finally: "It could be a big dead fish," she muttered. "Or some wood or something."

He nodded. They went trudging down to the shore until they were on wet sand, their feet beginning to sink in.

She pointed. True to his word, he vomited, turning away from her, being careful not to splatter his shoes.

"Jesus, Mary and Joseph," he gasped. "May the soul rest in peace."

"Ah," she said, beginning to weep, "ah ..."

He wiped his lips with a soiled handkerchief, then held her to him. For a moment they stood there, trembling, the two of them, strangers.

"Now look," he said finally, "will you do something for me?"

She nodded dumbly.

"You go back to the boardwalk. You tell Bobby—he's my partner—that we won't need the launch. The tide's coming in. But tell Bobby we'll need another car and the meat wagon. Got that?"

"Yes."

"And will you give your name and address to Bobby? And the name and address of that man of yours who went back?"

"Yes."

He looked at her, his face broken, the old porky Irish face shattered.

"Shit," he said.

"Yes," she nodded.

She plowed back to the boardwalk, did exactly as he had instructed. In for a penny, in for a pound, and she stood there, waiting for many minutes, while more police cars rolled up, and an ambulance, and men in boots with boathooks and a curious kind of stretcher. It was a drill. They knew what to do.

Eventually, the few people who had gathered around this operation dispersed to their warm homes; the thing was put into the ambulance, which growled away. The old cop came plodding up. His face was laced with grease and grief. He saw her standing there; he wasn't surprised.

"Well, now," he said, "where do you live?"

"Manhattan."

"Can we get you home?"

"No, thanks, I'll manage."

"Yes," he said, looking at her closely, "you'll manage."

He took her hand, clasped it tightly, turned away.

She folded up the fringed blanket, went stumping toward the bus stop, not thinking of anything. There were many cars screaming around the curve, heading across the bridge, speeding their way to Brooklyn and Manhattan.

There were two other people waiting for the bus: an old man with fishing tackle and a canvas bag that flopped, and an old woman carrying a Bible and muttering.

And then along came Charles Lefferts in his fire-engine-red MG-A, squealing to a stop. He leaned over, opened the door. She got in.

"I saw them," he said. "That's what it was."

She nodded. They drove toward home.

He drove slowly, never looking at her. At the tunnel he didn't have the right change, so he borrowed a nickel from her. Then he drove up the East Side, pulled up at her block. He couldn't stop right in front of the canopy because a big black Cadillac was double-parked there, a uniformed chauffeur leaning against the fender.

She turned to look at him then, his sharp Steinberg profile somewhat chinless, his gloved hands caressing the wooden steering wheel.

"What are you thinking about?" he asked, staring straight ahead.

Well . . . what she had been thinking about was curious. A few weeks ago she had passed a pipe and tobacco shop in the block where she worked. The shop had many pipes on display in the window, some inexpensive, some costly. Included in the display were hand-carved pipes in the visages of famous men. There was a Stalin pipe, a Winston Churchill pipe, a Franklin Roosevelt pipe, a Beethoven pipe. The tops of their skulls, naturally, were cut off cleanly, and you put the tobacco down into their heads, and then you smoked the pipes. She supposed that pipe stores all over the world carried similar pipes, hand-carved, and that was true.

But this pipe shop also carried a John F. Kennedy pipe. The top of the head was cut off cleanly. You stuffed the tobacco down into the briar skull.

She told Charles Lefferts about this because, after all, he had asked what she was thinking about.

He looked at her a puzzled moment, then looked away with a thousand-yard stare.

"Well," he said, "I don't know . . . I'm a cigar smoker myself."

19

1. Her period was due on Monday—a date circled in red on her office-desk calendar. She was on the Pill—but who can remember? By Wednesday she was—not worried exactly; she did have a cold. But still it nagged. Thursday morning she woke up grumpy and nauseous and knew it was coming. She snarled at Harry Tennant and poor Susie Carrar, who had hardly recovered from her abortion. So Helen went home by herself on Thursday night, grumbling. It started late Thursday evening. She inserted a Tampax and had two Rob Roys, four aspirin, a Librium and went to bed early. Her mind was beautifully blank. The bed felt good: two sheets and two blankets on a firm hair mattress. She rolled onto her right side, and that was it...

2. It was nine in the morning—Friday morning—when she opened her eyes. She knew at once it had been snowing.

The city had that swaddled quiet. She looked for Rocco, but he wasn't there. Then she looked at the window. A gray, slick, steely light. Pipes were knocking, walls were creaking as the heat came up. She darted out of bed, slammed the window shut, leaped back into bed again. She rolled around, tucking the blankets beneath her until she was in a cocoon of wool. She ducked her head beneath the covers until her envelope was warm with her breath, then came up, gasping for air. The hell with going to work. She'd stay home. She was entitled.

3. She lay there, staring at the fine cracks in the ceiling, wondering when the damned landlord was going to repaint. The room warmed; she moved the blankets down to her waist. She was sleeping naked. She reached down and flicked the fuse on her Tampax. It was there all right. She felt the insides of her thighs. On the left one, there was something that itched—like a little bite. So she scratched it.

4. It became warmer. She threw the blankets aside, swung her feet down to the floor. She sat on the edge of the bed, yawning, scrubbing her scalp with her knuckles. There seemed to be some scurf, so she decided she'd shampoo. She lighted her first cigarette of the day and coughed twice. She stretched her legs out as far as she could, holding herself on the edge of the bed, looking at her legs, twisting them. Not bad. But they could use a shave. Maybe she would. She'd take a long, hot bath with oil in it; she'd shave her legs and shampoo her hair. Except she always cut herself when she shaved her legs. She used a shaving cup with a soap biscuit in it, a shaving brush, and a safety razor. It took a long time if she didn't want to cut herself.

5. She sat farther back on the bed, brought one foot up onto her knee. She leaned far down and smelled it. It smelled okay. She looked at it, saw the toenail polish was flaking off. She would also paint her toenails. She would just have a nice, quiet, lazy day and do things. She crossed her other foot, picked gently at a small corn on the middle toe. She would also cut that off with a razor blade. What she liked about her feet was that her second toes were longer than her big toes. She had read somewhere that this was a mark of elegance. Anyway, her feet were good. No one could deny it.

6. She stood, finally. She put her hands on her naked hips, leaned far back, arching her spine, thrusting out her pelvis. Her spine gave a modest crack. She padded over to the big mirror, looked at herself. "Hello, pretty face," she said.

7. Her breasts looked distressingly flaccid to her, so she licked her thumbs and forefingers and twirled her nipples like someone dialing WQXR. The results were immediate and pleasing.

8. She scuffed into a pair of straw slippers. She went naked into the living room, still yawning, briskly scratching waist, hips, appendicitis scar, ass. She took the cover off the parakeet cage. He hopped up close to the bars and squawked, "Hello, pretty face!" She laughed delightedly. "You doll," she said, nuzzling her nose against the bars, "you absolute doll!" He started to peck at her nose; she drew away hastily.

9. Over to the window...the snow floating down in big pieces, like shredded Kleenex. It was steely gray all right. She wondered what could possibly happen if she didn't go to work. Nothing would happen. Nothing at all. She let the Venetian blind fall with a clatter. She yawned again.

10. She went slopping into the kitchen, opened the refrigerator door. It wasn't crowded, but she wasn't going to starve to death, that was for sure. She decided to perk some coffee instead of using the instant. She measured it into the pot, added the water, plugged it in, switched it on. While it was heating, she found a little can of tomato juice. And, oh, boy, a bottle of vodka with one hefty shot left. So, before she could consider the wisdom of this, she shook up a fast Bloody Mary with everything, including horseradish and a few drops of Tabasco. Everything mixed up very well, very cold. She took a cautious sip. It was like plasma; her eyelids flipped open wide, nerve ends began to tingle. By the time she finished the drink the coffee smell was driving her up the wall. She took the whole pot, plus cup and saucer, into the living room and poured the first cup of the day, black and steaming. She lighted another cigarette.

11. She opened her front door cautiously, retrieved the morning paper, relocked the door, put the chain on. She finally found her glasses on the shelf in the bathroom, came back into the living room, settled down with coffee and paper.

12. "A significant day for you," her horoscope read. "It may lead the way to an entirely new life." Very good, she nodded approvingly. She read some of the stories, some of the columns while she finished her first cup of coffee. She looked around carefully and then picked her nose—just a little and very quickly.

13. She poured a second cup of coffee, carried it and the newspaper into the bathroom. She sat on the toilet, hunched forward with her forearms on her knees. She held the cup and sipped while she did her duty. The newspaper was on the tiled floor; she flipped the pages slowly, reading some of the ads. Cartier's had a watch for $7,500.

14. Her toilet paper was puce imprinted with yellow daisies. It seemed a shame to. . . . She had finished her cup of coffee. She stood in front of the medicine cabinet mirror, opened her mouth wide, stuck her tongue out as far as she could. It wasn't very pretty. She took the washcloth, wet a corner of it, and wiped some of that stuff off her tongue, gagging a few times as she reached far back into her mouth. Then she brushed her teeth vigorously, washed her mouth out several times, spitting into the sink.

15. She spread her legs wide, bent over, examined herself. Everything seemed to be all right. She felt pretty good, now that her period had started. A pain in the ass—but what the hell are you going to do? She debated whether she should take that long, hot bath right now or maybe just a shower . . . or what. She finally decided to take a whore's bath—soaping up the washcloth, washing her face, hands, armpits, a quick swipe between her legs Then rinsing with a soap-free cloth. Then drying. She put on the terrycloth robe that was hanging behind the bathroom door—the robe that had "Killer Miley" embroidered on the back. She went into the living room, picked up the paper again, and started reading. There was about half a cup of coffee left. It was cold.

16. She finished the paper, took off her glasses, switched on the radio. She listened to "Pomp and Circumstance" for a few minutes; then a man came on and said, "Snow continuing throughout the day and possibly into tomorrow, mixed occasionally with rain and sleet." She switched off the radio, started to yawn, and suddenly a tremendous belch rumbled out of her wee stomach (the Bloody Mary,

no doubt). She clapped a hand to her mouth, looked about apologetically.

17. She lay back on the couch, feet tucked under her, put one hand inside her robe, fondled a tit.

18. She thought about Harry Tennant. She put a hand down between her legs and tapped herself there, just tapping the way you'd tap the ash from a cigarette. She didn't do it very long—just a few taps.

19. She lighted another cigarette, went back into the kitchen, stuck the coffee cup and saucer into the sink, let hot water run into them. She opened the refrigerator door again, began to consider what she could eat. The previous Saturday night Harry Tennant had been over for dinner. She had served London broil—but it was really flank steak (which is better), so tender it just shredded away. She broiled it with a thin pasting of oil, spices, parsley flakes. And they each had a baked potato with sour cream and chives. And she made a big salad with endives, tomatoes, cucumbers, onions, with oil and vinegar dressing. It was the first salad she had ever made that she tried to make *look* good. It was in a big, old wooden bowl her mother had owned. She put the quartered endives on the bottom, surrounded by chunks of tomato, surrounded by slices of crispy cucumber, surrounded by quarters of small onions. It *looked* nice. Harry Tennant said the whole thing was the best meal that had ever been created on God's earth. She thought so, too. Oh, one other thing . . . she brought a can of mushroom gravy and added a big dollop of red wine to it while it was heating. They had the rest of the wine with their meal. Well, what she had left in the refrigerator was about half the salad. It wasn't spoiled, but the endives were getting brown. Also, she had a nice slab of the flank steak left with a bit of that gravy. This was in the freezer. And she had one uncooked baking potato. It was not an Idaho; it was one of those California baking potatoes with the thin skin and delicate flavor. Now she considered her options. . . . She took the steak out of the freezer and unwrapped it to thaw. She put it on the little radiator in the kitchen. There is something so *formal* about a baked potato, so she decided she would slice the remaining one and fry it in butter. She had never heard of frying slices of a baking potato, but she didn't see why it couldn't be done.

What could happen? And she would also finish the salad.

20. The meat unwrapped and thawing, she went into the bathroom and began to run water into the tub, pouring some oil and some bubble bath into the steaming water. It smelled good. She went back to the kitchen, selected her biggest glass—really a lemonade glass—filled it with ice cubes and made a great big scotch highball. She put a Frank Sinatra album on her hi-fi, turned the volume up high enough to hear it in the bathroom. Then she went back and felt the bath water. Much too hot. She ran in some more cold, set her highball on the tiled floor alongside the tub, took off her robe and slippers. She gently eased herself in, going, "Ooh, aah, eee, ooh, wah," as she slowly, slowly dipped, came out, dipped, came out, slowly sank down into that hot soapy water while she supported herself with her hands on the sides of the tub, dipping her rosy ass into the steaming water until she could endure it, then slowly lowering herself, the water rising, she sinking, until she was up to her chin and with her toes turned off the faucets but still going, "Ooh, aah, eee, ooh, wah," the sweat breaking out on her scalp, forehead and upper lip. She reached over the side of the tub, found that big cold scotch, and took a long, deep swallow. Life was worth living.

21. She soaped up a nice fresh washcloth, went over her face, neck, shoulders, dug into her armpits, scrubbed between her legs, elevated her feet, soaped each and every toe, and finally pried into her belly button, inspecting it curiously. Unexpectedly, she farted; three bubbles slid up between her legs and came plopping to the soapy surface, going *bloop, blip, bleep* on an ascending scale. She looked about guiltily and smirked.

22. She lay back, far down in the water, the back of her neck on the edge of the tub. It was so good she didn't want to move. All her joints turned to melted soap, her fingertips getting crinkled. She slowly tousled the fine curls between her legs, tugging the hair gently, scratching gently. She touched herself softly, gasping a little. All hot and tender and swollen. Her eyes were closed. She did this for a while. Not long—but for a while.

23. She sat up in the bath, flicked the lever to let the water run out. She just sat there, watching the water slowly measure

down below her glistening breasts, below the flat stomach, below the bent knees, thighs, hips. She took another slug of that highball. Then she stood up in the tub, shaking herself like a wet dog. Rocco, Rocco, where are you now?

24. Without drying herself in the steamy bathroom, she got out her razor, brush, shaving cup. She put a towel over the closed toilet seat and sat on it. First she cut off her little corn, very carefully. It didn't bleed. Then she lathered herself up, began shaving her legs, her tongue sticking out the corner of her mouth. She went slowly and easily; she didn't cut herself once. She knew it was going to be a good day. Then she stood in front of the mirror, lathered her armpits (it tickled) and shaved those, too. No cuts. It was all going so marvelously that she bent down, stared between her legs, wondered if she should shave that also. For a moment she was tempted, but then she figured it would itch like hell when it was growing back in. Besides, her wispy triangle was blond, and it was nice to show men that her collar and cuffs matched.

25. She stepped back into the tub, adjusted the shower. Hot, but not too hot. She washed off all the dried soap and shaving lather. She had missed a little patch on her left calf, but she shaved that off under the shower. Then she was perfect. She stuck her head under the spray, soaked her hair, then shampooed it vigorously until the suds were dripping onto her shoulders and she was panting. She rinsed her hair, soaped it again, rinsed it, then rubbed it between her fingers. It squeaked satisfactorily. She turned off the shower, reached for a dry towel.

26. She shuffled into her straw slippers, went back into the living room, lighted another cigarette. She mixed a fresh drink, put that on the cocktail table. She turned on her portable TV set. She went into the bedroom, got a package of cotton balls, her manicure set, the bottles of stuff she needed. She felt a wetness on her thigh, looked down, realized that little string hanging out of her was soaked from the bath and dripping. She wrung it out.

27. It was a soap opera. She heard a man saying, "Marcia, we can't go on like this." But she didn't bother watching it; she just listened. What she did was put little balls of cotton batting between her toes, separating them so she could paint the nails without smearing. Then she painted all her

toenails crimson with that tiny brush that comes in the bottle, her tongue peeking out of her mouth's corner again. She did a good job, lay back, her legs in the air, waving her feet about to help the polish dry. It was such a complete job that, for some reason, she was dissatisfied and brought the left foot high upon the right thigh while she scratched a tiny ticktacktoe pattern on the nail of her big left toe with the point of a nail file. She didn't know why she did this, but it looked kind of funny and nice.

28. "Marcia," the man was saying, "we've got to face reality." Helen Miley replaced all the paraphernalia and tools of her trade. She went over to the cage and said, "Hello, pretty face," but the bird stared at her stonily. She had about half a drink left, but she suddenly felt drowsy. She put the drink in the refrigerator, high up near the freezer where the ice wouldn't melt too much. She switched off the TV, turned out the lights, went and got back into bed. She was asleep almost instantly. The snow had turned to a sleety rain.

29. She slept for almost an hour. She woke slowly, floating up out of a sweet, dreamless sleep, tucked naked, an unwrapped mummy. She realized she was holding herself. But that was all right. She wasn't doing anything, you understand—just holding. She yawned—a great jaw cracker of a yawn—and wiped the tears from her eyes with the edge of the sheet. She coughed, grunted a few times, tasted her tongue. Then she felt her hair. Practically dry.

30. She sat on the edge of the bed, yawned again. She stood up shakily, then bent down, and touched her toes— almost. She did this three times, then did three deep knee bends with her arms stretched out in front of her. Then she pressed her palms together in front of her chest, pressing as hard as she could for a count of six, until her arms quivered with the strain. She had read somewhere that this increased the size of the breasts. She tried to do this every day but usually forgot about it.

31. She went over to the mirror behind the bedroom door, looked at herself. She pulled her lower eyelids down, stared at her eyeballs. They were there all right and stared back at her. She got out her big tortoise-shell comb and combed out her curls. She went over to the window, looked down into the street. It was still raining; a few people were humping along, bending down into the wind. It didn't look

good at all. She went over to her dresser. Leaning her
elbows on the top, she carefully applied purple lipstick—a
little sample the man in the drugstore had given her. She
looked at herself in her magnifying mirror (on a small brass
stand) but didn't like the way it looked, so she took it all off
with three tissues. She dumped tissues and lipstick into her
wastebasket.

32. She decided she was hungry. After all, she'd had no solid
food all day. She pulled on her robe, went into the kitchen,
opened the refrigerator door—and there was that half a
drink she had stored before she took her nap. The ice cubes
had hardly melted at all; the glass was chilled through.
Boy, was that ever good! She mixed another right away in
another glass and put it in the refrigerator so the glass
would get good and chilled. She liked that.

33. She felt the hunk of steak thawing on the kitchen radiator.
It felt fine, beginning to get soft around the edges. She
leaned over to smell it; it also smelled good. She decided
she would have just a *nosh* now—not enough to spoil her
appetite for her big meal. So she had a bologna sandwich
on rye bread, a pomegranate, a stalk of celery and some
pickled herring. Also three chocolate chip cookies.

34. She put the dishes into the sink, ran some hot water over
them. Her cleaning woman came in every Monday and
Saturday; she'd do them. Then Helen took her fresh drink,
went back into the living room. The bird saw her, made one
little sound—a single, dignified chirp of protest. She saw
its seed cup was almost empty, and there was no water left.
She filled both cups—two trips to the kitchen. She put on
her horn-rimmed glasses, sat down at her maple desk. She
took a moment to turn on the TV and find a soap opera. A
man was saying, "Evelyn, when you told me that Mabel
was going to speak to Dr. Hanson about that night, I had
no idea you knew she would bring Frank's name into it. I
had promised Ralph that the incident with Sarah would
remain confidential, and only Mrs. Bradley would know
what had happened to Barbara."

35. Listening to the voices with her inner ear, Helen Miley
took out her checkbook and a thin bundle of bills held
together with a blue rubber band. There was the telephone
bill, the one from Con Edison, a life insurance bill, and also
her rent was due. She carefully wrote out the checks,

sipping her scotch highball. She got them all sealed in the proper envelopes. According to her records, she still had more than two thousand dollars in her checking account. She decided this was too much—the money wasn't earning any interest—so on Monday she would transfer one thousand dollars to her savings account, which paid 5 percent and would bring *that* account up to almost three thousand dollars—the most money she had ever had in her life. She wanted to get five thousand dollars in there. Then she was going to ask for a month's leave of absence and take a luxury cruise to Pernambuco. She already had the travel folders on it. Pernambuco. It sounded nice.

36.   She put her checkbook and savings account book on the desk top where she'd be sure to see them on Monday morning. Then she looked for stamps for the checks she wanted to mail. She found three good ones in a strip, then couldn't find a fourth. It bothered her. She went through the messy top drawer—pausing to read (for the sixth time) a moving letter Uck Faye had written to her after they had made it for the first time. He had signed it: "Always . . . Hamlet." She finally found a fourth stamp. It was an old airmail stamp. The glue was dusty, but the stamp itself was enough to carry the letter, so she stuck it on with tape from a holder she had swiped from her office. So there the four checks were, all addressed, stamped, very neat in their envelopes. She felt virtuous.

37.   She went back into the bedroom. Leaning on the dresser again, she put on a pair of false eyelashes. She had tried them once before, but she had trouble getting them on correctly, and they bothered her. But she put them on, peered at herself in the magnifying mirror, and batted them. They didn't, she decided, do a fucking thing for her. So she took them off and pasted them on her forehead, above her eyes. That looked funny. She went back into the living room to display her strange face to the bird. He cowered away in fright. She laughed, went back to the bedroom, peeled the lashes away.

38.   She took off her robe, letting it drop to the floor. She dabbed on perfume, putting it on the inner sides of her arms, a bit in her armpits, on her neck and shoulders, and finally just a touch on the inner sides of her thighs. It was a light, crisp scent—Moon Walk. She thought it smelled

great. She pulled her robe on and belted it.

39. She went back into the living room. There was a different soap opera on TV now. A woman was saying, *"Love, Clarence? What do you know about love?"*

40. Helen Miley went into the bathroom and took a leak. Then she went into the kitchen, wondering if she should mix a fresh drink. The way she remembered, she had had three drinks already—not counting that breakfast Bloody Mary, which was really like having tomato juice in the morning. She decided to mix just one more, a big one, but she would drink it very slowly—just sipping it—and make it last until it was time to eat. To tell you the truth, she was feeling buzzy. Not drunk—but a small, relaxed buzz.

41. She went back into the bedroom, brought her mending and sewing kit into the living room so she could listen to TV while she was sewing. She was gratified to note that she had no trouble threading the needle; she didn't stick her finger once, even though she didn't use a thimble. There really wasn't much to do—a tiny pair of bikini panties that had a little hole in the tail; a pair of opaque panty hose with a run beginning down one thigh that she could stop; the top button on her red wool coat. She was good at sewing, neat and precise. When she put up a hem, the stitches were quite small, and the hem was even all around. Sometimes she'd get ambitious and make a dress from a pattern. Once she made a silk blouse for Peggy Palmer.

42. She finished her mending, looked around. Now then.... There were other things she could do, and she did them: She gathered up her dirty laundry, stripped her bed, put on fresh linen, put a pillowcase of stuff near the door. She'd take that down tomorrow. For the dry cleaner there was her tweed suit; she had spilled a Rob Roy on the skirt. She did all these chores, walking steadily back and forth, never once lurching into a doorjamb, but sipping a little at her drink now and then.

43. She put on her glasses, sat down at her desk again, made out a list of things she wanted to do at the office on Monday: See about repainting the reception area: check the press releases on the Turgo account; order more marking pens; talk to her bosses about an idea she had for getting out a monthly newsletter to all media that would include items about all their clients.

44. She finished all these jobs, glanced at television—and there
     was Robert Armstrong telling Fay Wray that if she'd come
     on this mysterious expedition with him, he'd make her a
     great movie star. "Oh, boy!" Helen Miley said and sat on
     the couch, feet tucked under her, watching anxiously
     (commercials and all) right up to the final line: "No, it
     wasn't the planes that killed the beast. 'Twas beauty that
     killed the beast." Helen sighed with satisfaction, switched
     off the TV set.

45. She felt great—and very hungry. The apartment was
     getting dark now; she put on more lights. She decided to
     start preparing her big meal of the day and also to get
     dressed. No more of this *schlepping* around the house
     naked or in a robe and straw slippers. She made up her
     mind to *really* get dressed—something fancy. After all,
     someone might ring her bell. About a year ago she and
     Peggy Palmer had gone to a "singles only" night at an East
     Side disco. It was so awful, so depressing, that they never
     went again. But for that one occasion she had purchased a
     dress on sale at Saks—silver lamé with a fringed hem. She
     looked great in it—she *knew* —and that was what she
     would wear, with a pair of silver sandals. Also a
     broad-brimmed silver-gray hat, like a man's fedora. She
     went into the bedroom, leaned on the dresser, put on
     makeup carefully, combed out her curls.

46. Then she went into the kitchen. Now this is what she did:
     She melted some butter in her big enameled frying pan.
     Then she cut up her lone baking potato in quarter-inch
     slices, placed them in the pan. She had the gas at
     medium-high. As she watched, the slices of potato began to
     make a noise.

47. She went back into the bedroom, pulled on a pair of panty
     hose. They were in a silver-gray sunburst pattern. She
     hiked them up, slid her feet into the skinny sandals. Then
     she went back into the kitchen.

48. Those frying potatoes didn't seem right to her, so she got
     the chilled bowl of salad out of the refrigerator. She picked
     out all the quarters of onions that were left. She broke
     them into flakes and dropped them in the frying pan with
     the potatoes. Right away she knew she had acted correctly;
     this was going to be good. The onion slices had been
     soaking in the salad oil; that didn't hurt at all. She got out

her old charred wooden stirring spoon, messed up the potatoes and onions. Good. It began to smell good, and it sizzled.

49. She went back into the bedroom, stepped into the silver lamé shift, zipping it up the side. She looked at herself in the big mirror, poked at her hair a few times, went back into the kitchen. She looked at the clock in there, figured she'd give the potatoes and onions about twenty minutes on each side.

50. She went to the hall closet, got out that wide-brimmed hat, She used the hall mirror to adjust it, pulling it down over one eye. Very nice. Intriguing. Marlene Dietrich in the Casbah.

51. She went back into the kitchen, poked at the potatoes and onions which were browning just great. If you could have bottled that smell, you'd be a millionaire.

52. She went into the living room, to the corner nook where the plastic-topped dining table and four wire chairs were placed. She spread a cloth (red) over the tabletop, set a place for herself. She put out one dinner plate, one salad plate, one knife, one fork, one spoon. Salt shaker and pepper mill. Paper napkin. And then, on impulse, two small star-shaped candleholders she had bought at Woolworth's. She fitted them with pink candles she found in the top drawer of the sideboard. The candles had been used once before, but they still had a lot of good left in them. The table looked nice.

53. In her silver lamé gown, silver sandals, silver slouch hat, she went back into the kitchen. She stuck a fork into the potato slices, estimated another five minutes or so. The slices were getting a hard crust; the onion was browning. Everything smelled fine. She took out her little wooden cheese board and sawed the thawed flank steak into three thick, ragged slices. She put them on top of the frying potatoes and onions. so they'd warm through. There was a little blood and gravy left in the bowl which had held the frozen steak; she poured that into the frying pan, too. She washed out the bowl with a few drops of warm water, poured it into the pan. Everything looked good.

54. She went into the living room, turned off the lamp on her desk so the table would be dim. She lighted the candles. Okay. She wondered about what to drink. In the

refrigerator she found a can of ale, the last of a six-pack she had bought for Uck Faye. She opened it, poured it into a glass stein.

55. She put the old endives and what was left of the tomatoes and cucumbers into an enameled bowl and set that out. Everything seemed about done. She put a record on the hi-fi *(A Selection of Great Overtures.)* As the stirring strains of the "Light Cavalry Overture" came on, she filled her plate with steak, potatoes, onions, gravy (salad on the side), pulled her chair up to the table, and began to eat by candlelight.

56. Helen Miley believed that all music—and particularly what she considered good music—was written to tell a story. And she enjoyed listening to good music while imagining the story it was intended to tell.

57. She leaped to her feet, balled up her paper napkin, tossed it expertly into the wastebasket alongside her desk. She took a pink linen napkin from the top drawer of the sideboard. That was better.

58. She had a very definite idea of the story the "Light Cavalry Overture" was written to tell. In fact, it was a recurring dream she had, perhaps once a month. There was this very large sunlit meadow. Tall grass. The meadow was surrounded by a green wood. In her dream, a troop of cavalry came riding out of the trees on one side, trotting across the meadow, cantering occasionally, heading for the wood on the other side. The horses all were trim and sleek. Chestnuts. And the troop were even more handsome. Young men in some kind of Germanic uniform. All the men were Germanic, blond, juicy with life. Very young. Now, the troop—perhaps fifty or a hundred blond, Germanic young men in gray uniforms with glistening brass helmets with plumes—well, as they came out of the wood on one side, astride their fine, sleek chestnut horses, and began to ride across this open meadow, they changed. They began to change. The fine, strong horses stumbled, lowered their heads. The leather gear became worn and stained. The helmets tarnished. And the young men ... the young men ... they grew unaccountably older. Their shoulders slumped. Their faces sunk. They were hungry, defeated. In that short ride across the sunlit meadow, from one wood to another, the troop dissolved into something

infinitely sad. Men and horses drooping. All heads down. Uniforms torn and dirty. All hope gone out of them. They came out of the wood brave and shining. They passed across that sunlit meadow. They entered the far wood old and defeated. That was what Helen Miley kept dreaming about the "Light Cavalry Overture." At least once a month.

59. Oh, it was a good meal. There was nothing at all displeasing about slices of a baking potato fried with onion that had been soaked in salad oil. The steak was tender and good. Even the browned endives had retained their bitter flavor. Sitting there in silver (hat, dress, sandals), dining by candlelight, Helen ate slowly and with enjoyment.

60. When she finished—all dishes clean—she was listening to "William Tell"—something else again. She patted her lips with the pink linen napkin, looked about vaguely. Then she went into the kitchen and inspected the possibilities. There was a jar of instant espresso coffee, a Golden Delicious apple chilling in the refrigerator vegetable tray, and also, she remembered, she had just a bit left from that bottle of Grand Marnier Jo Rhodes had brought her when he came over for dinner. It all added up.

61. So she brewed coffee, poured Grand Marnier, sliced ice-cold apple, lighted cigarette, moved over to the living room couch, belched delicately, and lived. Don't knock it.

62. Eventually, it was done, all done. She pinched out the candles (licking her fingers first), took the dishes into the kitchen, dumped them into the sink. She returned the folded tablecloth to the sideboard drawer, put the soiled napkin into the bundle of laundry leaning against the wall near the outside door.

63. Then what? She changed her Tampax.

64. Then still wearing silver hat, gown and sandals, she mixed herself another scotch highball, the Grand Marnier having disappeared. She just sat there on the couch, smoking a cigarette, sipping her drink, lazy, beamy, not concentrating on anything. Until she thought it was silly to sit around like that. No one was going to ring her bell. She took off hat, dress, slippers, panty hose and got back into the terrycloth robe. She looked out the window. It wasn't nice out there.

65. She put on her glasses, began to flip through the latest issue

of *Tomorrow's Woman*. She didn't read any of the stories
or articles; she just flipped through the magazine, envying
those models who had never been constipated. They were
all twice as tall as she was, six times as beautiful, twelve
times thinner. She wondered if the strings on their Tampax
ever dripped after a bath.

66.   A lot of fire engines went by outside, sirens and buffalo
whistles screaming. They seemed to be stopping nearby.
She wondered if she should look out the window. She
decided not to. If her house were on fire, someone would
tell her.

67.   She put something on television. She mixed about one
good drink an hour. The age went, it went... She wasn't
drunk. Her movements were coordinated and sure. But she
was drifting, drifting... For one moment she wanted to
call Richard Faye or Harry Tennant or Jo Rhodes or
Charles Lefferts. But she didn't.

68.   It all went so fast. Suddenly it was late; the eleven o'clock
news was coming on. She watched that, then found herself
yawning. She went over to the cage and said, "Good night,
pretty face," but the little bastard wouldn't even look at
her.

69.   She checked the chain and locks on her front door. She
opened her window just a trifle. She turned off the lights.

70.   She took off her robe, sat on the edge of the bed. She
wondered if she should do some exercises, decided not to.

71.   She got into bed naked, turning the sheet and blankets
down to her waist. It was warm, warm... She was sleepy.
For a while she put her hands behind her head. But then
her arms began to get pins and needles, so she turned on
her side, hands tucked between her legs. She wasn't
thinking.

72.   She wanted to sleep, she really wanted to, but it wouldn't
come. She didn't want to take a pill, so she tried counting
slowly—one, two, three, four.... That didn't work. So she
tried a little scheme of her own—she added sums: 115 plus
47 plus 83 plus 196 plus 33... That worked; she could feel
the darkness rolling in, in waves. She knew it was coming;
she kept adding...

73.   She had not spoken to a human being, nor had she been
outside her walls, for fifteen hours. And yet... and yet the

hours had possessed a sweet sequence, her solitude had run a rhythm. If she was not happy, she was content.

74. She couldn't remember a better day in her life. She wondered what was happening to her.

20

THERE WERE NO lights in the bedroom; the only glow came seeping through the half-open door to the living room. It was dim in the bedroom; you could hardly see the big poster on the wall that said LOVE.

Helen Miley, fully clothed, sat on the foot of the bed. She was smoking a cigarette, flicking the ashes onto the floor. She was wearing her horn-rimmed glasses. She had a cold; every once in a while she'd sniff and punch at her nose with a knuckle.

She watched Harry Tennant wander around the room. He had his hands shoved deep in his pockets. His sad eyes were turned down. He passed in and out of the beam of light coming from the living room. Once he stood for a moment before the LOVE poster, staring at it. Then he resumed his pacing.

"What is it, Harry?"

"Nothing. It's nothing."

"Something's bothering you, sport. I can tell."

"I know I've been bad company tonight, babe. I'm sorry. It's just that . . . Shit, I don't know."

"Maybe you're catching my cold. There's a lot of flu around. Like the French say, maybe you got a chill on the liver."

He looked at her, smiling sweetly. "And maybe I've got a sliver in my soul."

"A what?"

"A sliver in my soul."

"What does that mean?"

"Aah . . . nothing. I'm just making words."

"What can I do?" she asked anxiously. "Can I do anything?"

He shook his head. "No, babe. But I do thank you."

"Do you want to go to bed? Do you want me to get undressed?"

He tried to laugh. He came over to the bed, sat close beside her. He picked up her hand, kissed her fingertips.

"Babe, you are really one sweet babe. You think dipping Cecil in the hot grease solves all problems?"

"It solves my problems," Helen said stoutly. "Most of them."

Harry put a hand on her bare knee. "See this?"

"What?"

"This here."

"My kneecap?"

"Oh, yes." He nodded. "When you walk toward me, I see this muscle here, right above your little pink kneecap— well, this muscle bunches and jerks when you walk. That's the sexiest thing I've ever seen in my life."

"You're over the edge." She laughed.

"I guess. But now, on the street, I catch myself looking for that little muscle to bunch up above the knee of every woman who's walking toward me. Harry, the sex fiend. Next year it will be elbows."

He unfolded to his feet, began stalking around the room again. He kept passing in and out of the glow coming through the open door. His long, stiffened body flickered—light and dark.

"I had this big argument with my brother last night," he told her. "I mean a *big* one. We came close to hitting each other. He's moving out. When I got up this morning, he was packing. We didn't say anything, but I guess he's going."

"What was the argument about?"

"He's got no call to move out. That place is big enough for both of us. We don't have to talk to each other. My God, babe, he was born in that apartment when we couldn't get Mom to the hospital on time. He was *born* right there. That's his home. Now he's moving out. He'll be gone by the time I get back. I know it."

"What was the argument about?" she asked again.

"Oh . . . the usual. This has been going on for years. When am I going to start doing something for our people? That's what he keeps saying . . . 'our people.'"

"Doing what, Harry?"

"Working with him, with all these outfits he's joined. Writing things."

"What kind of things? You want a cigarette?"

"Yes. All right. Thanks."

He paused in his pacing to take a cigarette from her, to hold a match for both of them. She was startled by the way his face looked in the match flare. Wrenched out of shape. Parts loosened, falling away.

"Well . . . he wants me to write booklets, letters, articles, proclamations, constitutions, posters . . . all kinds of things."

"And you don't want to do it?"

"Babe, I *want* to do it. And I want to fly and walk on the water. Haven't you ever wanted to do something you just couldn't do?"

"I don't know . . ." she said, puzzled. "Maybe. I can't remember. Mostly I do what I want to do."

"You're lucky."

"I guess so. What did you tell your brother?"

"I told him the truth. I just haven't got it in me. This race thing doesn't move me at all. I can't get involved. I know it's my fault. But that's the way it is. It's driving me right through the top of my skull."

"What did your brother say then?"

"He blew his stack. I told you this thing means a lot to him. It's his whole life. Did I tell you he got his head busted a few years ago? Yes, I guess I did. Well, anyway, last night when we had this big shouting contest, he started calling me names."

"Names? You mean he was swearing at you?"

"Not swearing, no. Names like Uncle Tom and Little Black Sambo. You know—like I had sold out. Shit!"

"Take it easy, Harry."

"He said I thought I was a white man. He said I was living in a dream. He said I better come out of it because sooner or later something bad would happen to me."

"Something bad?"

"He said they'd teach me I was a nigger. They'd put me in my place. And my brother said it would break me. He said I better forget my fantasy and realize who I was."

He bent suddenly, looked out the window. He stared down, hands in his pockets again.

"Still some snow," he said. "But light. Letting up. Looks cold out there. No good at all."

Helen pried off her shoes with her toes. She swung her feet onto the bed, sat with her back against the footboard. She raised her knees, hugged them. She put her cheek down on her bare knees, felt that little muscle he liked.

"Harry, I've got to tell you that I'm the wrong woman to talk to about this. I really don't know anything about it. I guess I should. I guess I should read the front pages of the newspapers. But this race stuff and politics and Vietnam and going to the moon—I mean, all that leaves me cold. I loved John F. Kennedy; he was so handsome. God, I cried when he was killed. But all the rest of it—well, it just doesn't interest me. I mean, I've got my job to worry about and my personal life and what's going to happen to me. I just can't get wound up with all those things. I just feel sorry for everyone, that's all. It's not easy. Being alive, I mean."

"I know, babe. Do I ever know! I feel cold. Feel my hands..."

He came over to Helen again, stood before her. She took his two hands, clasped them between hers. She raised his hands to her cheek.

"My God, honey, you're freezing. Come on, get under the covers for a minute. Just to get warmed up."

"Yes. All right. I *am* cold. We won't take our clothes off. We'll just get under the covers for a minute until I warm up."

He took off his shoes. She plumped the pillows, spread the sheet like a summer cloud, added the blanket. They climbed into bed. Fully clothed, they held each other. Their voices were wispy, floating in the dusk.

"Are you shivering, dear?" she asked.

"A little maybe. I don't know what's wrong with me. Suddenly I got real cold."

"You'll warm up in a minute. Move closer. Put your feet against me."

"My feet are like ice, babe."

"That's all right. Put them against me. There. How's that?

Isn't that better?"

They lay huddled in each other's arms. Hiding from the world. She moved closer to him.

"Harry."

"What?"

"Do you want to?"

"What? I..."

"Let me try."

"Oh, babe, babe... I can't tell you what all you've meant to me."

"Shh... Don't say anything."

She put her hands on him. He moved his hands down, but she pushed them away. She was serious. This was important to her. He leaned forward, put two wet, smoochy kisses on the lenses of her horn-rimmed glasses.

"Now I can't see," she murmured.

"Good. That's good. Don't see me."

He closed his eyes, and then only God could see. Helen did all she could, trying. Believing they were the whole everything in their secret place. It hurt no one. They were the only two and meant no harm.

But nothing worked.

"No use," he said.

"Don't even think anything. Just let me..."

It all went wrong—the way it does sometimes. His zipper caught in the fly of his underwear. An agonizing cramp in her left calf. A sneeze she tried to stifle. Suddenly, in him, a sour stomach and a terrible desire to belch. Too much warmth from the blanket. Sweat. No rhythm to it at all. No growing. Just trying. The motions.

"Stop it," he said loudly. "No use, babe. I'm no use at all."

He kicked his legs free of the blanket, sat up, rubbed his face with both palms.

Helen Miley lay there, still covered. She took off her smeared glasses, put them on the bedside table. She just lay there, her eyes following him as he began to pace the room again. His long shadow loomed around the walls.

"Oh, funny," he said. "That's funny."

"What's funny?"

"Me. I'm getting more like a whitey every day. Now I can't get it up."

"Harry..."

"Oh, boy," he breathed, "this is it. This is really something."

"It could be anything. A cold. The flu. A virus. Like I said, a chill on the liver."

"And like I said, a sliver in my soul."

"What are you going to do?"

"*Do*, babe? Oh, I don't know. Something. I'll think of something."

She swung her legs out from under the covers. She sat on the edge of the bed, toes touching the floor. She tried to light a cigarette, but her hands were trembling so much she couldn't make it. The match went out. She broke the cigarette in half, let it drop to the floor.

She hunched over, head down. Her arms were deeply folded; she was hugging herself. Harry Tennant took a few quick steps over to her. He looked down, shaken. He put one hand softly on her head.

"Helen, what are you doing? You're crying? Jesus Christ, babe, you're crying for me?"

She sobbed. "For all of us. All of us."

"Oh, babe, babe," he crooned. "It's not that bad. Come on now. Stop that. You stop that crying, y'hear? We'll get through it. We always have. Right? I'm going to be okay. I'll figure something out. It's going to be all right, babe."

"Harry, you promise? Everything's going to be all right?"

"Oh, sure. Now come on..."

He sat on the bed alongside her. He put an arm around her shoulders, cuddling her close. Slowly her sobs ebbed. She bent her head to his chest. She leaned against him like a small child safe in the arms of her father.

He touched her face. He wiped her tears away with his finger. He touched her hair. He coiled her blond curls, let them spring back. He touched her lips, chin, throat.

"Oh, God"—she sighed—"it's all too much."

"What happens," he declared, "what happens is that you never get a second chance. Do you? That is, we all play life by ear. You know? You get to be real old, and you shake your head and grin and say, 'I'll be damned. I did it all wrong. But I know better now. The next time I'll do it better.' But there is no next time, is there? You get it right the first time around, or you're shit out of luck. Am I right? Oh, yes. I'm right..."

They hid in each other's arms, seated on the edge of the bed. Still trembling...

21

"MILEY," RICHARD FAYE SAID, "you are one big erogenous zone."

What inspired this sincere tribute was that as Faye drifted his fingertips down Helen's naked spine and then lightly flicked the skin stretched tautly over her shortribs, she appeared to be trying to claw her way down through the mattress, her legs pumping, looking for all the world like a woman running for a bus.

"I just happen to be sensitive," she gasped. "I just happen to be sensitive all over."

He laughed and bent to bite her plump ass. Not a hard bite. Just a nip.

He got up, stalked naked around her bedroom. There was a time he would have covered himself with fluttering hands, a stout and hairy "September Morn." But now...

"Look at me," he bragged, smacking his stomach with his palm. "Down another five pounds. The gut is going. You've got to admit it, Helen, that gut is definitely going."

She flopped over, sat up in bed, pulled sheet up, pulled knees up, lighted a cigarette, leaned her arms on her knees, inspected him critically.

"Yep"—she nodded—"you're looking real good. What does Edith say?"

"She says I'm getting too thin. She says I don't eat enough."

"How are you two getting along?"

"All right. An armed truce. I'm looking for an apartment of my own; I told you. But they're hard to find."

"I know."

"By the way, she doesn't call me Dickie anymore. Now she calls me Richard."

"That's nice. Uck, you really should do something about those varicose veins in your legs."

"I will, I will—but first I'll make us a couple of fresh drinks. Okay?"

"Fine. Not so much water this time. I could hardly taste the booze."

He took their glasses, went trotting out of the bedroom. She just sat there, smoking her cigarette, her head tilted down on her forearms. She was really proud of him, of what he had done for her, and even prouder of his pride. Those loopy bags were gone from under his eyes. His can had assumed reasonable proportions. Sometimes you could almost see his ribs through the thinning layer of suet. She looked over to the dresser where she had arranged the bouquet of daisies and mimosa he had brought her, and she smiled.

He sat on the edge of the bed, handed her the drink. They just sat there, sipping. Then he reached under the sheet, clasped one of her thighs lightly.

"Give me one of your legs," he said.

"Why should I?"

"You've got two of them, and I don't have any."

"You have two of your own legs."

"I don't like them. They have varicose veins. I want one of your legs."

"You can't have it."

"And you call yourself a friend."

He got up, began to pace naked around the room. He carried his drink, gnawing on it occasionally.

"Miley," he said sternly, "we've got to change our way of living."

"How's that?"

"We never *do* anything. We never *go* anywhere."

"We went out to dinner tonight."

"Yes—but then what? Right into bed and sip, sip, sip. We never even go to a movie."

"You want to go to a movie, Uck? I'll get up and get dressed."

"No, I do not want to go to a movie. But we never go to concerts or the theater or the ballet or museums and all that crap. We do not, my dear Helen, live a cultural life. We're either eating or drinking or in bed—sometimes all three simultaneously. There's a whole, great world out there, Miss Miley," he orated, gesturing grandly with one naked arm. "There is beauty and truth and things to stretch the mind."

"And what do you suggest, Oh, lord of the manor?"

"Quiet," he commanded. "The lord will ponder."

The lord pondered, stalking up and down, his silly little whang banging against his thigh. He stopped suddenly, turned, faced her.

"Do you have any luggage?"

"Sure. I have three suitcases. One is a big suitcase, one is a medium-sized suitcase, and one is a kind of hatbox with a zipper all the way around it. They're all in light blue. Some kind of blue plastic that looks exactly like pigskin."

"Remember that seersucker robe you bought me that I've never worn? Do you still have it?"

"Of course. It's around here somewhere. What's this all about?"

He had that demonic gleam in his eye she recognized. She began to get interested.

"And do you have a ring—any kind of a ring—that will fit your third finger left hand, and even if it has some junky stones in it, you can turn it around so it will look like a wedding ring?"

"I guess so," she said faintly. "I guess I've got a ring like that."

He swooped over, sat on the edge of the bed, picked up her hand, chewed on her knuckles.

"Helen," he breathed, "I have this idea. And if you do not like this idea, and if you will not go along with it, I will never speak to you again as long as I live. And I should warn you that I intend to live forever as I am too mean to die."

"Okay, Uck—what's your idea?"

"Do you have any cash in the house?"

"Yes."

"How much?"

"Eighty, ninety dollars. Something like that."

"Splendid. I have about a hundred and ten. Now this is what we are going to do...I have all my credit cards with me. I am going to call an airline and book us two seats on a flight to Washington, D.C. I am going to call a hotel in Washington, D.C.—a very expensive, fashionable, luxurious hotel—and reserve the bridal suite, if possible. Then you are going to pack your medium-sized suitcase and the one that looks like a hatbox with a zipper all around. You are going to throw in whatever we may possibly need for one glorious day in the nation's capital. Then we are going to fly down to Washington, D.C., and stare at the cherry blossoms."

"Uck, for Chrissakes, it's November!"

"Well, we will look at the trees where the cherry blossoms will be when they come out. And we will visit the White House and the Capitol and the Smithsonian Institution (notice I say 'Institution.' Most people say 'Institute,' which is incorrect). And we will visit all the great public buildings in Washington, D.C., and absorb the heritage of our country and the art galleries and the libraries and the Washington Monument and the Lincoln Memorial. We will be properly moved and awed, and we will have a very cultural day. We will return tomorrow night. And that is what we are going to do. We are going to fly to Washington, D.C., right now."

She didn't hesitate a moment.

"Let's go!" she yelped, flinging out of bed.

While he was showering, she filled the bird's cups with water and seed. Then she got the two suitcases down from the top shelf of the hall closet and began to throw things into them. How much do you need for one day? She put in robes and underwear, a sweater and a knit suit she could roll up, all her makeup stuff. They still looked empty and felt distressingly light. So she threw in some books and a bottle of scotch so the bellhop wouldn't get suspicious.

Faye came rushing out of the bathroom; Miley went rushing in. When she came out, he was all dressed and had his little case of credit cards open on the desk in front of him.

"I just called Edith and told her I was spending the weekend with a friend."

"How did she like it?"

He showed his teeth in a shitty grin.

"She didn't like it."

He called and discovered they could get on the shuttle to Washington, D.C., if they could be at LaGuardia Airport by ten.

He called a hotel chain; they switched him to Washington; he made a reservation for two. The bridal suite was being occupied by an eighty-two-year-old Senator and his twenty-three-year-old bride, but the hotel promised him a very nice suite overlooking the White House.

They were downstairs with their luggage a little after nine thirty. Helen was wearing gloves over her fake wedding band. The doorman went out into the middle of the street and began whistling, two fingers clutched between his teeth. A cab pulled up.

"LaGuardia Airport," Faye said to the driver. "Right away. We've got to make a flight."

"Waddyaoutofyermind?" the driver demanded. "You want me to go out to LaGuardia at this hour? How do I know I get a fare back? I get on line, the regular guys break my head. You think I'm gonna—"

"Twenty dollars," Faye said.

"Put your luggage up front with me," the cabby said. "By that way you folks will have more comfort in the back."

Well, what happened on the drive out to the airport was that this cab driver had a nineteen-year-old son who had unaccountably fallen in love with a fifty-six-year-old widowed grandmother who owned three kosher butcher shops and a small booth in the Essex Street Market that sold dill pickles. Now the question was ... the question was.... No one ever got around to stating exactly what the question was, but all three offered logical answers—and the drive passed pleasantly with lively and interesting conversation by all.

They were in plenty of time. Plenty. They even went to the bar where Helen took off her gloves, and Faye said, "My wife would like a scotch and water, and I would like one also." The bartender didn't blink an eye. He didn't even look at Helen's hand which she had placed on top of the bar, the stones in her ring turned around so they dug into her palm, only the thin band showing.

Faye held up his glass, clicked rims with Helen.

"It's going to be all right," he assured her.

Nothing much happened on the flight down to Washington, D C., except that Richard Faye said something beautiful. Helen was looking out the window, counting the stars. She said, "I love to travel. I just love to go places. I'd like to go to every place in the world. Uck, if you had your choice, where would you like to be, right this minute?"

"At this moment?" he asked.

"Yes."

"Anywhere in the world?"

"Yes."

"I'd like to be lying naked between your naked thighs."

She smiled secretly and clasped his hand.

They were having very good luck with cabs, which Helen interpreted as a Good Omen. They were taken to their hotel by a cabdriver whose wife suffered from nasal drip. Faye registered at the hotel as Mr. and Mrs. Richard Faye of New York, as Helen casually placed her hand near the register, her ring showing.

They were conducted to their suite by a 343-year-old bellboy, who carried their luggage in, proved to them the lights worked, showed them how to open and close doors, flipped the Venetian blinds up and down, and smiled. Richard gave him five dollars.

"We would like," he said, "my wife and I would like a tub of ice cubes, four highball glasses, four small bottles of soda water, and four small bottles of ginger ale. In addition, we would like a tourist guide to Washington, D.C., with illustrations of the main attractions, including descriptions of points of interest and sights my wife and I shouldn't miss."

"A delight," the hotel guru said.

They looked around. It was a marvelous hotel suite. There was one room that was just for living. This had a couch and soft chairs, a cocktail table, a color TV set, a dining table with seating for four, and like a little bar where you could serve drinks. There were watercolor paintings on the walls of men on horses jumping over fences.

The bedroom had two big beds, plus a sort of small couch and two mirrored dressers, plus *another* color TV set. There was a big closet you could practically live in, with hangers you couldn't take off the rod. Over one of the beds was a steel etching of George Washington crossing the Delaware, and over the other bed was a steel etching of George Washington, his hand on a Bible, taking the oath of office. This hotel was called the Franklin Pierce.

Then there was this tremendous bathroom with the glasses wrapped in tissue paper, and facial tissues, toothpaste, aspirin, yards of soap, shampoo, everything. The toilet paper was scented. More towels than they could count. Free sanitary napkins.

"Oh, boy," Helen said, clasping her palms to her cheeks, "is this ever great!"

The Ancient One came back with their ice cubes, bottles of mix, and tourist guide. Faye offered him another tip, but he waved it modestly aside and bowed himself out.

Faye hung the Do Not Disturb sign on the outside knob. Then they mixed big scotch highballs, got undressed, and took a shower together. They didn't need it, you understand, but this hotel suite was so nice that they felt they should be clean and shining before going to bed.

So there they were, very serious and industrious, soaping each other up in the shower, all business, no hanky-panky (but copping a feel now and then), and drying themselves on those wonderful, fluffy towels, using twice as many as they needed.

Then they got into bed, the two of them using just one bed; they weren't fooling each other. Helen was wearing a shorty nightgown. Richard had on the seersucker robe Helen had bought him. She kissed him on the cheek and rolled over on her side, away from him. He put on his reading glasses, those funny half-lens glasses that make everyone— men, women, children and cocker spaniels—look like Benjamin Franklin. He switched on the lamp over their bed, began to leaf through their tourist guide to Washington, D.C.

"Now then," he said, "Washington, D.C., is the capital city of the United States of America."

"Mmm," she said, reaching around behind her to touch him, to feel him there.

"Its heritage," he went on, reading the guidebook, "stretches back many years to the days when the first settlers—"

He looked at her and realized she was gone. The shutter had come down. Already she was snoring. Not a deep, rumbling SNORE, but a little SNORE, like a droning.

Soon after, he turned off the bed lamp and also fell asleep, moving close to her, groaning with content.

She opened her eyes first, just a peep, then stared wide-eyed at the strange surroundings, wondering where she was and who she was sleeping with. Then it came into focus: It was Sunday morning; she was in bed in a Washington, D.C., hotel with old Uck Faye. They were going to visit buildings, see things, and have a cultural day.

She smiled and turned to him. He was curled into a blissful

ball, his legs drawn up, hands clamped between his thighs. She bent over him. He smelled nice and warm.

She carefully lifted the tail of his seersucker robe and fitted herself to his naked body, bending her legs where his were bent, moving tight to him until they were nesting spoons. Then she reached around and very slowly, very softly, very gently, grasped his piccolo in her warm fist.

"Hello there!" he said brightly.

"You're awake, Richard?"

"No, I am asleep. I am asleep and dreaming that a strange creature is nuzzling my ass and performing other chores that were never mentioned in *Woman's Home Companion.*"

She giggled and pressed closer, hugging him closer to her. This was really what she liked best. Not the sex so much. That was great. But what was greater was . . . was the being close, the nakedness, the kissing and all that stuff. She loved it when men would lick her and she would lick them. That was dear, so dear . . . The goddamned world, and there they were, just the two of them . . . That was what was best. The hell with it. We're all going to be dead someday. Right?

Well, as you can imagine, one thing led to another, and soon it was all sweat and grunts. They got all tangled up in his robe and her nightgown and the pink sheets. Finally they tore everything away like maniacs, gasping, panting, saying things they couldn't remember later—which was a blessing.

Then she was over him, he was over her, they were on the bed, they were on the floor, they screamed in merriment, they did very personal things to each other, guffawing, their hands, fingers, feet, toes, tongues and, yes even their eyelids were busy until they collapsed in a mutual roar of ease and pleasure, feeling their bones melt.

After a while Richard Faye rose from the carpet naked, staggered over to the window, looked out, and there was the White House.

Faye showered first, came out, put his robe on again. They didn't have slippers for him, but he padded around contentedly on his big splay feet; the rug was shag, thick and soft. Then Helen went in to shower; those towels were going fast. Meanwhile, Faye consulted the breakfast menu and called room service.

By the time the cart was wheeled in Helen was seated at the dining table in her robe, stroking her cheek with her left hand, the turned-around ring catching the light.

What a breakfast it was; what-a-breakfast! It seemed to be constructed around a kind of spicy pork patty that neither of them had tasted before. There were shirred eggs, home fried potatoes, muffins and wild blackberry jam. They started with cold melon and ended with wedges of warm apple pie covered with slices of American cheese. The menu said this breakfast was called the Cockadoodle Special, a name Faye said he personally found in rather poor taste.

"Would you pour me another cup of coffee, mine wife?" he asked, going into the bedroom for his glasses, ball-point pen and illustrated guidebook to Washington, D.C.

"At once, mine husband," she murmured submissively, pouring the coffee and floating just a little cream on top, the way he liked it.

"Now then," he said, resuming his seat. "I feel we should plan our cultural tour of Washington, D.C., logically and with care. After all, we only have about ten hours, and we must make every minute count."

He unfolded the map fastened to the inside back cover of the guidebook. She leaned toward him, smoking a cigarette, sipping her coffee. She looked at him as he peered through the lower halves of those nutty glasses, intent on the map. She put her coffee cup down for a moment so she could touch the back of his hand.

"Now then," he said, pointing, "this is the location of our hotel. This is where we are. I will put a little X there."

"Put two little X's—one for you and one for me."

"Very well—two little X's. Now Helen, it seems logical to me that the first place we should visit should be the White House. It's so close. See—right across this park."

"Well," she said doubtfully, "I don't know, I mean we just can't barge in on them, can we, Uck?"

"I thought of that," he said, nodding. "Did you see that candy store in the lobby when we were checking in last night? Well, I thought we might bring them a nice jar of hard candy."

"Very good," she approved. "Or maybe a box of toffee."

"We'll bring both hard candy and toffee," he decided. "After all, one of them might like hard candy, and the other one might like toffee. But Helen, we won't stay long; we'll make that plain from the start. No dinner or anything like that. They're very busy people. We'll just poke our noses in and look around and give them this candy, and we'll tell them we have to run. We definitely can't stay for dinner."

"What if they—you know, urge us? We can't be impolite."

"Well, we'll just have to be firm. Now then ... let's see what this guidebook says about the White House."

He read in silence while she nibbled on a piece of cheese and smoked another cigarette.

"What a fascinating guidebook," he said. "Some of these facts are really unusual. Listen to this: 'One of the most unusual rooms in the White House is the so-called Parcheesi Room. No visitor should miss this handsome and historic room located on the third floor. Many tourists believe it received its name from the fact that, since the beginnings of the Republic, the First Families have played parcheesi in this room, but such is not the case. Actually, the room was named for Aldo Parcheesi, a special envoy from the Duke of Tuscany, who choked to death on a slice of salami in this room at a state dinner held in his honor during the Presidency of Millard Fillmore. See footnote six.' Now let's see—where is footnote six? This is really interesting, isn't it, Helen?"

"Unbelievable," she said, shaking her head.

"Ah, here is footnote six. It says: 'Another little known fact about the state dinner at which Signor Parcheesi died is that it provided the first public appearance of James G. Blaine who later became a United States Senator despite the famous chant his political opponents devised for use against him. This was "Blaine, Blaine, the barefaced liar from the state of Maine." Of particular interest to historians are the facts that, far from being barefaced, Blaine had a long red beard and was actually not from Maine. But his political opponents pointed out that it was extremely difficult to chant 'Blaine, Blaine, the bearded liar from the state of Massachusetts.' Helen, it's really marvelous to learn all these little-known anecdotes about our nation's history, is it not?"

"Beautiful. Where are we going when we leave the White House, Uck?"

"Now let's take a look at the old map ... I'd say our next stop should be the Washington Monument. I'll draw a line from our hotel to the White House and then to the Washington Monument so we'll know the shortest route. I'll see what the book has to say about the Washington Monument."

"Uck," she said thoughtfully, "while you're looking it up, maybe I should mix us a couple of very mild scotch and waters. You know, just a little something to settle the old tum-tum."

"Excellent idea," he muttered, flipping pages. "Settle the old tum-tum."

She lay back on the couch in their living room sipped her drink, twiddled her toes, listened happily as he read from that wondrous guidebook to Washington, D.C.

For instance, he said, while most tourists believed the Washington Monument was sheathed in marble, actually this tallest phallic symbol in the civilized world was covered with sheets of linoleum in a marbleized pattern ("which tend to flutter in a high wind"). The original marble sheathing had been removed one moonless night in 1948 to cover the walls of a combination sauna and bowling alley in the basement of the Capitol.

Carefully, on the map, he traced their planned route from hotel to White House to Washington Monument to Lincoln Memorial to Ford's Theatre ("where the new Fords are shown each year") to the Supreme Court Building. He took a moment off to mix them another drink, somewhat stronger this time, and then returned to his labors. Immediately he exclaimed with astonishment and brought the guidebook over to Helen to show her a photograph of an enormous high-ceilinged room with marble colonnades and damasked walls decorated with fine oil portraits of dead tax collectors.

"Do you know what this is, Helen?"

"The men's room at the Library of Congress?"

"No, my dear. This is the famous Truss Room in the Capitol. Listen to what the book says: 'High on the must-see list of almost every tourist who visits Washington, D.C., is the traditional Truss Room, used by Senators and Representatives alike. The east wall of this imposing room is equipped with sufficient hooks to enable every member of Congress to check his truss when the exertions of office do not require its wearing. The room is under the supervision of Robert E. "Flannel-Mouth" Ravenel, a man who has become a legend in his own time and who has held his important post for more than fifty years, during the administrations of eight Presidents. In his famous book of memoirs, *Kiss My Truss,* Mr. Ravenel reports that the solid brass medallions issued to Congressmen who check their trusses have become the most popular souvenir of a visit to the nation's capital (they bear the famous inscription "In God We Truss") and must be replaced at least twice a year.' Helen, we've simply *got* to visit the Truss Room."

But meanwhile, he took off his glasses, brought his drink with him, lay down beside her on the couch.

"Skinny over," he said, "and give your husband a little room."

She skinnied over. After a while she said dreamily, "We're not going out at all—are we, Uck?"

"Do you want to?"

"Oh...not really. I'll do whatever you want to do."

"Mmm," he said, clamping his lips on the lobe of her left ear. "Anyway," he said, "we did get out of the house, didn't we?"

She reached over him to set her glass on the floor. She took his glass out of his hand, set that on the floor also. Then she struggled to get an arm under this neck. She pulled him close. He kissed her, smiling.

"Okay?" he whispered.

She knew what he meant. "Oh, yes," she whispered back: "As I've ever been."

"Why don't we get into bed and take a little nappy?"

"Is that what you want, Uck?"

"Just a short one."

"All right."

They finished their drinks on the short stroll into the bedroom. They put the glasses aside, took off their robes. They rolled between those smooth sheets, throwing off the comforter because the room had suddenly become quite warm.

They slept longer than they had intended; the light was weakening when they awoke. Faye slid out of bed first. He went into the other room to get their cigarettes and mix them a fresh drink. He held the bottle of scotch up to the light, calculated there were three drinks left for each of them.

When he came back into the bedroom, Helen was lying on her back, hands clasped behind her head, staring at the ceiling. But she changed position to take the glass.

"Sip, sip, sip," she said, smiling, not sore at all.

He got into bed alongside her. A mood came on him; he longed to thank her. But he knew how gratitude exasperated her, so he contented himself with kissing her shoulder.

"I don't know if I can make it again, Helen."

"Sure you can, baby. I know you can. I'll help you."

After a while they put aside their empty glasses and their cigarettes, and they did try. She did help him, but it was no good—which seemed a shame.

So they gave up. They just lay in each other's arms. They weren't embarrassed; it had happened before, but it did seem a shame.

"Uck," she said, speaking slowly and carefully, "what's going to happen to you?"

"Oh...I don't know. Something nice."

"You're not going to marry, are you?"

After a few moments he said gently, "No, dear. I am not."

"Why not?"

He shrugged. "I don't really know. I guess it's just something I don't want to do."

"But why not?"

He pulled away from her, turned on his side, propped his head on one hand, bared his teeth. "Did I ever tell you what Oscar Wilde said? He said—"

"I know, Uck," she said sadly. "You told me. Several times."

He was silent a moment, then muttered, "I only told you twice."

There was a long quiet before she said, faltering a little, "You're not afraid you'll—you know—go back...are you, Uck?"

His laugh hurt his ears.

"Now look," he started, "there's no natural law that says one man has to marry one woman. If you've ever researched the history of marriage you'd realize it was an historical imperative. That is, for the sake of the survival of the human race, one man married one woman and they had as many children as they could. It was the need to exist. Children died very young. Adults died at twenty and thirty. Disease, poverty—all that. The human race had to survive. That was the way to do it: marry and breed. It worked. But things are different now. Infants mostly live. People keep going to their eighties and nineties. It's all in the books. Now we've got too many people. Medicine and better living conditions. So maybe there are better ways. Maybe people should live alone. Maybe there should be double marriages— you know, two men and two women, or two women and one man, or communes. There are a lot of combinations. These are new times, and we need new ways of living. Man-and-woman marriage isn't the only answer anymore. There are plenty of other possibilities. We can—"

His voice began to drain; the Master Illusionist of Them All began to run down. She could hardly hear him: "New relationships... in transition... one man, one woman ...obsolete...new ways to...meaningful...we can..."

His voice dribbled away, just faded away, his eyes closed. Until, finally, he whispered (so low she could hardly hear him): "Yes. You're right, Helen. I am afraid..."

She loved him so much at that moment that she would have died, and cheerfully, if it would make him happy.

But all she could do was take him into her naked arms, murmur, hold him, stroking. He trembled at first. After a while he muttered, "It's not easy to..."

"I know, baby," she whispered. "I know."

She was afraid he might start weeping, but he didn't. He just lay there, quivering a little, responding to her long, thoughtful stroking. She thought of their first night in bed together—the night The Muscle showed up and said Edith Faye had suffered a heart attack.

But it was different this time. She stroked strength into him, still murmuring things he couldn't hear. It took a long time. The arm she had under his neck went to sleep, but she didn't remove it. It seemed to her they were more than naked right then: it was something she had felt a few times before, an inside-out thing that was sweet...ah, sweet! She wanted to cry, laughing.

She started to slide down in bed slowly, but he wouldn't let her. He caught her, held her. In all solemnity they tried something—whatever it was.

But they were reasonable people, and she really didn't begin giggling until he whispered in her ear, "Baby, it's smaller than both of us." Then they were heaving with loving laughter, coughing, sputtering, sweating in each other's arms, trying foolish and quite impossible feats of derring-do.

Something happened—neither knew quite what—but if not ecstasy, they felt at least a sense of accomplishment not to be denied. We can't all swing from chandeliers or stand up in hammocks.

At least it had the advantage of going on for what seemed to be a long, long time. The light darkened; the White House was lost in the night.

On the flight back to New York, just after they took off and were airborne for LaGuardia Airport, he stared at her, squeezed her hand. In a tone of great amazement he said, "You know, I think I'm going to make it."

"Damned right," she said fiercely.

22

My dearest Helen,

One of the sweetest things, to me, in our friendship, is our ability to talk *to* each other. Most people talk *at* each other. You know—one will say, "I went to the movies last night," and the other person will reply, "I saw Joan on Thursday." But when you and I talk, it seems to me so personal, of such consequence, that I hope I may write this letter to you with that same intimacy, and that you will understand and feel compassion for all the things I say and all the things I dare not say.

In the ordinary course of events, I would have said all this to you in person. But I have been called out of town unexpectedly, and I don't know when I shall return. So I thought it best to write you. I warn you, this letter will ramble on and on. But there is much I want to say to you, and I shall not blame you in the least if you read it in three or four easy installments!

First of all, darling Helen, let me assure you that when, at our last meeting, you told me you could not come away with me to my home in Italy, I understood. I was disappointed, naturally, but I could appreciate your realism. You are half my age, you have your own career and your own life, and while, as you said, it would have been a temporary delight, you obviously did not feel it had the potentiality of a lasting relationship. Now there, my dear, I must disagree. I am nothing if not constant!

I accept your decision since it was yours to make. But you will forgive me if I still hang on tightly to a few remnants of my dream—the two of us shopping for tripe and Provolone in the morning market, the donkey rides up into the hills, the Sunday mass at the little whitewashed church, watching the bare-legged women in the fields gather in the wild *gnocchi*—their largest cash crop. And those mad motor-scooter races on Friday nights, with everyone drinking harsh Sicilian wine from goatskins. How gay it all is! Ah, well...

Yes, it is true that I am on the "far side" of seventy. And I am certain you think of me as "a dirty old man." But is there a better kind? (My only hope is that in our more *personal* relations I have not been too demanding and caused you pain and anguish.) But there is much about growing old you do not yet know (how could you since you are so eternally young yourself?) that I must tell you about.

First of all, let me assure you that some of us who are fated to grow old (it was Maurice Chevalier who said "It is not pleasant—but consider the alternative") remain forever young in mind and soul. That is, I have the same dreams and hopes and loves I had as a boy of eighteen. The brain remains young and steaming, but something dreadful happens to the thing in which this wild spirit is sealed.

Suddenly, warmth and dryness become important. You wear rubbers in the rain, when years ago the possibility of ruining a pair of forty-dollar shoes seemed unimportant. You wear waistcoats and scarves. Blankets multiply. Hot-water bottles and heating pads are no longer a joke. That is, physical comfort begins to assume a more important, an overwhelmingly important, part of your life. Strolling bareheaded in the rain is for Vassar sophomores. Running and sliding gleefully on ice-sheeted sidewalks is for young maniacs.

But, mind you, while all this is happening, almost unbeknownst to you, the spirit—the *essential* spirit—remains young. That is, you still have sexual fantasies, you still react to young beauty, you still hope, and you still dream. Yes, it is true you have corns and calluses. You are a victim of quite unexplainable aches and pains. You wake one morning, and the second joint of your middle finger hurts like h——. No reason for it. And it passes. But your entire body is prey to these inexplicable and frightening agues.

Your shanks thin. The hair disappears from your legs, and the skin of your calves takes on a peculiar, shiny, white appearance. By this time, of course, you probably have glasses and dentures, perhaps a hearing aid and a cane. Your eyes begin to leak, and strange things appear on you—all kinds of things: bumps and knobs, growths, like lichen and moss on an old oak.

Certainly everything in your physical rhythm has slowed. You find yourself stepping hesitantly off curbs. You are more deliberate, moving with an "old dignity," even reaching for a drink with a carefully calculated movement so as not to knock over the glass.

But the spirit! Still young. Still dreamy and hopeful.

And with these physical changes comes a strange and sad vulgarity. You belch, cough, sneeze, hiccup, let go at the breech—all quite openly. And if it offends others, you couldn't care less. Obscene jokes lose their ability to shock, but not to amuse. The things that seemed troubling when you were young now appear to be such a natural part of living and not so important after all. Sex...

Not as important as a good eight-hour sleep, perhaps, or even a good bowel movement. Dear Helen, why is it the young always think they have discovered sex? They think it has never been like this for the human race before. No one has tried such positions. No one has felt such pleasure, such ecstasy in all history. They are embarked on a wonderful voyage of experimentation and revelation. It is only when they are properly aged—like good hams hung up in a smokehouse—that they realize it has all been done before. And probably better.

And no more fear of death. That is a comfort. It simply becomes a need. Like sleep.

The memory... Now there is something strange and curious. I have a theory about memory—but then I have a theory about everything! I believe we are all born at twelve noon on a Life Clock. We all start at the top and move in a circle, in a clockwise direction. At the ages of, oh, say between forty and sixty, you can't remember names of things that happened or poems or dates. Anyway, this is what happened to me. Then you're past the bottom, you've passed six o'clock, and you're coming up the other side. Suddenly you begin to remember things. The name of your third-grade teacher. The time your parents took you to Atlanta. When you got chicken pox and had to stay inside. You understand, Helen? You're coming up around the circle again. You're getting closer to twelve o'clock again. Twelve midnight. And everything in the beginning is that much closer.

Do you suppose this is why old people—people in their sixties and seventies and eighties—are so good with very young children? Grandparents and grandchildren. They can talk for hours together and play together. Because they are getting closer in this circle. The old people have come around to the top again, and they're getting closer to the young ones just starting down on the righthand side. I wish I had had grandchildren. But as I told you, Helen, my only son was killed in Africa in World War II. They found him dead at his machine gun, holding off an enemy attack to enable his company to regroup and launch a successful counterattack that shattered enemy forces. I have the clippings.

But enough of what happens to your body and what happens to your memory. What is important, as you grow old, is that the spirit still flames and flares. The dreams...

I recall your mentioning—do you remember? It was that evening we were shelling peas together—how much you disliked men telling you how grateful they were for your company. And especially, you said, that after being intimate with a man, you could not endure his gratitude which, according to you, "spoiled" the whole thing.

Dear Helen, I am afraid I must now offend you by thanking you for your many sweet kindnesses, for your enduring my nonsense, for the pleasure and happiness you brought into my life.

I think it best if we do not see each other again. Yes, you are correct; it is a hopeless situation.

But meeting you and knowing you have been, for me, a complete vindication of keeping the spirit young and flaming, no matter how decrepit this sad sack of a body becomes.

With all my love always... with all best wishes and hopes and prayers for your future happiness... with appreciation for your wit and beauty and kindness... with all my heart, I remain

Lovingly,

/s/ Jo Rhodes

P.S. That recipe for rock cornish hens you asked about calls for two teaspoons of thyme added to the melted butter and the lemon juice. Baste frequently while broiling.

23

"HELLO?"

"Helen? This is Uck—Uck Faye."

"What's wrong? Is anything wrong?"

"No. I—I—Helen, I'm not—not interrupting anything, am I? You know."

"Uh—you're interrupting my sleep. What time is it, Uck?"

"It's after three. It's almost three-thirty."

"Jesus. Are you drunk, Uck?"

"Oh, no. No. I just couldn't sleep. I've been lying here since midnight. I turn on one side; then I turn on the other. God, how I want to sleep. But I can't. I just lie here, and my brain is churning."

"Maybe you're overtired."

"Maybe. I don't know, I want to sleep so badly, and I just can't. And I keep hearing sounds, Helen. Like there's someone in the house. You know—like footsteps."

"That's silly, baby."

"I know, I know, I got up twice and looked around. I turned on all the lights. There's no one here. All the windows and doors are locked. Then I get back into bed again, and I hear the sounds. Little thumps and thuds. I'm sorry I called you."

"That's all right, Uck. Listen, why don't you take one of those pills I gave you?"

"I don't have any. I used them all up. Can you get me more?"

"Sure. I'll get them for you tomorrow."

"Helen, can I talk to you? Just for a few minutes? I feel so—so shattered. I'm so scared. My heart keeps pounding. Maybe I'm having a stroke or something like that. I'm all sweaty. It's too hot in here. I've thrown off all the blankets. I'm just lying here naked, sweating."

"Take it easy, baby. Wait a second while I turn on the lamp and light a cigarette...Okay, I'm all set now. Did you work hard today?"

"Oh, yes. Yes, I did. Maybe you're right; maybe I'm overtired. I've been researching a thing on blindness and the problems of the blind."

"That's nice. Did you have a good dinner?"

"It was all right. Pot roast. Edith is a lousy cook. Whoever made up that crap about 'mothers' homecooked meals' never tasted my mother's cooking. She can't boil an egg right. Listen, Helen, I'm really sorry I woke you up, but I had to talk. I had to talk to *you*."

"It's okay, baby—I told you. Not to worry. Did you drink a lot today?"

"No. Very little. Two martinis at lunch and three scotches after dinner. That's not very much."

"No. Very little. Did anything happen at the office or at home? You know, like an argument or anything? Anything that upset you?"

"I can't think of anything. But I'm just lying here sweating and thinking of things."

"What are you thinking about, Uck?"

"All kinds of things. The noises in the house. The research I'm doing on blindness. Edith. The way I live. Jesus, I'm depressed. I wish I had one of those pills, Helen. A hundred of those pills."

"Take it easy, baby. Just take a deep breath. Do you still hear the noises?"

"Wait a minute... No, I don't hear them anymore. I guess I was imagining them."

"Maybe it was windows rattling. You know—the wind. Or maybe the heat going off. The woodwork shrinking and creaking. Listen, sweetie, would you like to pull on some clothes, grab a cab, and come over and sleep here?"

"Oh, no. No. Oh, God, yes, how I'd love to. How I'd love to be with you right now—all safe and sleepy. But I can't do that. I couldn't do that to you. This isn't so bad. I'll get through this night. It's just that I wanted to hear your voice."

"I know, baby, I know..."

"Helen, I feel so—so—"

"I know, I know."

"I keep thinking about dying, about what's going to happen to me—never being anymore. Just disappearing. You understand? And life going on. The world. Like I had never been. Holy Jesus Christ."

"Take it easy, Uck. Just calm down. Light a cigarette."

"That's another thing; I'm out of cigarettes."

"Maybe there's a long butt somewhere. Take a look around. Maybe you can get a few puffs."

"Yes. That's a good idea. Hang on a moment, Helen. I'll look around... okay, I found one. I'll probably burn my lips. Oh, boy, that helps. Are you there, Helen?"

"I'm here, baby."

"Listen, on this blindness thing I'm doing—how do blind people dream? Do you know?"

"I don't understand what you mean."

"Well, you know we all dream. And it's all in scenes. It's places. Where we've been and people we've known. It's all in visual scenes—like a movie. But if you've been blind from birth and you've never seen anything, how do you dream?"

"I don't know, Uck. I can't imagine."

"Not even in colors. If you were blind from birth, you couldn't even dream in colors because you wouldn't know what colors are. So how do the blind dream?"

"Maybe they don't dream."

"Everyone dreams. I dream all the time. Only it's usually when I'm awake. But that's one of the things I've been thinking about—dying and how the blind dream. Oh, God, what an awful night this has been."

"Are you calming down—a little?"

"A little. Yes, I think I'm calming down a little. My cigarette butt is going out. Should I smoke the filter?"

"Now I know you feel better, Uck. At least you can joke."

"Sure. I do feel better. But it was talking to you. Did I tell you I love you?"

"Not today you didn't."

"I love you today."

"Sweetheart. Now put out your cigarette filter and turn on your side and pull a blanket over you. Don't sleep all uncovered. That's how you catch cold."

"Yes, Mother."

"Don't call me that, you son of a bitch. Now just lie there and take deep breaths and don't think about dying or how blind people dream. Just think about me. Okay?"

"Okay. Yes. That's what I'll do. I'll cover up and snuggle down and think about you. And everything will be all right."

"You bet your ass, Good night, Uck."

"Good night, dear."

"Good night. Good night."

24

"PEGGY PALMER," Helen said, her eyes filling with tears, "do you realize this is probably the very last time you and I will be alone together before you're an old married bag?"

"Oh, Helen," Peggy moaned, blinking hard, and the two women clasped hands tightly in the crowded restaurant.

"Two champagne cocktails," Helen called commandingly to the drowsing waiter. "Peggy, this is my own special lunch for you. I don't want to hear any shit about dividing the bill or you get the tip or we divide the cab or anything like that. This is my farewell lunch for you—just the two of us."

Now sweet Peggy was sobbing openly, jabbing at her eyes with the starched napkin.

"We'll see each other," she sniffed. "Promise me we will. You'll come over for dinner at least once a week. You can bring Uck, or I'll get Maurice to bring a fellow from his office. You won't stop seeing me, will you, ducks?"

"Well, baby," Helen said, patting her hand, "you know maybe it would be smart to play it cool for a while. Just for a little while. Until you and Maurice get settled. I never believe in thrusting myself upon newlyweds, sweetie. Give 'em a chance to get tired of each other, I figure. So let's wait awhile—maybe a couple of weeks after you get back."

"A very good idea," Peggy agreed, wiping her eyes. "But as soon as we're all settled, I'll give you a call. First we'll have lunch—just the two of us. That's when I'll tell you all about it. Then you come over to dinner. We're going to Puerto Rico—did I tell you?"

"Puerto Rico? Oh, baby, that's marvelous! Just think, all that sunshine and hot sand! You'll be strutting around in your purple bikini, and I'll be sloshing around in this damned snow and sleet. Where are you going to stay?"

"Somewhere just outside of San Juan. It's like a tour with the plane tickets and the hotel room included. All you can eat. Maurice is making the arrangements. Did I tell you he doesn't want me to call him 'Morris'? He wants me to say 'More-eece.'"

"So? What's so bad about that?"

"Nothing. I just wondered if I had told you. 'More-eece.' I've got to remember that."

Their champagne cocktails arrived. They clinked rims, smiled at each other before they sipped.

"Peggy, I'll never find another friend like you."

"And I'll never find another friend, ever, in all the world, like you, ducks. Jesus, we've had fun."

"Yes." Helen nodded. "Fun. Listen, Peggy—I've got to tell you. I sent you a wedding present to the Camel's . . . oh, God, I'm sorry. I know I shouldn't call him that anymore. I really am sorry, baby."

"Oh . . . that's all right. I have to catch myself sometimes."

"Anyway, I sent a wedding present to Maurice's apartment. That's okay, isn't it?"

"Oh, sure. That's where we're going to live until the place in Forest Hills is ready. We'll be there about a month after we get back from Puerto Rico. What did you send?"

"Well, I figured everyone would be sending toasters and electric frying pans and crap like that. So I found this marvelous glassware at Tiffany's. It's pure crystal, and it's six on-the-rocks glasses and six highball glasses and six cocktail glasses and six beer steins. They're all in the same pattern with real heavy bottoms."

"Oh, ducks, how wonderful!"

"I really flipped when I saw them, and I figured no one else would buy you glassware."

"Are you ever right! You know my stuff is all chipped, and all Maurice has are empty cheese jars and stuff like that. This is something we can really use."

"Well, listen, baby, if you don't like them, if you want something else from Tiffany's, just take them right back. The man said you could return them with no trouble at all. Boy, was he ever cute! I've got the bill, so if you want to return them and get something else, you go right ahead. I mean, you won't be hurting my feelings or anything like that."

"I'll never return them," Peggy Palmer said loyally. "Never. But, Helen, you shouldn't have done it. I mean— Tiffany's. You probably spent a lot of money."

"Don't be silly. Waiter! Two more of these, please."

They lighted cigarettes, smiled at each other, looked around the crowded restaurant, didn't speak again until two more champagne cocktails were brought.

"Do you know how to make these?" Peggy asked. "Are they ever great!"

"Well, what you do is put half a cube of sugar in the bottom of the glass. Then you add about four or five drops of bitters. Then you add the champagne and put in a slice of orange or lemon or whatever you want."

"They're really great," Peggy said enthusiastically. "This is all I'm going to drink in Puerto Rico. Champagne cocktails. I'm going to live it up."

"Here's to living it up," Helen said, raising her glass, "and to you and Morris."

"Morre-eece."

"More-eece. I'm sorry, Peg."

"That's all right. Sometimes I can't remember, and he gets sore."

"Listen, kiddo, will you excuse me for a minute? I've got to call the office. Harry Tennant didn't show up this morning. He didn't even call in. Susie Carrar called his home, but there was no answer. I want to call Susie and see if he came in or if she heard from him. Susie wanted to go down to Gimbel's—they're having a coat sale—but she had to have her lunch sent in and can't get out. I'll just be a minute."

"Take your time. No rush."

"That's right." Helen grinned, sliding from her seat. "I had forgotten that you are now a lady of leisure."

She was back in a few minutes.

"That's funny. Susie hasn't heard from him and can't reach him at home. This is the first time he's pulled something like this; it's not like him. Listen, sweet, should we have another drink or should we order?"

"That's up to you, ducks. I've got all the time in the world, but I know you've got to get back to the office, especially if Harry isn't coming in."

"Well, look . . . let's have one more drink, and at the same time we'll order what we want. This Special for the Day sounds good. It's chicken Kiev. That's chicken breasts, boned, with a lot of butter."

"Oh, God, I'm getting so fat."

"Aren't we all? Well, how about it?"

"All right. With French fries and buttered asparagus."

"Very good. I'll have the same. Waiter!"

They each had two more drinks and tucked away their meal with no trouble at all. Then they ordered two café expressos and—virtuously—no desserts. But Helen insisted they have Strega on the rocks with a little twist of lime, and Peggy Palmer said okay.

Then Helen said, "Listen, honey, I told you I'm sending a wedding present to your guy's apartment. But that's official. I've got something else for you. This is just from me to you."

She reached under her chair, brought out a small shopping bag. Within the bag was a flat, elegantly wrapped box, the paper decorated with little hearts and voluptuous cupids. Helen handed it across the table.

"Just from me to you, baby." She smiled.

"Oh, Jesus," Peggy said, her eyes gleaming over again. "You shouldn't have. You're so sweet."

"Goddamned right." Helen nodded. "Open it up. But just sort of peek in. I mean, don't hold it up where everyone can see."

Peggy untied the ribbon, opened the box carefully with nervous fingers, peeked in. It was a blue bra-and-panty set, decorated with white lace, very delicate, very fragile, very lovely.

"Oh, my God," Peggy gasped. "Oh, my God."

"Do you like it?"

"Oh, my God."

"Something old, something new, something borrowed, something blue. This is your something blue—from me to you."

"Son of a bitch." Peggy sobbed. She leaned across the table to press her wet face against Helen's cheek. "Oh, is this ever beautiful!"

"I got it at that French place up on Madison Avenue. I'm sure it's going to fit. And you know what I wish for you? I wish you wear it on your wedding night, and your man snorts and growls and rips them right off, rips them into rags. I don't care. That's what I want him to do."

"Are you kidding?" Peggy said indignantly. "If he puts a hand on these, I'll smack his face."

They huddled over the box, examining the lace and stitching on the lingerie, pointing out to each other how artfully the bra straps had been attached, how the panties were cut in such a seductive design. But then the waiter came with their coffee and liqueurs; they put the box away, lighted cigarettes, leaned back, sipped coffee, breathed deeply, looked around, tongued their Strega... and dreamed.

"Do you remember," Helen Miley said thoughtfully, "do you remember that night we went to Palisades Park and met that nut with the Rolls-Royce?"

"The guy with the plaid cap?"

"That's the one. And we went to his apartment."

"Wow," Peggy Palmer breathed, "did you ever see such paintings? We were lucky to get out of there alive."

"You can say that again."

"Do you remember," Peggy Palmer said dreamily, "that bar over on Lex? The two guys who told us they were brothers?"

"Do I ever!" Helen said mournfully. "My guy stole my wristwatch. And do you remember that night in the Village at the discothèque, and all those people we met?"

"When we went up to the loft on Houston Street?"

"That's it. For some reason they were cooking pot in a frying pan over a gas jet. Remember? That was the first time I ever tried pot. It didn't do a thing for me."

"Me neither. Remember the two young Marines—when we went back to your apartment and had the scene?"

"Peggy Palmer!" Helen gasped, clasping palms to her flushing cheeks. "We said—we *swore!*—both of us *swore* we would never ever speak of that again! Don't even mention it!"

"Was it so bad?" Peggy asked gently.

"I don't want to talk about it. I don't even want to think about it."

"Was it so bad?" Peggy insisted.

"That's beside the point," Helen said stiffly. "Waiter! Our check, please."

They stood outside on the sidewalk, under the restaurant canopy, huddling within their fur coats. A greasy snow was falling—not really falling but being blown on gusts of an angry wind.

"Well, baby"—Helen smiled—"I guess the next time I see you, you will be at the altar. I don't have to say, 'I wish you the best of everything.' You know I want the whole world for you."

"Oh, ducks," Peggy said, beginning to cry again, "you've been so great...so great. Thank you for the lunch and the official wedding present and this—" She held up her little shopping bag. "Everything has been just wonderful."

"Sure. Now I've got to get back to the office. See you at the wedding, sweet."

Suddenly Peggy Palmer was embracing her, holding her tight, trembling.

"I'm scared," she whispered. "Honest to God, Helen, I'm scared. I don't know what to do. I'm just all—I don't know—I'm all confused. Tell me, am I doing the right thing?"

"Take it easy, baby. It's going to be all right. Everything's going to be fine."

"You won't forget me, will you, Helen?"

"No darling, I won't forget you."

They kissed, on the lips, and parted.

Helen saw right away she wasn't going to get a cab. And walking over to Fifth Avenue for a downtown bus seemed silly. So she started sloshing back to the office, her chin buried in her fur. She was wearing the boots Richard Faye insisted she wear the last time they went to bed. (Boy, what a nut!) They buckled high on her calves and kept out most of the slush and snow, but her feet got cold and felt wet. She was certain her nose was going to freeze hard and fall off. She'd be left with nothing but two holes there—two holes right in the middle of her face; no nose.

But in spite of all these pains and discomforts she had to admit it wasn't bad. Plowing through all that stuff. People with their heads bent down, grumbling through the sleet. She was warmed with food and drink, chuckling when she thought about Peggy Palmer's misgivings. Helen Miley just slopped along, snow on her eyelashes, slipping and skidding, her purse slung over her shoulder, gloved hands dug deep in her pockets. It wasn't all that bad. She liked it. Sunshine and heat were great—but she wouldn't want them all the time. This wasn't so bad.

She walked all the way down to the office. By the time she got there her teeth were chattering, her bones felt brittle. She figured she'd have a black coffee sent up. She'd swipe a belt from that bottle of brandy Swanson kept in the lower drawer of his desk. Maybe she'd take two aspirin. And what could happen?

The elevator starter shook his head sadly at her, and she knew her number of the previous day was a dud. Oh, well. She took off her fur coat, shook it free of melted snow. When she entered the office, she was carrying it over her arm. She remembered all these details later.

What an odd sight. On that Grand Rapids Swedish Moderne couch in the reception room—the one with the bare wood arms and legs and the orange plastic cushions—two men were seated, upright. One was black, and one was white. Both were perhaps thirty-five or forty-five, around there. Both were neat, closely shaved, wore overcoats, and had placed their naked hands on their knees. Both were wearing rubbers. Both wore hats— similar gray fedoras. They looked like bookends in a pop-art gallery. When Helen entered, both rose, removed their hats.

Susie Carrar didn't look up. She sat at her desk, her fingers poised over the keyboard of her typewriter. Yet she did not type.

"Miss Miley," she muttered. "Uh. These. Uh. Gentlemen. These, uh, gentlemen. Would like to talk. To you."

The black gentleman took a half step forward, opened his pink palm. There was a little leather folder—some writing, an official seal, a shield.

"Detective Samuel B. Johnson," he cried. "This is Detective Rollin H. Forsythe."

The white gentleman stepped forward, performed the same smooth juggle, his palm opening, the little leather folder revealed.

"May we speak to you, Miss Miley?" he asked. His voice was unexpectedly high-pitched—almost a woman's voice.

"Sure," she said, puzzled. "Come on in here."

She led the way into her office, closed the door behind them.

She hung up her coat. They stood there, heads hanging, both of them with clasped hands, holding their hats, covering their privates.

"Sit down?" She gestured, but they paid no attention. So she remained standing.

"What's all this about?" She tried to smile. But she wasn't getting warmer; she was getting colder.

"Harry L. Tennant?" the white detective asked in his screechy voice. "An employee of this company?"

"Yes," Helen said nervously. "Of course. Yes, he's an employee. He works for us. He hasn't shown up today, but he's been working for us for months. What's wrong? Is anything wrong?"

The two of them exchanged a quick glance. Then they seemed to dissolve. That is, they seemed to become softer inside their wooden overcoats. They slumped a little; their faces slumped, and they no longer looked like bookends. They looked like human beings. The black had a pimple on his chin. The white had a Band-Aid around his thumb.

"Sit down, Miss Miley," the black one said gently. "I do really believe you should sit down."

So she sat down, behind her desk. But they just stood there, staring at her.

"What happened was—" the white one started. "What happened was—"

"He committed suicide," the black one said. "Harry L. Tennant committed suicide. He's dead."

Outside there was a siren—a squad car or a fire engine or an ambulance. There was something keening through that snow.

"Dead?" Helen Miley said, wondering what the "L" stood for. He had never mentioned that, never told her.

The team simultaneously whipped out identical little notebooks.

"Discovered at eleven-eighteen this morning..."

"Empty bottle of what appear to be barbiturates on bedside table..."

"No visitors reported..."

"No record of previous suicide attempts..."

"Body removed to New York City Morgue at twelve twenty..."

"His cleaning woman," the white detective explained. "This was her day to clean. She came in to clean, and she discovered the body. She called the police."

"But it was too late," the black detective explained. "He had been dead for hours. Well, we don't know that for sure. There will be an autopsy. But the ME thinks he was dead for hours. Was he on drugs?"

"What?"

"To your knowledge, was the man you know—*knew*—as Harry L. Tennant addicted to drugs of any kind?"

"No, sir," she said formally. "To my knowledge, the man I knew as Harry Tennant was not addicted to drugs of any kind."

The white one turned to the black one.

"You know, Sam," he said wonderingly, "that's a funny way for a black to pull the Dutch Act. I never heard of one doing it with pills—did you?"

"Rolly, you're right," the black one said wonderingly. "I don't think I ever heard of a black pill case. Mostly we go out a window or off a roof."

"Will you stop it?" Helen Miley shouted at them. "Will you just stop it?"

"Well," the black one said briskly, "he left a note addressed to you. Here it is."

He whisked it out of his overcoat pocket. It was in a small Swanson & Feltzig envelope.

Helen reached for it with a steady hand. She put on her glasses, looked at it.

"You opened it," she cried angrily.

They both shrugged, looked away.

"Ma'am, we had to," the black detective muttered. "That's what regulations say. If there's a note, we open it to make sure it's a suicide. You know . . . we got to investigate. To make sure it really is a suicide. We made a Xerox of this, but you can keep it. Can you give us a sample of his handwriting?"

"What?"

"A sample of his handwriting. So we can be sure he wrote this."

She didn't answer. She was reading. It said: "Babe. Don't blame yourself. It wasn't you, it was me. I thank you. You tried. Harry."

"What did he mean?" the white detective asked.

"You opened it," she yelled again.

"We had to," he explained patiently. "We got to open suicide notes and read them. Miss, we don't like to do this, we assure you."

"We assure you," the black detective nodded.

"Oh, I don't know," she said dully. "I don't know what he meant."

They said Harry's brother had been notified; he would take care of the arrangements. Helen bobbed her head. She dug up some samples of Harry's handwriting. She gave the notes to the detectives. They thanked her.

There didn't seem much else to say. They shuffled around a little, then started toward the door. They paused, looked back toward her.

"This isn't so nice for us," the white detective screeched.

Helen nodded.

"Well..." the black detective said.

Then they were gone.

Between the private office of Swanson and the private office of Feltzig was this tiled room. It had a toilet and a sink, but no bathtub or shower. It was just a convenience, where you could take a pee or wash your face—a little place like that.

So Helen went in there, took off her glasses, kneeled on the tile floor right in front of the toilet, bending over like someone at a religious font or something like that. She threw up—everything coming out of her—the champagne cocktails and the chicken Kiev and the buttered asparagus and the French fries and the café expresso and the Strega and then, finally, a thin white thing, like a rope. She just emptied herself out, making animal sounds, whooping and jerking and coughing and sneezing with stuff coming out her nose...and she couldn't stop.

God, she must have been in there for almost half an hour, just jerking and whooping, her whole body shuddering, all this stuff coming out of her...she couldn't stop.

But then she heard Susie Carrar banging on the door, and she could gasp, "All right. All right. I'm coming out. I'm all right."

On her knees in there. Her forehead pressed against the cool of the toilet rim. Her breath coming in great gaspy sobs. "Babe. Don't blame yourself." That's what he said. She heaved. "It wasn't you, it was me." Her tongue felt thick and hot. "I thank you. You tried." She wanted to vomit more, wanted to, but there was nothing left. Nothing. "You tried. Harry."

She dragged herself upright, grabbing onto a towel rod for support. She was halfway to her feet when the towel rod came off the wall, just broke loose from the tiled wall. She staggered but didn't fall. Then she was standing upright, holding a towel rod in her hand. She looked at it, opened her hand, let it fall.

She washed her face with cold water. She didn't have a toothbrush, but she ran a finger around her teeth and gums, washing them with cold water. She looked at her face in the mirror. Not so good.

After a while she came out, looked around vaguely. She put on her coat, hat, gloves and went out. In the reception room Susie Carrar was bent over her desk, face and arms all cradled down on the top of her desk, shoulders shaking. Helen knew she should say something. But she couldn't. She couldn't touch Susie, couldn't even pat her. She just walked past her, out the door. Well...

There it was—the world. People bending against the wind, snorting in the snow. Cabs and trucks. Arguments and screaming. The buildings still there. Advertisements. Special sales. Discounts. Everything. Still there.

She walked home, almost strolling. Once she turned her face up to the sky, stuck her tongue out. Snowflakes fell on her tongue and melted. She hadn't done that in years. An elderly woman walking by looked at her, smiling, nodding.

Cabs splashed her. A messenger with a big box bumped into her. But she walked home slowly, trying not to think of anything but the falling snow, the bang of Manhattan in early winter—all charged with life and hope.

Then there she was. Up in her own apartment. The door double-locked and chained. No Rocco there. An insane bird chirping for no reason and mouthing obscenities. But mostly Helen Miley in her very own apartment, alone. She figured, Oh, boy, this is it. If I get through this night, I'm home free. The first thing she thought was that she wouldn't call anyone—not Peggy Palmer, not Richard Faye, not Jo Rhodes, not Charles Lefferts— no one. This one was hers. Hers alone.

25

A few weeks after Harry Tennant killed himself, Helen Miley was meandering down Park Avenue on a Saturday, enjoying a bright, hard December afternoon, and there was St. Bartholomew's. For a moment she was tempted to go inside, sit down in that haunting chapel, and say a word for Harry.

But she hadn't gone to church regularly since her mother died. She usually went on Easter and Christmas, but that was to see the shows. To go into a church now, when she wanted something, seemed indecent to her, ignoble—like a soldier who had never prayed in his adult life until someone fires a gun at him, and then he screams, "Oh, my God!"

Helen Miley's relations with God were distant; they were practically strangers. She used words and phrases like "goddammit" and "God damn it to hell" and "for Christ's sake" and "oh, Jesus Christ." But these were just things to say, as we all do. Once in her life she said, "God fuck it!" when a shoelace broke, but she never said that again.

But she believed in God. That is, she believed in a Supreme Being. Because if you didn't believe, how the hell could you figure out what everyone was up to? It all became a nothing, and what with her laundry and dry cleaning every Saturday, she didn't have the strength to face that.

So, like most of us, she was willing to go along with the vague idea of Somebody Up There—a big guy who looked like Charlton Heston with a cotton-candy beard and who patted little children on top of their heads. This Guy—who might have some kind of a Divine Nuttiness that no one could understand—made things happen or let them happen without interfering. He let or made Harry L. Tennant kill himself. But if you looked for any kind of reason or logic, you'd wind up in the giggle factory. Right?

That was about the extent of Helen Miley's religious feelings; it was very similar to that of most people she knew. But it wasn't all that important. What was important was that you had to work and earn a living, you were lonely, waiters snarled at you, they tried to cheat you at the deli. But still, when something happened like Harry up there in his Harlem apartment gulping down those pills, washing them down with a glass of tepid water from a rusty sink, then you thought about things. For a while.

Helen thought about them for a while, not forgetting to cut over to Madison Avenue so she could get around Grand Central Station. Once she stopped in a drugstore to buy a pack of cigarettes; once she stopped in a lingerie shop to look at some black lace bikinis, but she didn't buy any.

She leaned forward a little, trudging up Murray Hill, and thought about Jo Rhodes not so far away on Thirty-eighth Street. After that letter she had called him twice, but there was no answer. She had written him once, but there was no answer. She decided to buy Jo Rhodes a small bottle of Grand Marnier in a liquor store. Then she would go to see him. If he wasn't home, she'd have the Grand Marnier, and she could sip it or cook with it; it wouldn't go to waste.

When she rang his bell, a woman answered the door—elderly, not crinkly old, but not middle-aged either. Helen Miley wasn't shocked, startled or even surprised. She knew immediately this was Jo Rhodes' wife. Helen smiled, thinking she had known all along, even if she had never admitted it to herself. She did this all the time—knowing things but not admitting them.

"Mrs. Rhodes?" she asked.

"Yes."

"I'm a friend of Jo's. My name is Helen Miley. I came to visit but if..."

"Oh, hell," the woman said, opening the door wide. "Come on in."

She was big, much taller than Jo, and husky, wide-shouldered. She had a black mustache—faint, but there it was. She had that kind of complexion older women sometimes get—soft rose velvet. You wanted a copy of *Against the Grain* bound in skin from her shoulders. She was holding a cigarette and martini (straight up) in one hand (no mean trick). She was wearing a—well, it was like—like pajamas in some kind of a Persian design, everything floppy.

"Sit thee down," she said to Helen in a voice that was heavy and coarse, almost masculine. "I'm having a martini. You?"

"I brought this," Helen said, thrusting the small bottle of Grand Marnier at her.

Mrs. Rhodes took it, inspected it, nodded. "He's been going through his Escoffier period again, has he?" she asked amusedly. "Surely you don't want this?"

"Oh, no. That's for you. I'd like a scotch with a little water, please."

"Very good." The old woman nodded approvingly. "My name's Martha."

Helen sat down, put on her glasses, lighted a cigarette. She felt very good. She wasn't embarrassed or anything. She felt very good about this meeting, liking the wife immediately, feeling instinctively the wife liked her.

Martha brought in the scotch—a big one—and handed it to Helen. Then she sprawled in a soft chair, her plump, silk-sheathed legs spread wide open in front of her.

"He went to an exhibition," she said. "Some art gallery way up on Lexington. Probably won't be back for hours."

Helen nodded, sipped her drink. It was strong.

"I was out in Kansas City," Mrs. Rhodes explained. "My youngest daughter was having her second, and I stood by. Then Jo came out to visit and fly back with me."

"How many daughters do you have, Mrs. Rhodes?"

"Martha."

"Martha."

"I have three daughters."

"No sons?"

Martha tilted her head back and inspected the ceiling.

"You mean the son who was killed in World War Two when he instructed the crew of the bomber he was piloting to bail out, and then he dove his plane with its load of bombs into an important German arms factory and thus shortened the war by at least a year? And Jo's got the clippings."

"Yes." Helen nodded. "That's the son I meant."

They grinned at each other.

"Sorry," Martha said. "No sons. Three daughters."

She opened a little tin can, selected a dry Dutch cigar. Helen got off the couch to come over and hold a match for the older woman.

"Thank you. Tell me something, Helen..."

"Sure."

"Where was it going to be this time? A small stone cottage in Ireland? You could watch the sea pounding against the rocky cliffs. The women with faces like walnuts bringing you the poteen they made in their smoky kitchens, and the shamrock puddings. The fishermen going out in their cockleshells, braving the elements, bringing in the schmaltz herring. Was that it?"

"Well...no," Helen said thoughtfully, looking at the glowing tip of her cigarette. "First it was France. On the Riviera. Near Spain. But later it became Italy. He forgot."

Martha sighed.

"Jesus. Last year a young thing showed up here. So young she still had dimples in her ass. Red hair down to her waist. A real beauty. She had an armful of furs. She was ready to spend a glorious month at his dacha just outside Moscow. He had told her they'd do nothing but drink vodka and watch the natives harvest the wild blintzes— their largest cash crop."

"Martha, he's not—well, you know—he's not senile, is he?"

"*Senile?* Oh, you tot. Don't you know that *all* men are senile—from the day they're born?"

"I didn't know," Helen murmured humbly.

"Clowns," Martha said, shaking her massive head. "There should be a law requiring all men to dress in clown suits with false noses and funny hats and baggy pants."

She heaved to her feet and stretched, flinging her arms wide. An old woman, you understand, but still strong, still vigorous. That mustache. Those cigars.

She went into the kitchen, came back with fresh drinks for herself and Helen. They took sips, slumped down in their chairs.

They thrust out spread legs, stared at the ceiling once again.

"I guess you're right, Martha," Helen said finally. "I know this freak who thinks he's Mister Orgasm himself. As a matter of fact, he's a pretty good acrobat. But this nut wants to make a career of it. He thinks he's going to float through life on a hot sheet and make a lot of money."

"Sure, tot. The fantasy. They all have them. And mostly sexual fantasies."

"Sexual fantasies," Helen said dreamily. "Yes, that's true."

"Did you ever know a prostitute? I mean did you ever become friendly with one, and did she ever tell you what her job was like and what the clowns asked her to do?"

"No. Not really. I never knew a prostitute that closely."

"Tot, you wouldn't believe. They could tell you stories . . . the scenes they have to play. But did you ever hear of a woman who insisted her lover dress up like Little Boy Blue and come running into the bedroom rolling a hoop? Of course not. Because they're the dreamers; we're the realists."

The light was leaking out of the room, but Martha didn't bother switching on lamps. Helen didn't suggest it. They just sat there, nibbling their drinks, chopping up men, feeling fine.

"About Jo," Martha started, "he may lie occasionally but—"

"Oh, no," Helen protested. "Not really."

"Not really," Martha agreed. "It's only because reality doesn't come up to his expectations. He must improve on it, bring it closer to his—to his—"

"To his dream?"

"Well . . . yes. To his dream. But understand, there is no malice in him."

"Malice?" Helen Miley shouted. "In Jo? How can you say that? He's the dearest, sweetest man who ever lived."

"I did not say there was malice in him. I said there was *no* malice in him. Helen, you are just not listening."

Helen took this rebuke with a grin. In truth, she was getting a mite steamed. The drinks were tall. And husky.

"He's very nice," she assured the other woman. "Jo is . . ."

"Of course he's nice," Mrs. Rhodes rasped, lighting another cigar. "My Jo-Jo is a saint. He's exactly what you said he is—the dearest, sweetest man who ever lived. He's also one big pain in the ass."

"Do you love him?"

"What did you say, tot? I didn't hear you."

"I asked if you loved him. Do you love Jo?"

"Do I love him? Do I love him? That's a good question . . ."

"Well, I love him," Helen said defiantly.

Martha Rhodes looked at Helen a long moment.

"You don't love him," she said gently. "You feel a very great affection for him. That's nice. I like that. But it's different from loving. All the tender young things Jo meets have a great affection for him. The man has charm. I'd be the last to deny it. But love him? Helen, he didn't screw you, did he?"

Helen blinked, twice.

"No. He didn't."

"Of course he didn't. He would never do anything like that. It would spoil everything. He would wake up and have problems. Besides, he can't. But me"—she took a deep breath, those monumental lungs swelling under the Persian silk—"*me* he fucked. So I'm entitled to love him. You're not."

She walked slowly into the kitchen to fetch refills. Moving regally, her head high. Helen decided that if she tried to match this woman drink for drink, she would need a stomach pump.

When Mrs. Rhodes returned with their drinks, she also brought a bowl of pistachios and a paper plate. They gnawed contentedly, cracking the nuts in their teeth, spitting the shells onto the paper plate. Their fingertips got red.

"You see," Martha Rhodes said, chewing away, "when Jo and I first met, years and years ago, when we were sleeping together, when we were so young we thought we had invented it all, well, then, I loved Jo, truly loved *him*. I wish you could have known him then—the wit, the charm, and almost as handsome as John Barrymore. Have you ever seen photos of Cole Porter or Noël Coward in the south of France during the 1920's? That's the way Jo dressed in warm weather. White linen suit. A Norfolk jacket. That's the kind with a belt. He carried a rattan cane. And a wide-brimmed hat with one side up and one side down. Like Jimmy Walker. Oh, God, men were so elegant in those days. If they had the money. And Jo had the money. Because beneath the clothes, the wit, the charm, was a very clever, talented and hard-working man. Oh, yes, tot, he worked very hard and made a great deal of money. And just threw it away on me. Clothes, perfume, travel—whatever I wanted. One winter night—I think it was before the Crash—we took a ride in a closed brougham through Central Park. Most people call them hansom cabs, but they're really broughams. And we fucked in there, the horse just clopping along. Have you ever done that?"

"No," Helen said enviously, "I never have." Then she brightened. "But this man I knew—he's dead now—but when he was alive, he took me to a little Italian restaurant and taught me how to eat biscuit Tortoni. What you do is order Tortoni and a big cup of black coffee— maybe even expresso. Then with your spoon you scoop out about two spoonfuls of the Tortoni, including those chopped nuts on top, and you carefully float them onto the coffee. The ice cream melts, and those nuts are there. Boy, is that ever good! Harry L. Tennant taught me how to do that."

"Listen," Martha Rhodes said, "I remember once when Jo and I were in Paris. Oh...years ago. We went to the Folies Bergère. Then we went back to our hotel, and he decided he wanted to drink champagne out of my slipper. Well, he had bought me this lovely pair of gray silk evening slippers with open toes. They must have been the first open-toe evening slippers ever made. Anyway, I told him he couldn't drink champagne out of my slipper because the toe was open. But he insisted. So he lay down on the couch and opened his mouth, and I poured champagne into the heel and it ran down the slipper, out the toe and into his mouth."

"Listen," Helen Miley said, "I was with this guy out in Ohio. It was in his rooming house. We were making it in his bed, and he was on top. Well, this was a folding bed—you know, one of those things with wheels that fold in the middle, and you can push them into a closet or out of the way. Anyway, we were banging away on this crazy bed and the catch broke and the whole damned thing began to fold up. I mean I began to bend in the middle. My head and shoulders went up in the air and my legs. And he began to bend backwards, his spine bending backwards. He started to holler, and I started to laugh. Jesus, was that something. We finally fought our way out of the damned thing. It was like a bear trap."

"Listen," Martha Rhodes said, "once I was with this man, very famous, and I won't tell you who he was, but his initials were J.B. Anyway, I went back to his hotel room with him, and right away he wanted to bang me. He didn't even want to waste time taking our clothes off. He threw me down across the bed and made a grab for me. I was wearing a string of pearls, and he broke them with the first grab. Pearls spilled all over the hardwood floor. Every time he tried to press into me he'd skid on those pearls. He was like a man trying to run a mile in one place. He pedaled and pedaled, not getting anywhere, the pearls just rolling back under his feet. I was giggling, and he was roaring like a maniac. Finally he gave up and just flopped down on top of me. He told me his father had been killed in the assault on San Juan Hill."

"Listen..." Helen Miley started. Then stopped. The two women sat there in the deepening light, smiling, saddened. Then they straightened up, sipping their drinks as ladies should.

"So tell me," Helen said finally. "After you and Jo made it in that carriage in Central Park, what happened then?"

"Well, that's when he proposed—over tea at the Plaza after he bounced me in the brougham."

"Did you say yes right away?" Helen asked eagerly.

"No. Not right away. Not for almost three months. By then my feelings about Jo had changed. I still had a great love for him, you understand. But I knew a little more about him, knew how he made up these incredible fantasies and how he was incapable—absolutely *incapable*—of loving just one woman. To Jo, women are vitamins. He cannot exist without them. He needs them as much as he needs cold lobster and warm brandy. They replenish him. So I was no longer only in love with *him*, but I was in love with love. With the idea of loving. It seemed to me the most important thing in the world, and I didn't want to lose it."

"Oh, yes, yes..."

"Besides, I was pregnant. So I told Jo I would marry him. He was surprised. I think he had forgotten he had asked me. But very gallantly, he married me. I hope he has never regretted it. I certainly haven't. Another drink?"

"Well. Yes."

Helen Miley sat there alone, head slowly wagging. She was determined to keep her wits. It was a marvelous afternoon. She didn't want it to end. But she didn't want to do anything foolish either, like gibber or get sick or something like that. She was enormously hungry.

Martha Rhodes came in with their fresh drinks, not bringing any food. She handed the scotch to Helen, flopped down in her soft chair again, heavy legs spread out in front of her. She lighted another cigar.

"And then," she said, taking a sip of her new martini, "and then, after you have loved one man, and then you begin loving the *idea* of loving, then you progress and you—and you—"

She stopped. Twirled her glass. Looking down at it,

perplexed. She looked up at Helen, peering at her through the dusk.

"Well, it just expands. That's the only way I can say it. You start by loving one person, one man. Then you begin to love the idea of love. Then it expands to take in the whole ugly, beautiful, good, evil human race. There's no one you can't love. You want them all to suck your big titty so you can hold them close, the sad, sad creatures. In your mind you know exactly what they are—so awful, so lonely. But that's not important. What is important is that by loving one person and then by loving the idea of love, you finally come to the point where, when you meet someone, you want two raw souls rubbing against each other."

"Oh, yes," Helen breathed.

"Two raw souls rubbing against each other," Martha Rhodes repeated slowly, looking at her. "That is what I think," she added loudly, although no one had asked her.

Warm silence came down on them.

"Children help," Martha offered. "They help. You don't have children?"

"No."

"Married? Ever?"

"No."

"You want children?"

"Yes," Helen said, tears coming to her eyes. "Very much."

"They help." Martha nodded. "How old are you, tot?"

"How old?" Helen asked, confused. "Oh, thirty-three or thirty-six. Around there. I've lied so much about it, I don't really know. No one ever sends me a birthday card."

"Do you know when your birthday is?"

"Yes, I do. It is May the fourteenth."

"I'll send you a birthday card," Martha Rhodes said. "Every year."

Helen got to her feet. Went over and kissed the old woman's cheek.

"You're great," she said. "Jesus, are you ever great!"

Martha reached up, clasped Helen in her strong arms. She pressed her tight.

"Stick in there, tot," she murmured.

Helen nodded dumbly.

She went home right after that, not finishing her drink. She went home, kicked off her shoes, went to bed immediately. She fell asleep instantly. She slept almost two hours.

When she awoke, she rushed to the refrigerator. She ate two

stalks of celery, a whole tomato, three slices of salami (folded in half; each slice between two pieces of Ry-Krisp), half a cucumber (salted), two hard-boiled eggs, a chunk of Cheddar cheese, drank a whole can of chilled pineapple juice, ate a cold shank of fried chicken, two macaroons, and half a bar of chocolate (with almonds) that was gray from being chilled.

She ate all this standing up at the sink, not bothering to put out a plate or set the table. She just snagged everything down, furious with hunger.

Finally, she wandered into the living room, bloated but feeling better. She sat down at the desk and woofed, patting her stomach. She lighted a cigarette, smoke disappearing inside her somewhere.

After a while she calmed, smiling to think of Martha Rhodes.

What a nice, gabby old woman. And Martha Rhodes would send her a birthday card. Helen was certain of it.

She thought about Martha's life with Jo. Then she thought about her own life. She figured Martha was happy—or at least as happy as anyone had a right to expect. So?

So Helen took out a sheet of yellow paper and a ballpoint pen. She was going to make out a Personal Balance Sheet, listing her good points and her bad points. She had read in a women's magazine that this was the thing to do when you were dissatisfied with your life, when you wanted to change things. You made out this ledger, being absolutely honest. Then you eliminated the negative and accentuated the positive. And then you would be happy.

She drew a rough line down the middle of the sheet. The left-hand column she headed Bad Things, the right-hand column Good Things.

She decided to start with Bad Things. Get them over with right away. She wrote:

—I drink too much.

—Swear too much.

—Go to bed with too many men.

—I don't write my brothers and their families often enough.

—I am jealous of Peggy Palmer.

The last one hurt her, a little, so she went into the kitchen, mixed a big scotch and water. She brought it back to the desk, sat down, wrote:

—I drink too much.

Then she realized she had already mentioned this, so she changed a word, making it:

—I smoke too much.

Then she became fiercely honest, began writing as fast as she could scribble:

—I should have helped Harry, but I didn't.

—Sometimes I am mean to Uck.

—I think Charles Lefferts is a jerk.

—I hate the bird and don't take care of him.

—I should take more baths and use a deodorant.

—I should go to church regularly.

—I should give to charity.

—I could adopt a kid in a foreign country somewhere through one of those charities. It doesn't cost much, and I could do it out of my salary if I stopped drinking. Or if I don't go to Pernambuco.

—I take too many pills.

—I don't do my exercises every day.

—I should read good books and improve my mind.

She paused a moment to gnaw at the top of her pencil. She took a long swallow of her drink. Then she added:

—I drink too much.

Groaning, she crossed it out. But she wrote:

—I dress too sexy for my age.

—I lie about my age.

—I should go to more museums.

She couldn't think of any more Bad Things, but the list seemed incomplete. She had probably forgotten something. Finally she added:

—I should pray more.

...And let it go at that. She read over the list. It seemed sufficient. She sipped her drink, reading the list again, and counting. There were twenty-one Bad Things.

Before she started on the Good Things, she mixed a fresh drink. Then she came back to the desk, sighed, picked up the pen and ... Well ...

—I am attractive.

—Men like me, and I like them.

—I am generous, in several ways.

—I am always clean and neat.

There were four Good Things right there. It had hardly taken a moment. She took another swallow of her drink, started out again:

—I am good at my job and work hard.

—I try to help people.

But this last was too much like Number Three ("I am generous, in several ways") so she crossed it out, sadly. But then she wrote:

—I loved Rocco and took good care of him.

—I really did what I could for Harry, no matter what happened.

—I have helped Uck. I know I have.

—I haven't been mean to Charles Lefferts even if he is a jerk.

—I was very nice to Jo Rhodes and liked his wife.

She had ten Good Things. But they were coming harder now. It was important to her that she should get twenty-one of them, to match the list of Bad Things. Suddenly she realized that the one she had crossed out ("I try to help people") wasn't *exactly* like Number Three ("I am generous, in several ways"), so she put back in:

—I try to help people.

She took a swallow of her drink, added:

—I love children and want to have some.

That made twelve Good Things.

She sat there, lighted a cigarette. She leaned forward slowly, wrote:

—I don't wish anyone any hurt.

That didn't seem much of a Good Thing, but she put it down anyway, needing it. That made thirteen. She sat back, sipping her drink. She couldn't think of more. For a moment she was tempted to write: "I am a good lay," but she was ashamed.

But she wrote:

—I have a good sense of humor and can make jokes.

That one was all right. But still, the list of Bad Things was distressingly longer. She stared at her Personal Balance Sheet, feeling awful. There *had* to be more Good Things, but she just couldn't think.

Finally she added:

—I have nice hair.

Then she slowly tore the sheet into strips. Two strips, four strips, eight strips. Then into little squares. Then into the wastebasket with all of it. The whole thing was silly and stupid. She should have had more sense.

She turned on the TV set, went into the kitchen to mix a fresh drink. When she came out, there was an old movie with Doris Day and Cary Grant. He was trying to seduce her, but she broke out in this rash. Helen Miley settled back on the couch contentedly. She just knew it was going to have a happy ending.

26

"HELEN," HE MURMURED, "what's this?"

"What?"

"Here. This scar. I never noticed that before."

"You haven't been down that way lately."

"What is it?"

"Appendicitis, baby."

"Did it hurt?"

"No. It felt good."

"Silly. Silly Helen."

"Ahh. This is going to be a good night. Right, Uck?"

"Right."

"I have a feeling this is going to be a great night."

"Mmm."

"We won't let anyone or anything crap it up. Right?"

"Mmm."

"Cold, baby?"

"A little."

"Move closer. Better?"

"Yes. My ass is cold."

"Jesus, it *is* cold. I'll rub it up a minute. How did your ass get so cold?"

"I soaked it in ice water before I came over."

"Nut."

"You feel so good. I'd like to crawl inside of you."

"Why not?"

"I mean all of me. I'd like to get inside of you and sit in a big, soft leather chair in robe and slippers and smoke a pipe. Maybe read *Fortune* magazine."

"Ear. Chin. Nose. Lips."

"Helen, Helen."

"Ah, no. Let me do the work. Be my guest."

"Okay."

"You just lay there."

"May I breathe?"

"No. Oh, boy, is this ever great!"

"God."

"You like that, Uck?"

"I love that."

"This?"

"Yes. I love that."

"This?"

"Yes. Everything. It's always the first time with us."

"Really? Honestly?"

"Really and honestly."

"It's going to be great, baby."

"I know, I know. And we're sober. I'm completely sober. Aren't you sober?"

"I'm completely sober. We just had that little glass of wine at dinner, so I'm completely sober."

"Let's go slow."

"Yes. Slow. I'll go slow. Uck. Old Uck Faye."

"Oh, oh, oh."

"If I hurt you, just scream."

"Eek. Like that?"

"Sure. My teeth are very sharp. Last year my dentist had to file down my teeth, a little."

"Where did—oh, God. Where did you learn to do that?"

"Do what?"

"That. What you're doing."

"I'm an old hand at this game, baby."

"I know, I know. I'm just a child. A child."

"Shh. Relax. Just relax."

"Helen, I'm going to sneeze."

"So sneeze already."

"Ah—ah—no. It passed."

"Pinch your nose."

"No. It's all right. It passed."

"You're cold. Pull the covers up, Uck."

"I'm warm. You're warming me up."

"Like this?"

"Yes."

"And this?"

"Jesus. Oh."

"You taste good, baby. And you smell fresh."

"I sprayed my crotch with Lysol room freshener before I came over."

"Idiot. Hey. Want to feel something funny?"

"Funny?"

"Something you never felt before."

"What?"

"This. Like this."

"Oy-vay! Where did you learn? How did you learn?"

"I studied. I applied myself."

"Helen, it's an art."

"Damned right. I'm an artist. Uck, turn a little."

"Like this?"

"Yes."

"Mmm..."

"Ticklish?"

"No, I—*yes!* There. Who isn't?"

"I'm ticklish all over."

"Let me see."

"No, Uck. Don't."

"Yes. Let me. Here?"

"Yes."

"And here?"

"Oh, God. Yes."

"Here?"

"Uck, you're killing me."

"Good. Here. And here. And here."

"Oh. Oh. Oh. Stop, Uck. Please."

"No. It's my turn. Ear. Chin. Nose. Lips."

"Mmm."

"Helen, I—"

"Baby, let's—"

"Wait till I—"

The phone rang.

"Should we answer, Uck?"

"I don't know. I don't know."

The phone rang.

"I'll answer, Uck. If it's for you, I'll say you're not here."

"That's no good. She knows I'm here."

The phone rang.

"What should we do, Uck? Let it ring?"

"It won't stop. She'll never stop."

The phone rang.

"I better answer, Uck."

"What? All right. If it's for me, I'll take it."

"Hello? Yes. Yes, he's here. It's the Muscle, Uck. He wants you."

"All right. Hello? Yes. Again? When?"

"What's wrong, Uck?"

"No. No, I won't. I don't give a damn. I just don't care. I told you."

"What's happened, Uck?"

"For the last time, no. Tell her that. Ah . . . go to hell."

"What was it, Uck?"

"He said Edith had another heart attack."

"Again?"

"He said they were playing Hearts. He said they called the doctor."

"'They?'"

"Three of them. He said it's serious this time. Really serious."

"Do you believe him?"

"He said she's calling for me."

"Do you want to go?"

"I."

"Do you want to go to her, Uck?"

"Well."

"Do you believe him? Do you want to go to her, Richard?"

"What? *Richard?* No. I don't believe him."

"Sure?"

"Of course I'm sure. It's the same old game."

"Do you really want to stay, dear?"

"Damned right. This isn't going to make any difference."

"Darling. Darling."

"Bitch. Pulling the same stunt again."

"Uck, you've got to stop running when she calls. Stop now."

"I will. It's the end. Old Marse Miley freed the slave."

"Good boy. Mmm. Good man."

"I don't want to think about...anything."

"But this?"

"Yes."

"And this?"

"Oh, yes."

"Uck! How nice! A surprise for me!"

"I hope you like it. I didn't have it gift-wrapped."

"I love it. Wait just a sec. Okay. Now come over here."

"Here?"

"Yes. Like this."

"Ali-kazam!"

"And?"

"Yes. Am I too heavy?"

"Oh, no, man. Man."

"Geronimo. Dear old Geronimo."

"Do you want me, Uck?"

"Where are you now, Thomas Alva Edison?"

"Do you need me?"

"Tiberius Claudius Nero Caesar, I love you."

"Say it. Say it!"

"I want you. I need you."

"Wait. Wait."

"No."

"All right then."

"Yes."

The balloon went up.

A few hours later Dr. Franklin called to tell Richard Faye his mother had just died, still asking for him.

27

THE CAMEL WAS stunned. He plodded after Peggy through the mob of reception guests, flinching as men shook his hand, women looked at his nose and giggled.

"What's wrong with Maurice, baby?" Helen whispered to Peggy. "He acts like he was shotgunned into this. After all, it was his idea."

"He'll get over it, ducks," Peggy sighed. "As soon as I get him alone, I'll straighten him out. Is Uck here?"

"Not yet. After what happened last week, I don't even know if he'll show up. Poor bastard. I've been calling and calling, but I can't get him. I better have another drink."

She had several glasses of champagne, rapidly, and ate a dead shrimp impaled on a blue plastic toothpick. The reception grew noisier. One woman took off her shoes. One man put his toupee on backward. Everyone laughed.

The groom cornered Helen near the bar.

"You're her best friend," he said accusingly, "you got any idea what a new bridge costs?"

Helen admitted she hadn't.

"It's expensive," he stated gloomily. "After all, I'm not made of money. I'm not a millionaire, you know."

Helen told him she didn't believe that Peggy thought he was a millionaire.

"I know, I know," he said frantically. "But still, I mean, right off the bat like that? We leave the church, and POW! she needs dental work. Is that fair? I ask you, is that fair?"

She stared at him, shrinking down inside her white lace gown (the one with the pointy hem), suddenly saddened, almost defeated by what it meant to be alive. Cock, cunt and the grave. That's about it—innit? But then Carrie Edwards bustled over to tell her that Richard Faye was outside, asking to see her.

She hurried into the hall. Faye turned. His face looked like a slashed portrait stuck back together with tears. She thought of the little boy, the skinny maid with dirty heels.

She cried, "What are you doing out here, darling? Why don't you come inside?"

"I've got to t-t-talk to you. Just for a minute."

She put her arms around him, found herself embracing a post. His watery eyes slid away, followed a crack across the ceiling.

"I'm gassed," she told him. "I've been drinking so much, waiting to hear from you. It was a lovely wedding. I cried. Peggy looked so beautiful. I thought you'd call. About your mother, Uck . . . I mean, you know how I feel. I'm sorry. For her and for you. I . . ."

"Oh, that's all right," he said vaguely. His fish eyes filled, brimmed over. "Mother died calling for me. And I was—I was—"

"I know, I know. But you shouldn't blame yourself, dear. You *shouldn't.*"

"I can't help it. I can't help myself. I keep thinking if I had left when he called, if I had listened to him, if I had believed him . . ."

"You can't—"

"You just don't understand. I know I shouldn't blame myself, but I do. I *do.* It's there. Maybe it doesn't make sense, but it's there. What am I going to do, Helen? What?"

Then she thought of Harry. Maybe he had been right. Maybe Harry L. Tennant had been right on. For the first time in her life she thought seriously of killing herself. She was weary, of Faye's problems, of hers, of the climb. She was weary of the complexity of things, people as tangled as a basketful of snakes—not the "raw souls rubbing against each other" that Martha Rhodes talked about, but damp souls sliding off each other. She was so entangled.

The waking, the washing, the eating, the working, the sleeping. And that goddamned laundry and dry cleaning every Saturday. Lifts for her shoes. The toilet to be scrubbed out because the cleaning woman refused to do it. Every-month cramps. All the million details of nothing, just existing, but if neglected could sweep her away.

To endure these, to conquer these trials of existence—right out of a burlesque show—was not enough. Because they drained the strength and the spirit. And what was left for love and passion? What was left to fight a clawed old woman, a lonely, mushy man? It was all too much. The hell with it.

"It's all a crock of shit," she said wonderingly.

He wasn't listening, but he repeated exactly what she had been thinking...

"It's all too much," he said. "I can't fight it anymore. Maybe I could have beat the other thing. But not this. I don't blame you. It's my fault. I've been doing research for an article on the Andreas Fault. California is going to fall into the sea. It's the way I feel. Cracked open. Every time I'd look at you I'd remember. How could we go to bed again? How could we love? All the logic in the world won't change it. The Andreas Fault. My Fault."

She wanted very much to hurt him.

"Edith probably did it deliberately," she said. "She probably figured she had to do it to win. So she did."

"Helen."

"Oh, yes," she nodded. "I think she'd do that to keep you."

"Helen."

"But the funny thing is that she didn't have to. That's the funny thing. You'd have gone back to her sooner or later. Because you don't want to change. You were lying. You like the kind of man you are. You don't really want to change at all."

His mouth hung open. She examined him critically. The soft, tear-swollen bags under his eyes. The sagging chops. The wilted body.

"But you're not a man at all," she said, deliberately cruel.

"That's the really funny thing. You're a blob. A lump."

"No," he said slowly. "No more. No more."

He backed away from her, hands raised, palms outthrust, dwindling down the hallway, watching her warily. Then he turned, ran down the stairway.

"You promised we'd watch the eclipse together," she yelled after him.

Finally, she went back to the wedding reception. She stood in the doorway, looking at the crowd.

Not enough men, she thought dully. Never enough men.

She went into the bathroom and wept for exactly ten minutes, sitting on the closed toilet seat, rocking back and forth. Then she washed her face with cold water, put on fresh makeup. She went into the bedroom, called Charles Lefferts. No one answered. She didn't like Maurice's apartment. There were bullfighter posters on the walls. She eased into the living room mob, found a drink.

Carrie Edwards grabbed her arm.

"Beautiful." She sobbed.

"Yeah." Helen nodded. "Beautiful."

Peggy and Maurice were standing side by side behind the buffet. They were about to slice the cake (four layers). A photographer was yelling, "Close it up, close it up! Make like lovers!"

Helen went back into the bedroom, called Charles Lefferts. No one answered. She wandered into the living room for another drink.

"Beautiful." Carrie Edwards sobbed.

It was, Helen Miley finally decided, more than human flesh and blood could stand. She went into the bedroom, called Charles Lefferts. No one answered. She finished her glass of champagne in two stomach-flopping gulps. She grabbed up purse, coat, gloves. She left the apartment, not saying good-bye to anyone.

There was a young Swedish-looking cop at the corner of Lexington Avenue. That is, he looked at if he went skiing every weekend—or maybe he just rubbed snow on his face. Something like that. He had beautiful blond hair, rosy patches high on his cheekbones. Helen teetered up to him, stood directly in front of him. He looked at her gravely.

"When I first came to New York, I was a grape," she told him. "Now I'm a raisin."

"There, there," the cop said.

"I was at this party," she said. "Wedding reception. Girlfriend. She got married."

"That's nice," the cop said.

"Peggy Palmer," she muttered. "She bites her nails and washes her hair in beer. But *she* got married. Are you married?"

"Sure," the cop said. "Isn't everyone?"

"Wise guy," Helen Miley mumbled. "Isn't everyone? Wise guy."

"Want a cab?" the cop asked.

"No, I do not want a cab."

"I get off at midnight," the cop said, unblinking.

"I'm going for a long, long walk," she told him. "I may never come back."

"Now, now," the cop said.

"Do you think I'm attractive?" she asked him. "Not beautiful, mind you. Just reasonably attractive?"

"Sure," the cop said.

"My figure's not bad, is it?"

"I get off at midnight," the cop said.

"May be," she said shrewdly, "but son, you ain't getting *on* at midnight."

"Move along," the cop said. "You're blocking traffic."

She wandered down Lexington Avenue, looking in the windows of hardware stores. There was a medical supply shop that had bedpans in sky blue and blushing pink. Thin clouds were shining before the glow of the moon like oil on water.

She walked all the way down to Fifty-third Street, giggling once or twice. She veered over to Second Avenue. And there was that welcome sign of the Everest, with enough of the neon defunct so that it read "rest ar & ril."

She paraded in like a duchess, aloof, quite steady. It was too early for the regulars. There was only one young man at the bar, near the door. He took off his hat when Helen came in. She strutted down to the other end of the bar, hoisted her butt onto a stool.

Thack came trundling over, his beer belly hiding his belt. He wiped the bar with a damp cloth, then set out a little cocktail napkin with a drawing of a rooster on it.

"Helen," he said.

"Peggy Palmer got married," she told him. "She was that girl I used to come in here with. She got married today."

"God bless her," Thack said, "and may all her troubles be little ones."

"Thack, I feel awful. I think I'm going to die. I should go home. But I *can't* go home."

'What have you been drinking?"

"Champagne and scotch and some green stuff in a little glass. And I ate a shrimp."

He considered a moment.

"Now what I would suggest," he said finally, "would be an ice cold bottle of lager. Served to you in a chilled glass. To put you back on the tracks, as you might say."

"Oh, yes. Yes."

He dug deep in the cold cabinet to bring out a frosty bottle and glass. He poured for her, watched approvingly as she drained half the glass without stopping.

"I may live," she gasped.

"Easy," he advised. "There's more. Would you like some juke?"

She dug in her purse, gave him two quarters.

"But none of your lousy Irish reels," she called after him, suddenly feeling sweet and mournful. "Play something I can cry to."

The first thing he played was an old recording of Bing Crosby singing "Just a Gigolo," and Helen cried.

The second recording was Marlene Dietrich singing "Falling in Love Again" in German. Helen cried again and finished her beer.

Thack had returned behind the bar. He was talking to the young man seated near the door. The young man was lifting his highball glass with his left hand. His right arm hung straight down at his side. At the end was a thing like a hand, half-clenched, covered with black leather.

Thack came back to Helen.

"The young gentleman at the end of the bar wishes to know if he might purchase you a drink?"

Helen turned to look. Thack bent forward.

"He's straight, Helen," he whispered. "Of the neighborhood. Comes in now and then. Never a trouble."

She straightened on the barstool.

"Convey my thank-you to the young gentleman at the end of the bar and tell him I will be happy to accept his offer of a drink, and I would take it as a curt kindesy—a kind courtesy—if he would care to join me down here."

So there he was, seated next to her. A formal, secret look to him, like a doctor, lawyer or corsetiere. He had a neat brown mustache that looked like a little brush used to clean suede shoes.

"You've lost an arm, haven't you?" she asked him immediately.

"Well, I'll be damned," he said, looking down in amazement. "So I have."

She laughed and touched his cheek.

They talked about Bing Crosby and Marlene Dietrich and where was the best place in the neighborhood to get anchovy pizza.

"What is your name, sir?" she asked him formally.

"Clark."

"Are you Clark Kent, a mild-mannered reporter who goes into phone booths and becomes Superman?"

"No. I am Clark Bannon, an evil-tempered insurance statistician. What is your name?"

"My name is—"

For one awful, heart-grabbing moment she forgot her name. Then she remembered and said, "My name is Helen Miley."

"Was this the face that launched a thousand ships?" he demanded. "And burnt the topless towers of Ilium? Sweet Helen, make me immortal with a kiss."

"Okay," she said happily, and kissed his ear.

It startled him. He looked at her with new respect.

"And what do you do, Helen?"

"What do I do?" She considered. "What do I do? I chew nails, and I spit tacks."

"Very good." He nodded approvingly.

"And now, Clark, I would like to buy you a drink. If I may?"

"You may."

"Thack, could we do this again? And also, Thack, I would like to buy *you* a drink so we may properly celebrate Peggy Palmer's marriage."

"No doubt about it," Thack said.

He poured their drinks, took a beer for himself. They hoisted glasses and shouted, "To Peggy!"

"Who's Peggy?" Clark Bannon asked.

"A very dear woman-type friend of mine," Helen told him. "Would you pardon me a moment, please?"

When she got back from the toilet, she asked Thack, "Where's Clara? Isn't she on?"

"She'll be in later. I sent her down to the Bowery to get a leech."

"Thack? A leech?"

"She had a mouse you wouldn't believe. I can't have her looking like that, and a raw steak is just a waste of good meat. A fat leech is what she needs. Sucks out all the bad blood. You can get them at this place on the Bowery. She'll be back soon."

"What's going on?" Clark Bannon asked, lost.

"Peggy Palmer, this friend of mine, she got married today," Helen explained.

"To a fat leech?"

"Well... sort of. Anyway, that was the Peggy we were drinking to. Are you married?"

"No."

"Ever been?"

"No."

"How come?"

"Never trust a bachelor who keeps a cat and smokes a pipe."

"Do you keep a cat and smoke a pipe?"

"No," he said, catching on, "I keep a cat who smokes a pipe. I smoke a fat leech."

They had another round of drinks. And another. He'd pay for one round, and then Helen would pay for one round, and then Thack would buy a free round. It was a good arrangement.

They played some music. Helen and Clark danced to two of the records. He could hold her hand out with his left hand, but his right sleeve dangled. She didn't care. After a while she was pressed up against him, her hands around his neck. His left hand was against her back. That was nice.

Then they were back at the bar, and life was going. The old regulars were in now. Thack had turned on the TV. A cat was chasing a mouse.

Helen changed her seat. She made sure she sat on Clark's left side so she could hold his hand occasionally. When he wasn't lifting his glass.

"I'm from Ohio," she told him, beaming.

"I'm from Montana," he told her.

"Well, that certainly gives us something in common, doesn't it?"

He nodded happily, and she thought he was coming along just fine.

Thack gave them potato chips and salted peanuts. They had

more drinks. They didn't want to play the juke because that would annoy the old regulars who were watching TV, which was now showing a film on the sex life of sea lions. It was interesting.

But they whispered to each other. Their ages, movies they liked, places they had been, what they had done. Things. Stirring it up.

He was all right—tall, pleasant, reasonably wide. He was wearing light-brown shoes with a dark-blue suit— but what the hell.

He looked at her, sitting on that little barstool. Her lacy hem was hiked up above her yummy knees. She perched there, glowing, all jaw, leg and horn-rimmed glasses.

"Listen," he said to her, leaning close. "Listen, Helen—may I ask you a very personal question?"

"Of course," she waved grandly. "Ask away."

"Will you have dinner with me tomorrow night?"

"Hell, yes," Helen Miley said, giving him a raunchy smile. "Why not?"

LAWRENCE SANDERS

__THE TIMOTHY FILES	0-425-10924-0/$4.95
__CAPER	0-425-10477-X/$4.95
__THE EIGHTH COMMANDMENT	0-425-10005-7/$4.95
__THE DREAM LOVER	0-425-09473-1/$4.50
__THE PASSION OF MOLLY T.	0-425-10139-8/$4.95
__THE FIRST DEADLY SIN	0-425-10427-3/$4.95
__THE MARLOW CHRONICLES	0-425-09963-6/$4.50
__THE PLEASURES OF HELEN	0-425-10168-1/$4.50
__THE SECOND DEADLY SIN	0-425-10428-1/$4.95
__THE SIXTH COMMANDMENT	0-425-10430-3/$4.95
__THE TANGENT OBJECTIVE	0-425-10331-5/$4.95
__THE TANGENT FACTOR	0-425-10062-6/$4.50
__THE TENTH COMMANDMENT	0-425-10431-1/$4.95
__THE TOMORROW FILE	0-425-08179-6/$4.95
__THE THIRD DEADLY SIN	0-425-10429-X/$4.95
__THE ANDERSON TAPES	0-425-10364-1/$4.50
__THE CASE OF LUCY BENDING	0-425-10086-3/$4.50
__THE SEDUCTION OF PETER S.	0-425-09314-X/$4.95
__THE LOVES OF HARRY DANCER	0-425-08473-6/$4.50
__THE FOURTH DEADLY SIN	0-425-09078-7/$4.95
__TIMOTHY'S GAME	0-425-11641-7/$5.50
__LOVE SONGS	0-425-11273-X/$4.50
